Growing Up Filipino II

More Stories for Young Adults

Collected and Edited by:
CECILIA MANGUERRA BRAINARD

PALH
2010

GROWING UP FILIPINO II: More Stories for Young Adults
Collected and edited by Cecilia Manguerra Brainard

First Edition, 2010

ISBN: 978-0-9719458-3-8

Library of Congress Control Number: 2002104406

Published by
PALH
PO Box 5099
Santa Monica, CA 90409
U.S.A.
http://www.palhbooks.com
Email: palh@aol.com; palhbooks@gmail.com

Cover Design by Rica Hernandez Gomez
Layout by Studio 5 Designs

Special thanks to the following sponsors whose donations have made possible the publication of *Growing Up Filipino: More Stories for Young Adults*:

John and Elizabeth Allen
Christopher Brainard Law Offices – www.christopherbrainard.com
Emmanuel Gonzalez
Barbara Lim
In memory of Arcadio, Maria, Sylvestre, and Celerina
Carol Ojeda-Kimbrough
Marily Ysip Orosa
Remy's on Temple Art & Garden – www.remysontemple.com
Tony Robles – www.tony-robles.com
Milagros Santillan
Studio 5 Designs
Carolyn Williams, Director, Writers House, Rutgers University
    - http://wh.rutgers.edu/

GROWING UP FILIPINO II
More Stories for Young Adults

What They Say About The First Volume
Growing Up Filipino: Stories For Young Adults

In this fine short-story collection, 29 Filipino American writers explore the universal challenges of adolescence from the unique perspectives of teens in the Philippines or in the U.S. Organized into five sections--Family, Angst, Friendship, Love, and Home--all the stories are about growing up and what the introduction calls "growing into Filipino-ness, growing with Filipinos, and growing in or growing away from the Philippines." The stories are introduced by the authors, who illustrate the teenage experience as they remember it or as they wish to explain it to the reader--whether the focus is the death of a grandparent, budding sexuality, or going to the mall. The cultural flavor aspect never overwhelms the stories, and readers will be drawn to the particulars as well as the universal concerns of family, friends, love, and leaving home...The stories are delightful!

—Frances Bradburn, Booklist

These 29 short stories offer a highly textured portrait of Filipino youth and an excellent sampling of creative writing. Thematically arranged, most of the pieces have been written since the turn of the 21st century. Each story is introduced by a thumbnail sketch of the author and a paragraph or two about some element of Filipino culture or history that is relevant to the story. Authors include those born and continuing to live in the Philippines, émigrés, and American-born Filipinos. Tough but relevant topics addressed include a gay youth's affection for his supportive mother, the role of religious didacticism in the formation of a childhood perception, consumer culture as it is experienced by modern teens in Manila, and coping with bullies of all ages and stations in life...There are more Filipinos living in the U.S. than most people realize, but finding literature reflective of their experiences is difficult. The high caliber and broad but wholly accessible range of this collection, however, makes this title a solid purchase for multiple reasons.

—Francisca Goldsmith, School Library Journal

Emerging and established award-winning writers are the authors of this fine collection of 29 stories about what it means to be young and Filipino in the Philippines and in the United States. Filipinos in America are now the second largest in the umbrella group of Asian Americans, yet there is a scarcity of books by and for Filipinos. This impressive array captures the complexities of both the Filipino culture and history and the realities of the lives of young adults no matter what their ethnic affiliation. Each story is assigned to one of five universal themes: family, angst, friendship, love, and home.

—Glenna Sloan, BookBird

A wide range of views and insights into growing up Filipino are compiled in this anthology of short stories and memoirs. As one who grew up experiencing politically and socially what it means to be part of an ethnic group that has been known as the forgotten Asian Americans, I identify closely with the experiences conveyed by contributors to this volume. On the one hand, Philippine-born writers such as Mar V. Puatu and Anthony L. Tan reminded me of stories my relatives and friends from the Philippines would tell; on the other hand, American-born writers such as Edgar Poma and Vince Gotera struck a personal chord with my experiences as an American-born Filipino.

The term Flip, the penchant for singing songs in front of relatives and friends, social conflicts among American-born and Philippine-born Filipinos, experiences of being gay, and experiences working in migrant camps are among the more significant cultural, social, and political realities depicted in this collection. Because the writings focus on issues related to childhood and adolescence, with a style that appeals to teen readers, this book is highly recommended for young adults.

—Sam Cacas, Multicultural Review

The challenge of reading and writing Filipino literature is what makes this anthology exciting...Growing up Filipino is a valuable addition to Asian American literature.

—Pearl Ratunil, MELUS

This collection is the first anthology that focuses exclusively on children and adolescents and is directed towards a young adult audience. By addressing the issues of childhood and adolescent culture, aside from ethnic affiliation, the anthology can also speak to a wider audience.

—Rocio G. Davis
Associate Professor American and Postcolonial Literature
University of Navarre

Cecilia Manguerra Brainard has collected a dazzling and impressive array of 29 stories about the saga of what it means to be young and Filipino... This is a powerfully achieved and memorable book by authors who know their craft, and who also have a profound understanding and love for the Philippines and things Filipino.

—Roger N. Buckley
Professor of History and Director
Asian American Studies Institute
University of Connecticut

OTHER BOOKS BY CECILIA MANGUERRA BRAINARD

Acapulco at Sunset and Other Stories

A La Carte Food & Fiction (Coedited with Marily Ysip Orosa)

Behind the Walls: Life of Convent Girls (Coedited with Marily Ysip Orosa)

Cecilia's Diary 1964-1968

Contemporary Fiction by Filipinos in America (Editor)

Fiction by Filipinos in America (Editor)

*Finding God: True Stories of Spiritual Encounters
(Coedited with Marily Ysip Orosa)*

Fundamentals of Creative Writing

Growing Up Filipino: Stories for Young Adults (Editor)

*Journey of 100 Years: Reflections on the Centennial of
Philippine Independence (Coedited with Edmundo F. Litton)*

Magdalena

Philippine Woman in America

When the Rainbow Goddess Wept

Woman with Horns and Other Stories

ALSO PUBLISHED BY PALH

Growing Up Filipino: Stories for Young Adults

Contents

Preface

In 2003, I edited the first volume of *Growing Up Filipino: Stories for Young Adults.* The warm reception of this collection surprised me. In both America and the Philippines, the anthology garnered excellent reviews; educators are using the book in their classrooms; libraries keep copies of this title; and the public has been enthusiastic about the collection.

Even though that first volume had 29 stories, and was therefore somewhat substantial, I felt that not all the stories about "growing up Filipino" had been told. In fact, after the horrific events of 9/11, when life as we had always known it drastically changed, I wondered what sort of new experiences Filipino youths had gone through. Have the wars in Afghanistan and Iraq affected them? Have the bombings in Manila malls, the heightened security in airports and buildings, the shootings in American schools–the sense of dread and uncertainty–affected our youths?

I decided to edit a second volume of *Growing Up Filipino* with the idea of gathering contemporary stories. I came up with 27 stories written by Filipino writers in the Philippines, the United States, and Canada. Many of the contributors are established and well-respected writers. The stories are topnotch works of fiction selected primarily for their literary merit. The stories deal with experiences about growing up Filipino in the Philippines, America, and Canada.

The majority of the stories are about the usual concerns of the young (coming of age, family, relationships), but a few stories deal with heavier topics, which should inspire discussion. While the subject matter of this anthology focuses on Filipino or Filipino American youths, the readership is not limited to young adults. The stories included in this collection are high caliber literary stories that can be enjoyed by anyone, regardless of age. Educators will find this book a useful tool in their classrooms as well, considering, in particular, the scarcity of books about Filipino youths.

Special thanks to the contributors for their cooperation, to Tony Robles for his help in copyediting, and to Marily Ysip Orosa at Studio 5 Designs for her assistance and support. Thanks also to Rocio G. Davis for writing the Introduction to this collection, as she did for the first volume of *Growing Up Filipino*.

~ Cecilia Manguerra Brainard

Introduction

Children's Culture and the Metaphors of Growing Up (Filipino)

by Rocio G. Davis

Cecilia Manguerra Brainard's second volume of *Growing Up Filipino* expands and deepens the paradigms presented in the first book. In my introduction to that volume, I noted how the stories "repeatedly highlight diverse metaphors of Filipino-ness, as they suggest that growing up Filipino implies negotiating the consequences of history and family eccentricities, navigating cultural contingencies and personal choices, and enacting individual strategies of self-formation and self-representation" (ix). This new collection retakes the first volume's constitutive strategy and many of the themes but, importantly, extends some of the concerns. In particular, as a post-9/11 collection, we are given access to how child or adolescent characters deal with potentially violent new configurations of transculturality, and the ways race, ethnicity, class and religion blend (happily or not) in the representation of private or public identities.

It has often been uncritically argued that to read a literature is to encounter a country. This new volume's deliberately plural emphasis challenges that assertion's static connotation as it reflects how multiple forms of recent Filipino/American fiction interrogate the forces that direct shifting discourses of ethnicity in the Philippines and for Filipino Americans. When read collectively, these stories become an embodiment of the Philippine mosaic, to highlight the fluidity of Filipino/American identity. The stories' commonality lies in their intention to translate the Filipino/American's transcultural image, particularly in the context of mainstream American discourse, as "others" into a self-defined multilayered specificity. Their difference lies in the myriad of processes that lead to diverse conclusions. Indeed, the pause between being (the child narrator/protagonist's current position) and becoming (the panorama of possibilities) signals the crucial point of dramatic tension in many of the stories.

If writing in today's postcolonial, postmodern world involves the intense reworking of questions that refer to issues such as oppositionality, marginality, boundaries, displacement, and authenticity, the child's point of view contributes significantly to the understanding of the process of the creation of the transcultural subject. The use of the child character has become a powerful means of defining the responses of a country's artistic minds to its evolving cultural climate. The appropriateness of the theme of childhood in Filipino/American texts is self-evident. The dynamics of the child character make it a vivid metaphor for the quest for a definition of the ethnic pluralism that incorporates personal contingencies and cultural legacies, while adapting to the practices that govern the creation of literary texts. Peter Coveney's germinal work, *The Image of Childhood*, has emphasized the advantages of the child as the protagonist in texts that center on the consequences of cultural pluralism in the modern world: "If the central problem for the artist was in fact one of adjustment, one can see the possibilities of identification between the artist and the consciousness of the child whose difficulty and chief source of pain often lie in adjustment and accommodation to environment. In childhood lay the perfect image of insecurity and isolation, of fear and bewilderment, of vulnerability and potential violation" (31-32).

The links between history and memory, race and culture, imagination and current mood inspire those who write about growing up Filipino. The voice of the child serves two fundamental concerns in the presentation of the transcultural subject: how identity develops and how meaning may be established. Further, we have to consider the literary techniques used by these writers, which help establish the simultaneous differences and interconnections that makes Filipino/American writing such a potent source of insight into ethnic configurations of self. The two elements that shape the stories in this volume—childhood and ethnicity—must therefore be understood both independent and interdependently. For children today, issues of history, heritage, peer communities—cultural and scholastic— and the possibility (or imperative) of self-formation serve as impetus for processes of empowerment and agency. As Carole Carpenter argues, in contemporary writing we must reject the assumption that children are merely receivers of culture, to present them as "creative manipulators of a dynamic network of concepts, actions, feelings and products that mirror and mould their experience as children" (57). Though children's existence and experience as cultural beings must be negotiated critically by writers and readers, meaning in effective literary texts lies, at least in part, through the traditions and experience of collective children's culture which each of them experiences individually (Carpenter 56).

Meaning arises, therefore, from these stories' involvement with the nature of childhood, more than simply with the experience of ethnicity. Hence, the child narrator or protagonist should not be conceived of or presented merely as the bearer or learner of culture. In this light, we may argue that the idea of a "children's culture," defined as "the dynamic matrix of processes and products that to varying degrees young people experience and share simply by their being children" structures the texts (Carpenter 54). Though children's existence and experience as cultural beings must be taken into account, meaning in effective literary texts develops, to a significant degree, through the traditions and experience of collective children's culture which each of them experiences individually.

The children in these stories, in many cases, aim to become protagonists of their own lives, resisting outside impulses that require their passivity. As we attend to the narrative voices of the child characters, for example, we note an increased complexity in play: the voices do not only tell stories, but communicate all that notions of childhood and identity themselves connote. As each of the child narrators or protagonists of the stories struggle to make sense of the situation they find themselves in, writers negotiate patterns of self-representation for children in diverse situations. The children in these stories, which focus most generally on extended families, academic achievement, and peer relationships, navigate the personal and cultural codes that establish their place and possibilities. Herein lies the value of the stories, in their representation of the myriad possibilities and truths of childhood experiences.

The other integrative factor in this volume on growing up Filipino, reminds us that the stories, ultimately, literary reflections on ethnicity, contribute to the continuing definition of what it is to be, or become, Filipino/American. The narratives thus present the forces that shape ethnic identity and reveal possibilities for identification. More importantly, however, these texts offer models for writing and learning about ethnicity. Francesco Lorrigio's ideas regarding literary configurations of ethnicity may be usefully deployed in this context. He notes that ethnic writing involves two generally interrelated processes: on the one hand, the development of a perspective that "occurs when ethnics assume voice, speak about themselves, when there is vision from within, writing with inside knowledge"; on the other, "ethnicity presupposes an indirect act of reference...that relies on the figure of the author, and, more specifically, his or her social identity, for mediation" (55). Thus, when the text contains material directly related to the markers of ethnicity—race, culture, language, religion, among others—the writer's identity carries the burden of its authenticity: "The events, the characters in the possible world depicted by the text, resemble those in our actual world because they are narrated by someone who can vouch for that resemblance: ethnic authorship is authoritativeness" (Loriggio 55). By evoking personal ethnic identification—all the writers included in this volume are Filipinos or identify as Filipino Americans—the writers deliberately originate a particular kind of cultural discourse which, consciously or not, increases the text's literalness: rather than distancing the author, it draws him or her nearer. This factor, as I will argue, functions strategically as part of the process of creating and maintaining collective and cultural memory for a community, promoting ethnic identification and a sense of belonging.

These literary engagements with particular forms of being Filipino helps build and communicate ethnic identity, which then provides means of connecting with a community that may be physically dispersed but which acknowledges the other as members. Stories, a way of knowing and preserving culture, are also therefore means of survival for the group as characters share a cultural history illuminated through recurring metaphors and promoted through the publication of more stories. Metaphors are powerful because they provide ostensibly simple access to multilayered concepts and allow us to think through the ways we function and create meaning. When William Blake invited us to see the world in a grain of sand, he clarified one of the most valuable lessons we learn from literature: the power of words to capture a world, our experience, our need to understand our past, our hopes for the future. The intersecting metaphors in the stories allow readers to unveil some of the constitutive elements in the patterns of growing up Filipino and, concurrently, give the community sustaining stories.

Thematic similarities and recurrent metaphors link the narratives as they reveal unique perspectives and ideas. The traditional markers of both childhood and Filipino culture are explored imaginatively in these stories. Specifically, for example, the representation of family structures and negotiations with their particular forms, such as close parental supervision and the inevitable multitudinous family reunions, inform several stories. The family, whose symbolic connection to the idea of the nation is heightened in texts by diasporic writers, gives characters like Filipino Canadian Liana in Dolores de Manuel's "Someone Else" a sense of belonging, though she may roll her eyes at the thought of numerous Titas and Titos that have to be greeted. The most dramatic aversion to family reunions is portrayed in Dean Alfar's understated "How My Mother Flew." Funerals, in particular, become the central focus of family meetings or even children's imagination, as in Amalia Bueno's "Perla and Her Lovely Barbie," where the elements of the funeral ritual become a selfish manipulation of a younger sister's guilelessness.

Several stories focus on the relationship between parents and children: Tony Robles' "Son of a Janitor" contrasts lessons learned from a father with academic knowledge; Veronica Montes's "My Father's Tattoo" and Cecilia Manguerra Brainard's "Vigan" show children trying to understand the complicated tangle of adult love and commitment. Divorce marks many of the children's lives: Rita, in Paulino Lim's "Nurse Rita" struggles to raise her daughter after a divorce and the realization that her father's impositions have limited her professional opportunities; Tomas and Gabe, in Brian Roley's "Old Man" find themselves caught in the trap of their father's fickle and selfish love. In one of the most poignant stories, Rebecca Mabanglo-Mayor's "Yellow Is for Luck," young Juana holds on to her father's lessons about flowers and the hope he will return from war.

In the context of Filipino/American family relationships, three metaphors carry the weight of both personal and cultural belonging. One of the most vivid metaphors is, of course, food. This image, perhaps more than any other, symbolizes a child's awareness of family situation and cultural context. Filipino/American children's favorite food include nilaga ("Double Dutch") and purple ube frosting ("Old Man"), while the manongs in "Clothesline" are comforted by Filipino food cooked for them. Also, cooking rice serves as a reliable background to the action in many narratives. Many stories in the volume refer directly to mealtimes and particular dishes, as sources of intense pleasure and familiarity, or repulsion and cultural embarrassment. Descriptions of home or family reunions are made more vivid by references to the ways female relatives cook too much and serve the same meals at reunions, a fact that simultaneously irritates and gives the children a powerful sense of knowing their place.

A second pervasive metaphor is religion, particularly the Catholic faith and the ways the teachings and practices of the Church may be viewed as either liberating or limiting. The rites of religious practice provide many of the characters with a community and ideals of belief and behavior while others only see a set of impositions. Juana, in "Yellow is for Luck" finds comfort in planting primroses around the Blessed Mother's statue; the maid Auring, in Marily Ysip Orosa's "Auring's Dilemma," is compelled to do penance to atone for her affair with Felipe. The border between institutionalized religion and native Filipino practices is crossed in other stories. Marianne Villanueva's "Black Dog" and Brainard's "Vigan" have protagonists who carry the memory and burden of possible magic by native manghuhula, which may or may not have led to violent deaths. In Jonathan Siason's "Old Witch of San Jose," imagined magical attributes shape the young character's perception of an old lady and his grandfather.

The third crucial metaphor for Filipino/American children is their name. The stories make repeated references to idiosyncratic Filipino naming practices; and reflections on their names becomes one of the ways the children acknowledge connection with a cultural tradition and family. Specifically, for example, Liana, in "Someone Else" thinks about her "evil twin," a cousin who looks just like her and has the same name—but different nickname—as her, whose rebellion (Chechi has run away to join a Vietnamese gang) disturbs her hard-won complacency about her own life and achievements. In a diverse society, names become signifiers of more than merely individual or familial identity, and gesture towards membership in a particular racial, ethnic and/or cultural group. The protagonist of "Double Dutch," for example, hates the fact that her parents gave her two first names, the fact that her middle name is her mother's maiden name. "It sounds so strange. Maria Elizabeth Rañola Ramos. Two first names and two last names." "But that's what Filipinos do," her mother explained.

As in all stories about childhood, retrospective points of view, as in Geronimo Tagatac's "Hammer Lounge" or Kannika Peña's "Be Safe" highlight the painful perspective offered by hindsight, while Katrina Atienza's "Neighbors" reminds us that sometimes we can't go home again. Other stories focus on traditional rites of passage for boys and girls, such as Aileen Suzara's "Period Mark." Jaime An Lim's "Outward Journey" illustrates the importance of friendship for one's sense of independent self. Some of the stories offer character portraits from the perspective of childhood. In Oscar Peñaranda's "The Price" and Max Gutierrez's "Uncle Gil," young boys pay homage to eccentric uncles who functioned in ways contrary to family expectation, insisting on living their way; and Dean Alfar's "The Music Teacher" is a portrait of potential brilliance destroyed by artistic impotence and regret.

Several stories engage the consequences of immigration on class and interethnic relationships. Edgar Poma's "Clothesline" focuses on a boy's appreciation of a Filipino old-timer. Rashaan Alexis Meneses' insightful "Here in the States" delicately portrays a daughter's frustration at her awareness of how her family's social position has diminished with immigration. The protagonist, Alma, considers how her mother, a history professor in the Philippines, now works as a nanny for a family that lives in a house similar to the one they left behind, just as her friend June's father, an artist, now bags groceries. The dark side of the American dream appears here in stories that show the effects of racism, such as "Hammer Lounge," which describes the frustration of the second generation who cannot transcend the trap of social class. Perspectives and positions regarding interethnic relations also shape the experience of Filipino/Americans. Maria Elizabeth's excitement, in "Double Dutch," over a new friend and her fascinating ways, is destroyed by her parents' overt racism, showing her how skin color becomes a metaphor for belonging or rejection. Interestingly Charleson Ong's "A Season of 10,000 Noses" uses the mode of humorous fantasy to describe interethnic (mis)understanding and the insidiousness of stereotypical views of the other.

The world after 9/11 in both the US and the Philippines is explored in M.G. Bertulfo's "Shiny Black Boots," where a veteran's son in Chicago struggles to decide whether to enlist in the US Army and María Victoria Beltran's "The Veil," the story of a Muslim adolescent girl in the Philippines in the weeks immediately after the bombing. For these characters, like many of the others in the collection, making choices that often challenge parental and/or cultural norms serve to mark, as I mentioned earlier, that pause between being and becoming that serves as a vital structure in writing about children in general and Filipino/American children in particular.

As the stories in this collection illustrate, to read the interconnection between children's culture and ethnic affiliation leads us to consider how writers participate actively in producing texts that help identify a community, providing models for cohesion. Ethnic narratives often interpellate an implied audience for culture and history. And, in the encounter between text and reader, Marianne Gullestad observes, "readers create the text while interpreting it, and, to some extent, they find their own truths in the texts" (31). This idea requires us to unravel what the existence of a community of readers might mean in the context of Filipino/American literary and cultural discourse. You create a reader when you present texts that offer perspectives on shared experiences. The community that receives these texts grows conscious of how these works support the creation and sustenance of the community by providing the narratives of cultural or collective memory needed to validate their history, their positions, and even their political agendas. In this context, questions that historian Carolyn Steedman asks about the making and writing of the modern self resound: "Who uses these stories? How are they used, and to what ends?" (28).

Collective memory is our passport to membership in a group and these narratives may transcend the individual to speak of and for a wider community. The stories in *Growing Up Filipino II* should therefore be read as active interventions on existing historical or cultural records as they provide supplementary material for the cultural understanding of the Filipino/American self. Importantly, the anthology's presentation of a multiplicity of these texts facilitates what Gillian Whitlock calls "connected reading," a strategy vital to the process of creating cultural memory (203). By eschewing the entire truth within a single text and "making links between and across various narratives, tropes, sites, figures, movements," readers participate in a process of "supplementation rather than completion, for complexity rather than closure, for the making of truth rather than its revelation" (Whitlock 203-204). This plural and palimpsestic approach privileges association as a creative reading strategy that configures a wider scope for the enactment of transcultural subjects. It also evidences a reciprocal process: as a text or a group of texts empowers a community, the community also validates the authors and produces more texts.

Indeed, anthologies like *Growing Up Filipino* show us how transcultural identity may be narratively enacted to create a dynamic community that uses these texts to empower their history and cultural location in society. These stories about childhood, read collectively, play a pivotal role in the construction of this kind of cultural memory because of the way they validate each other and expand the meanings of similar experiences. The collective memory of Filipino/Americans is thus textually mediated by creative writing and enhanced by the connective reading process. These texts, therefore, which function on diverse levels—on that of childhood culture, as negotiations of transculturality, community identification and formation—superlatively illustrate how literary engagements with the complex process of growing up may signify culturally. What these writers negotiate, ultimately, in their narratives, are models for authentic personal and transcultural identity.

Works Cited:

Carpenter, Carole H. "Enlisting Children's Literature in the Goals of Multiculturalism." *Mosaic* 29. 3 (September 1996): 53-73.

Coveney, Peter. *The Image of Childhood*. Rev. edn. London: Penguin, 1967.

Davis, Rocío G. "On the Edge: Growing Up Filipino." Introduction to *Growing Up Filipino: Stories for Young Adults*. Ed. Cecilia Manguerra Brainard. Santa Monica, CA: PALH, 2003. ix-xv.

Gullestad, Marianne. "Modernity, Self, and Childhood in the Analysis of Life Stories." *Imagined Childhoods: Self and Society in Autobiographical Accounts*. Ed. Marianne Gullestad. Oslo: Scandinavian UP, 1996. 1-39.

Loriggio, Francesco. "The Question of the Corpus: Ethnicity and Canadian Literature." *Future Indicative: Literary Theory and Canadian Literature*. Ed. John Moss. Ottawa: University of Ottawa Press, 1987. 53-69.

Steedman, Carolyn. "Enforced Narratives: Stories of Another Self." *Feminism and Autobiography: Texts, Theories, Methods*. Eds. Tess Cosslett, Celia Lury, and Penny Summerfield. London & New York: Routledge, 2000. 25-39.

Whitlock, Gillian. T*he Intimate Empire: Reading Women's Autobiography*. London & New York: Cassell, 2000.

Rocio G. Davis has degrees from the Ateneo de Manila University and the University of Navarra, where she is currently Associate Professor of American Literatures. Her publications include the book *Begin Here: Reading Asian North American Autobiographies of Childhood* (University of Hawaii Press, 2007) and a special issue of the journal *MELUS* on "Filipino American Literature" (2004).

Perla and Her Lovely Barbie

Amalia B. Bueno

I told my younger sister Perla that she should not love Barbie so much. I never loved Barbie when I was her age. I didn't even like Barbie. She didn't look real to me. Her big blue eyes so empty and cold scared me. I didn't like Barbie's skinny legs, too. They reminded me of how short and ugly my brown legs are. In fact, nobody in my family looks like Barbie. None of my cousins, none of my neighbors, nobody in my homeroom class looks like her. Nobody in my whole school—except for Elizabeth Watson—looks full-on haole like Barbie.

Now that Perla is 8 and I'm 12, we were old enough to do special things to Barbie, I told Perla. When she asked what kind of things, I said like giving Barbie a hot bath in very hot water. But Perla wouldn't do it. Even when I said that I wouldn't really boil the water, just make it very hot on the gas stove upstairs. I even told Perla I would bring the pot under the house where we played so that nobody would see us. A hot bath wouldn't hurt Barbie because her skin is very hard, I said. But Perla wouldn't believe me. She didn't want to be part of the experiment to see if Barbie's skin would slowly get soft or if it would melt right away.

The Barbie doll that Perla plays with used to belong to our older sister Marina, who goes to high school now. She's 16 and doesn't want anything to do with us anymore. She tries to ignore us, but we like to keep up with whatever is going on in her life. Marina had only one Barbie. Marina passed that Barbie on to me when I was six. I passed her straight on to Perla, who was only two years old at the time. Perla loved that Barbie more and more each year, even though she was given other Barbies by our relatives. This year I noticed that Perla was starting to act more and more like Marina. Like wanting to wear dresses instead of pants and eating less and smiling more. Perla also didn't want to go outside and play in the sun as much, because she didn't want to get her skin darker. Just like Marina, who always put on sunscreen and wore a hat even if it wasn't sunny outside.

I would usually be spending more time with my best friend Joshua, but he is in summer school for the first time. Me and Joshua used to go everywhere after school and during the summer. We played war games under the house, explored the neighborhood streets and drainpipes, caught the Ala Moana bus to the beach by ourselves, and set up camp in his backyard for sleepovers and scared each other by telling spooky stories. But Joshua is taking pre-algebra and band classes this summer. Elizabeth Watson, the only pure haole girl in our school, is in Joshua's band class. And even though he won't admit it, I think Joshua is in love with Elizabeth. I told him last week I was tired of hearing about Lizby this and Lizby that and Lizby said this and Lizby did that. I noticed Joshua's ears turned red when I was saying those things, so that's when I knew he liked her.

And what kind of name is Lizby, I asked? He didn't answer. Her name sounds like a type of lizard, I laughed. I made my voice sound like the *National Geographic* guy on TV and announced, "The Lizby type of gecko lives in Kalihi Valley and plays the flute in the summer." I was only teasing, but Joshua didn't laugh. He didn't say anything to defend her and he didn't say anything back to me, which made me feel funny. So I told him that Elizabeth Watson looks just like a stiff Barbie doll.

Now, Joshua hardly comes over any more. When he does, he is really polite and doesn't want to do anything that will get his clothes dirty or make him sweaty. I miss Joshua and the things we used to do. When I'm bored and there's nothing to do, I hang out with Perla.

One day me and Perla were downstairs under the house, our favorite play spot. Perla was brushing Barbie's hair. Barbie had her Silken Flame outfit, the 1998 reauthorized edition. That's what the box it came in said. Her clothes, even if they were almost seven years old now, looked okay except that the white satin skirt was discolored in some places. The red off-the-shoulder silk top fit over Barbie's big cheechees like a tube top, only it was shaped like McDonald's arches in front. The gold purse and gold belt had some of the shiny stuff come off in some places, but it still looked nice. The black shoes were still good.

Perla had put Barbie in her make believe bed. When she noticed I was playing with matches, she came over to help me. I had found some pieces of our Lola's dried tabako leaves that she left on top of her old Singer sewing machine, preparing to roll them into her fat cigars. Perla watched me twist a small piece of tabako, light it, and twirl the leaf to make spiral smoke. We did this for a little while until it got boring. I told Perla we should stop already because Lola would probably smell the tabako pretty soon and come down and scold us. So we looked for some other things to burn.

We dug a small hole in the ground and decided to herd the stinkbugs into it using the lighted end of the matchsticks. But the stinkbugs would only dig deeper in the hole and go under the dirt. This gave me an idea. I convinced Perla that we should pretend we were at a funeral. We made the hole bigger and looked for things to put inside. I told Perla to go look around the yard for any dead animals. I went upstairs to get some chicken bones from the kitchen trash can.

When I came back to the hole, Perla was already there and she told me she didn't find any dead animals so she got rotten mangoes and white plumerias with brown edges. I told her to go look for some white rocks to line the sides of the hole while I would make a Catholic cross with some Popsicle sticks. We arranged the bones like a whole chicken and buried it. We carefully covered the bones with a thin layer of dirt and put some small gray rocks around the edges because Perla couldn't find any white ones. We put our palms together, kneeled down on our cardboard mat and said an Our Father.

Perla said we should do a novena even though we didn't know how to say the Filipino words. I agreed. We pretended we had just finished the ninth night of prayer and was doing the ending part called Santa Maria, Santa Maria, Santa Maria. I told Perla that I would be the priestess leader and she could be the audience and repeat after me. "Santa Maria, napno ka ti gracia ni Apo Dios," I said very fast and very serious. Perla copied me. Next I said, "Saint Mary, napno ka ti paria and apple juice." Perla laughed when she realized that the Virgin Mary was full of bitter melon and apple juice. But Perla wouldn't repeat after me. I said the Filipino version three times, then the mixed

English version three times. I ended with, "Mother Mary, you are full of bitter melon" and pushed the cross in at the far end where the chicken's head was buried. Perla gasped, surprised at the force I had to use because the dirt was hard.

We dug another hole and put in four rotten mangoes and five dead plumerias. We used the leftover dirt we had from digging the chicken's grave and made a burial mound of dirt like an imu. The dead mangoes and dead plumerias were double dead now. Three big mango leaves straight up in the middle of the mound completed the graveyard scene. I pushed the stems of three fresh plumerias in front of the long green leaves. It looked like a happy mound.

Then I had an idea.

I told Perla wouldn't it be fun to dress Barbie up in nice clothes and then bury her for a few days? Perla didn't want to at first. I told her, Perla Conchita Domingo Asuncion, you said so yourself that you do real things to Barbie, like feed her, and sing to her and comb her hair. Well, I explained, another real thing that happens is people go away and people die. We could practice burying Barbie as just another real thing that people do. We could pretend Barbie died, say a Mass for her and then bury her. Perla still looked hesitant.

So I said we could dig Barbie up nine nights later. I could tell Perla was thinking about it. So, I said, as a bonus, on the tenth day we could pretend that one whole year had gone by and we could have a one-year death anniversary party for Barbie. At that, Perla smiled and said okay. But only if we dressed Barbie really nice and gave her all the things that you are supposed to put inside a coffin. To that, I responded, "No prob-lem-ma."

We were going to make sure that Barbie got everything she needed to live in heaven. I made a list of all the necessary stuff that has to go inside a coffin: money, soap, toothbrush, toothpaste, shoes, change of clothes, non-gold jewelry, needle and thread, wallet, comb, slippers, socks, sleeping clothes.

I hunted around in our mother's clothes drawers and finally found a small, shiny, black satin handkerchief. It was too small to cover all of Barbie but it would cover her from the waist down. The black would look nice against her red top, I thought. I found a dollar bill in my dad's ashtray of loose change. I found a new toothbrush in the medicine cabinet. I put a little toothpaste on it so that I wouldn't have to take the whole tube of toothpaste. Perla brought down Barbie's pajama set and pink plastic shoes. She also took a pair of shorts and a T-shirt set from her California Girl Suntan Barbie. We borrowed a pair of fake silver and diamond earrings that Marina didn't use anymore. We knew she wouldn't miss it because she left it on the crowded bathroom counter. We found a needle and some thread in Lola's sewing machine drawer. The only thing we needed was socks.

I told Perla that since this was Hawaii, we didn't need any socks because Barbie was going to Hawaii heaven where it was warm all year. But Perla insisted and would not bury Barbie without sending her off with a pair of socks. I told Perla the container was too full already and if we added one more item then it would look like Barbie was suffocating. Perla wouldn't budge and said that it was her doll and she could bury her any way she wanted to.

When I returned under the house where Perla was waiting, I brought a larger, round Tupperware container and a pair of tiny booties. It had belonged to our 10-month old brother, Marcelino, who had outgrown them. I had hoped this would satisfy Perla's need and it did, especially when I said that one bootie would keep both of Barbie's feet warm at the same time.

While Perla dressed Barbie in her Silken Flame outfit and arranged all the coffin items inside the Tupperware coffin, I dug a round hole with the shovel my grandpa kept in the corner tool shed next to the avocado tree. When it was deep enough, I lined the hole with one of my dad's old stained T-shirts which I found lying around in the garage. He used it as a rag, so I figured nobody would miss it. I was already calculating how much or how little trouble I would get into for each of the missing items.

We buried Barbie by doing all the serious things we saw adults do at a funeral. I said a few words about how much happiness she brought to Marina, and Perla, and many girls around the world. Perla said how much she loved Barbie and how she wished to be like Barbie when she grew up. Then Perla pretended to cry and chant and howl like the old Filipino women at the funerals. I started laughing but stopped when Perla gave me the stinkiest eye I ever got from any six year old. I joined her in the howling and chanting about Ken, about Barbie's parents, about the Mattel Company, and how we would all be together soon.

For the next nine days we were supposed to wear black and pray. We decided that as long as we had something black on us, like a piece of black thread hanging over the waistband of our shorts, it was okay. We also decided that it was okay to laugh out loud, to go out to play with our friends, to sweep the floor, and to watch television comedy reruns like *Gilligan's Island*. We made our own rules because it was our funeral. And we got to decide how much the relatives of the dead person should be sad or relieved or happy.

On the ninth day, Marina asked us if we had taken her new toothbrush. Our mother had already asked us about her satin handkerchief and I had to pretend I only saw a white scarf in the living room. Our Lola had also asked us about a needle she was sure she left in her sewing machine drawer. We were planning to put everything back on the tenth day after we dug Barbie up and had her one-year death anniversary party.

The next day, exactly 10 days after the burial, Marina asked if we had seen her earrings. It just so happened that me and Perla answered her at the exact same time, using the exact same words, "No, we didn't see it." That was probably why Marina didn't believe us. She threatened to tell our dad something about us digging a big hole under the house, her missing toothbrush and earrings, and a Barbie doll she hadn't seen Perla play with in over a week.

After we dug up Barbie, we didn't feel like having a one-year death anniversary party. Perla was disappointed that Barbie did not seem that pretty anymore. And her beautiful clothes were a little dirty. After not playing with Barbie for more than a week, she didn't seem to miss her as much as she thought she would. Now she mostly puts Barbie up on the shelf by her bed.

Perla takes Barbie down once in a while to let Barbie sit quietly next to her. I knew she would end up not loving Barbie so much. 🐟

Double Dutch

Leslieann Hobayan

*E*ight years old. Woodlake Drive. Alicia's driveway rolls uphill, stretches in a yawn alongside the dark brown-shingled house. A few of her friends from the public school have come over to play. They've got an extra long jump rope. Someone grabs both ends. Another hugs the opposite loop behind her, around the waist. They begin turning—one side turns into the center, then the other—an alternating fashion that reminds Maria Elizabeth of her mother's hand mixer when she makes that chiffon cake she loves so much. And that butter icing. Yum. *One, two, buckle my shoe...*Alicia and her friends begin singing. Maria Elizabeth watches with excitement. The only kind of jump rope she's seen has been in the church parking lot during recess. Here, they're jumping with two ropes instead of one. She takes note of the girls' footwork, memorizes it; she's always been quick. Her nun teachers are impressed with her consistent A's, but they say it's because she's Asian—she's supposed to be studious and dedicated. Her eyes are locked on the twirl. She catches the rhythm of the song, the slap of ropes on asphalt. It's contagious.

The second verse. One girl leaps out of the spiraling ropes. The others call out—*Maria Elizabeth, come on! You can do it.* She hates the fact that her parents gave her two first names, the fact that her middle name is her mother's maiden name. It sounds so strange. Maria Elizabeth Rañola Ramos. Two first names and two last names. But that's what Filipinos do, her mother explained. *Maria Elizabeth, let's see what you got.* She stands at an angle, near one of the rope-turners, like the others have, to enter the magical dome. She nods her head in rhythm. *One, two, buckle my shoe...*She jumps. Step, step. Step, step. This is more like dancing. Nothing like jump rope with her schoolmates, hopping stiff in navy uniforms and Buster Browns. Step, step. Step, step. This is more fun. She can't wait to show her friends at school. She wonders where to get an extra rope.

She jumps out so another can jump in. Alicia slides in and calls to another girl. Now two are caught in the spinning ropes, stepping in time. A new song starts. *Eenie Meenie Douce-A-lini Oop Pop Pop-pa-lini.* They hop on one foot, then switch to the other. Then quick steps, a clap beneath a raised leg. Switch. Turn. Hop. Clap. Step, step. Twist. Turn. Switch. Alicia steps out, two more step in. Three! Three girls slapping against blacktop inside the twirl. Clapping of hands. Step, step. Skin on shirt, on sneaker, on skin. Step, step.

We can't tell you where it started

We don't know where it's been

But have no doubt, the word is out

Double Dutch is in.

After a few more songs, the girls grow tired. They drop the ropes, plop down on a small patch of grass near the garage. *Let's braid hair.* Someone produces a box of ponytail holders with marble ends. Alicia crawls over to Maria Elizabeth, settles behind her, and begins to section off black coarse hair.

"Your hair is a tree, just like mine—let's tame it. My ma does it for me all the time." She pulls and tugs. Maria Elizabeth's face winces just a little but she makes no sound. She likes it when people play with her hair. The other girls have paired off—one braiding or re-braiding another's hair. They're all talking at once. *You hear 'bout Malcolm? Got in trouble for running in the hall. Fool. Oh yeah? What 'bout Rachel?* The conversations move from school gossip to dreams of the future. *When I grow up, I wanna be a model. Oh yeah? Keep dreamin 'cause you ain't skinny enough for that.*

The sun begins to set. It's time for her to run home—four houses down. She hops onto her banana seat bicycle and waves sideways to Alicia and her friends as she pedals down the street to the little white house with red shutters. Handlebar streamers fluttering in the wind of her speed, she wonders what they're having for dinner tonight. She hopes it's nilaga, her favorite. She wonders if her father will be home for dinner. This has been a great day.

She throws down her bike on the driveway and bursts through the red front door. She sees her mother setting the table and immediately helps her. She is excited about this new thing she's learned. Her tongue slack with new slang, she begins to tell her mother all about it.

"Ma! Me and Alicia—" Before she even gets to the part about dancing, her mother slaps her mouth and pinches her ear.

"'Ma'? What is this 'Ma'? Who are you talking to? I am your Mommy. Don't ever talk like that again, hah?"

"But—"

"I don't want to hear it. If your dad hears you, hala," her mother warns. Maria Elizabeth is confused. She rubs the side of her mouth as if to erase the sting. "And what is that in your head? It looks ugly. Pangit na pangit." Maria Elizabeth runs to the bathroom to look in the mirror, to see herself in braids. There are footsteps approaching the kitchen. Her father sits down at the table. She's not sure why, but she doesn't want to leave the bathroom. Her mother calls her to the table. She must go.

At the kitchen table, her father is focused on the food, scooping rice with impeccable precision. Not one grain of rice out of place. Once he has a little bit of every dish on the table, he looks up from his plate. He gasps.

"What is that in your head?"

"Braids. You like them?" Maria Elizabeth glows.

"Ay, pangit talaga." He repeats her mother's opinion. The braids are ugly. "What's the matter with you? Why do you want that hairstyle? Are you trying to be Black?"

Maria Elizabeth shrugs.

"She was playing with that girl in the brown house," her mother says.

"I don't want you playing with that Black girl anymore," her father commands.

"But—" Maria Elizabeth knows better than to interrupt her father. Still, she doesn't know why she can't play with Alicia.

"And you should respect your mother. What is this 'Ma'? What's next? You'll call me 'Da'? Humph!"

"But—" She doesn't know what she did wrong.

"That's it. No more."

"But Dad, I—"

"I said no."

"But we didn't do anything."

"Ay, tigas ng ulo mo—your dad said no already. Huwag magsasalita." Her mother intervenes before Maria Elizabeth pushes too far, before she tests her father's short-lived patience. The kitchen is silent for a long moment. Then the clank of spoons and forks against dishes resumes. Nothing more is said on the matter.

Soon, because the silence is uncomfortable, her mother begins to speak to her father in Tagalog, asking him about his day at the hospital, if he had any new patients. This is not a conversation meant for her. Maria Elizabeth looks over at her younger brother who has no idea what just happened. He is only five and is content with his spoon, pushing his rice around the plate, making piles and then mashing them down. Suddenly, she's no longer hungry. She looks down at her plate, stares at the bite-sized pieces of beef soaking in broth and soy sauce. She is reminded of something.

Yesterday, she and her mother were at the grocery store, in the meat section. She remembers her mother struggling to get the attention of the fat man with a white coat—a coat much like her father's hospital coat; he looked like Santa Claus. His face was scrunched up the entire time her mother spoke to him; she was asking for ox tail. Maria Elizabeth didn't like ox tail. The man talked loudly and slowly to her mother, as if she were deaf. *Whaaaat do youuuuu neeeeeed?* She noticed her mother's voice drop when she repeated her request—she sounded like a boy.

Santa didn't seem very nice; he only talked louder and more slowly. Then, her mother grabbed Maria Elizabeth's hand and they left the store quickly. They never did get the ox tail.

"Maria Elizabeth, finish your food." She's brought back to the kitchen. She's still not hungry. She forces herself to finish what is on her plate so she can be invisible. A clean plate grants permission to leave the table, to disappear. So she does.

The next day, she doesn't tell her school friends about double dutch, doesn't mention the spiraling ropes, the dancing. Nothing. She says nothing all day. Walking home from the bus stop, she tries to avoid Alicia. Her walk picks up into a sprint. She looks away from Alicia's house as she races past. For a long time, Maria Elizabeth stays inside the little white house with red shutters, watches TV, says nothing. 🦋

Here in the States

Rashaan Alexis Meneses

"Alma, can you help?" I hear Nanay call from my little brother and sister's room. It's Friday morning, and we're running late 'cause Frankie peed in his pants and Nanay has to help him wash. I hide in the hallway, trying not to let Nanay see me. She peels my brother's pants off, one leg at a time. I can smell the pee from where I'm standing. It's a sour smell that reminds me of the hospital Tatay works at. We hardly see him anymore 'cause he's always at work.

I go to the kitchen instead, which is as far away in the apartment as I can get from that smell. Nita, Frankie's twin, is at the table drowning a waffle in a pool of syrup.

"Morning," she says before taking a big bite.

All I can think about is how I'm supposed to be at school 20 minutes earlier than usual 'cause we have a field trip. When Ms. Janairo announced we raised enough money to go somewhere before our last year of middle school, we thought it'd be Disneyland or Universal Studios, but when she told us we were visiting the LA Museum of Art, everyone groaned. We said we'd rather stay in Long Beach. Even though I'm not interested in seeing a bunch of stuffy paintings, today's the big day and I don't want to be late.

"Alma!" I hear Nanay call again, but there's no way I'm answering. Nanay should've remembered my trip. She should know I have to leave soon.

Ever since we moved to the States, I've had to look after my brother and sister, clean their messes, cook their food— do everything! Back in the Philippines, our house was tidier. The meals weren't burned at the edges or left frozen in the middle. Our housekeeper, Amalia, would cook breakfast, merienda and dinner. Now we're even lucky if Nanay comes home in time to make something. Usually I end up having to and I hate cooking.

I turn to the clock and watch the second-hand race. Nanay says the twins are too young to walk to school alone, so I have to sit and wait while Nita spoons butter into her mouth and Nanay helps Frankie find a clean pair of pants. This wasn't at all what I thought it'd be like when we came here.

Underneath the clock is an old picture of Nanay. She taught history at the University of San Carlos in Cebu. I remember she'd come home with arms full of books and stay up late reading students' papers marking them with a red pen. In this picture, Nanay stands proudly next to some men she worked with; everyone's dressed in fancy suits. All these professors used to come over on weekends and holidays for formal dinner parties that Nanay liked to host. Nanay's face was young and fresh then. She didn't have any of the worry wrinkles she has now. I have to look away 'cause Nanay's face then doesn't match what I see today.

Finally, Nita drops her spoon. "I'm done," she announces.

"Let's go!" I say, getting up.

Nanay and Frankie are at the door now. Nanay's helping him with his backpack.

"I've been calling you, Alma. What were you doing?" she asks. Her hair hangs loose past her shoulders. She still has to put it in a bun the way she always does. Nanay looks tired when she doesn't have any makeup on. She wears tennis shoes to work now instead of those shiny pumps she used to always buy. She yawns loud, her mouth gaping. I know I shouldn't be, but I'm glad she feels bad. She deserves it.

"I was with Nita," I say, looking her straight in the eyes.

"I needed you," she flashes anger at me, and I feel like kicking something but I can't.

Instead, I say, "I'm not supposed to take care of Nita and Frankie all the time. You're the mom, you should do it."

Soon as those words come out, I expect Nanay to smack me but she just stares back with a look of surprise. It's this look more than anything that makes me feel like I'm shrinking, like I could disappear right there and then if Nanay wants me to. I don't expect it when she grabs my arm and gives me a quick, angry jerk.

"What's the matter with you?"

Frankie and Nita stand there in complete six-year old fear. Their eyes are wide and they are speechless. All I know is I was mad and I wanted Nanay to know just how much. Frankie lets out a whimper, confused and scared by what just happened.

Nanay turns to him. "It's okay, sweetie," she says, giving him a reassuring hug. She eyes me again and I look away wishing I was at the museum already.

I make the kids race me down Santa Fe Avenue, their little legs move as fast as they can to keep up. I try my best not to think of Nanay. Part of me feels good for saying what I've been wanting to for a long time. It's a tiny part, but enough for now.

After dropping off my brother and sister, I make it just in time for the headcount in the parking lot.

"Alma!" my best friend, June, calls from the line. I steal a place next to her and ignore the nasty glances from Marta and Becca.

The bus ride is bumpy and loud like always. Five minutes into it and I'm already carsick. June is probably the most excited. Her dad was an artist and made a lot of money back in Manila. Here in the States, he works as a cashier at Vons. He gives us the double coupon discount every time.

June keeps talking about the different works we're going to see. Her family goes to museums when they can. According to June, their last trip to L-A-C-M-A, that's what she calls it, was a year ago.

"You don't understand. It's a good time to go. Modigliani's there."

"What's a Mogdilio?" I try not to let her see me roll my eyes.

"He's a famous Italian painter—wait, no. He's from France, I think. Oh, I forget," she waves her hand in the air and leans back in our seat.

"Whatever," I say looking out the window to see the endless gray concrete that makes the 110 Freeway. The bus ride takes forever. The highway is packed with cars. Everyone is going to work. Eric Padilla and Dexter Bustamante, who sit behind us, start kicking the back of our seat out of boredom.

"Knock it off!" I yell without turning around.

"Whatsa matter, Alma, you on your period?" Dexter teases while Eric laughs.

"Shut up!"

June turns to them, "How do you even know what a period is?" she asks.

"My mom's a nurse!" Dexter says kicking our seat again.

"How come she tells you about girly things? Guess she doesn't think you need to know about guy stuff, since you act like a sissy."

Dexter's smile disappears and June promptly turns around with a satisfied grin.

Things quiet down after an hour. Some students fall asleep. We're in L.A. City now. I can tell 'cause there are tall buildings in the distance and the sky's covered with a light-brown haze. I can't help but think of this morning and how I ran out on Nanay. Everything was left a mess, dirty dishes on the table, and Frankie's pee-stained pants still on the floor, stinking up the apartment.

Life in the States has been smaller and grungier compared to what we used to have. In Cebu, we had a swimming pool in the backyard and a jet stream bathtub that could fit three people. Nanay used to let me bathe in it on weekends. Frankie and Nita never did 'cause they were too small. They have no idea about the Philippines, but I remember it all. I remember the smell of the rains. The soft-sucky feel of the mud as you walk on it. I remember eating ripe banana and mangos that Amalia would bring every morning with fresh pan de sal. I miss the sweet creamy taste of coffee she let me drink when Nanay was at work.

Finally, we turn off the freeway and enter a neighborhood. Everyone's grumpy 'cause it's taken a lot longer than expected. The undersides of my legs are sweaty and stick to the plastic bus seats. I try pulling them off slowly but it hurts and I know there will be marks left on the back of my legs.

"Oh my God!" Marisa, the girl sitting across from us says, "Look at these."

Everyone turns to their windows and we see huge estates, one giant mansion after another. There is a house with Roman columns and a horse-shaped driveway in front. Another house is made completely of glass; from floor to ceiling, it's just all windows. But it's not like June and I haven't seen mansions like this before. It's not like we never lived in our own back home. We both turn to the front of the bus and stare at the road ahead of us. I know what June's thinking but she doesn't say anything. We never do anymore.

Then I see her. How can I not? She's on the sidewalk, and we're driving by her. I almost want to jump and yell, "Nanay" but for some reason I don't. I sit still and watch 'cause she is there pushing a fancy stroller, the nice kind with cherry-patterned cloth all over and a canopy. It's not like the rickety hand-me-down we got for the twins. Ours was so flimsy it could pass for a toy. Skipping next to Nanay is a little blonde girl. I think her name is Amy. Her hair is in golden pigtails, and she's wearing the cool new sneakers my friend Tanya came to school in last week. When I asked Nanay for the same pair, her face soured and she ordered me to set the table.

Nanay doesn't see me. She's too busy fussing over the baby. Amy is twirling on the sidewalk doing some silly ballet performance for no one but herself. She stops and points to something across the street. Nanay barely acknowledges. She's still rearranging the blanket for the baby. The bus stalls long enough for me to see Amy give my nanay a forceful tug of the arm, and Nanay doesn't snap or give that mean, angry look I know I'd get. Instead her lips curve into something I guess is supposed to be a smile but I know isn't and Nanay tries to politely get out from Amy's grip. Then the bus lurches forward before I can see what happens next.

At the museum, June leads me around showing me her favorite pieces. She has a lot. She tries to explain Impressionism, which was a bunch of French guys who went out on a limb to create watery paintings. I can't wait until this day is over. I didn't care about this dusty museum before. Now I just want to hide under the bed sheets and never come out.

I keep wondering where Nanay is and what she's doing. I know she's out there somewhere cleaning Amy and that baby's mess. I take a deep breath but my insides are burning. I wish I was home right now with Nanay telling me to put away the dishes or do my homework. I wish I was with Nanay on that walk instead of Amy. I feel raw like a pumpkin that has all its seeds and pulp scraped out. I can't shake how that little girl pulled my nanay's arm and the look in my nanay's eyes.

After hours of stupid art, we finally go home. The drive back doesn't take as long. Everyone is tired. Eric and Dexter give one good kick to the back of our seat but end up falling asleep like the rest of the class. I don't say anything to June about Nanay. There isn't any point. It wasn't like her dad wasn't doing the same thing. He used to be a great artist. Now he bags groceries.

~

When Frankie, Nita, and I get home, the house is quiet. Only the tick of the living room clock and the steady beat of the kitchen's leaky faucet fill the apartment. I shut the door and the kids race to the TV.

I sit in the kitchen. I know I should start dinner but I don't feel right. I keep picturing Nanay in those maid's outfits with the black dress, the white apron and those stupid hats. It makes me mad, but there's nothing I can do about it.

"Aren't you gonna make the rice?" Nita comes into the kitchen and heads for the fridge. I just shake my head.

"Want me to do it?" she asks.

I watch her reflection in the window as she pours a glass of milk. I turn to her and she gives me a little smile before taking a long gulp. She chugs that milk and sets the glass on the table so loud I think it might crack. She is breathing heavy now like she has just come up for air from swimming underwater.

"Go 'head," I mumble. I kind of want her to leave me alone but at the same time I'm glad she's here. She runs to the plastic bin where we keep our Calrose and sings to herself as she fills the bowl, then rinses the grains in the sink three times before setting it in the rice cooker. With a flick of the switch the machine is on and the rice is cooking.

"All done," she smiles, before going back to the living room. I sit some more staring at the floor. It's getting dark outside. I can hear voices from the alley. Cars drive by, and our apartment starts to smell of exhaust. Finally, I hear keys rattling and the front door creaks open. All of a sudden, I'm scared Nanay will still be mad at me, that she'll know I saw her when I wasn't supposed to.

"Hi, Nanay!" the twins greet her. I know they won't bother to get their butts off the floor, that Nanay will have to stoop over and ask for a kiss. Without seeing any of it, I know that's what's happening. I hear her go to the bedroom first. She is taking her shoes off and putting her hair down. She will have that long, tired expression on her face like she always does when she comes home from work, smelling of Pine-Sol and rubber gloves.

"How was your day?" she asks turning on the light. She doesn't seem upset and I wonder if she's forgotten about this morning or is too exhausted to deal with it.

"OK."

"Just OK?" she opens the fridge and the door hinges give a high-pitched screech. Tatay still needs to fix it but hasn't had the time.

"We went to an art museum."

"Was it fun?"

I shrug, "June really liked it." I keep waiting for Nanay to say something about how I acted earlier, but she doesn't. She is pouring soy sauce and white vinegar into a pot.

"Nanay," my voice sounds like it's far away, like my ears have popped and I can barely hear myself. I play with the empty glass Nita left. A milky residue still clings to its insides. Before I know it, I ask the one question that's been gnawing at me, "Is this what you thought it would be?"

Her back is turned against me as she cooks. She stops what she is doing.

"What do you mean?" she mutters in that dismissive way, when her thoughts are someplace else I sense she doesn't want me to be.

I hesitate. I don't want her to get mad, but I know what I saw and I know I'll never forget it. I get up from my seat and stand next to her. She is at the stove now stirring cornstarch into the pot so the sauce will thicken. I can tell she's really tired by the way she breathes, leaning over the food, like she could fall asleep right there.

"Did you think we'd end up like this?" I ask. This time my heart is beating so fast, it feels like it's throbbing in my ears.

She lets out a long sigh, relaxes her shoulders then looks at me. "I'm not sure what I thought," she says leaning over to give me a gentle kiss.

I smile back at her, not knowing what to say next. Instead, I raise my right hand over the stovetop like an offering and ask, "Want me to help?" 🌺

Nurse Rita

Paulino Lim Jr.

*H*er chilled face whiffed garlic and pepper as she entered the living room, softly lit by a lamp beside the sofa with an Ifugao blanket folded on its back. Shutting the door, she slipped off her shoes and dragged herself to the kitchen.

"Pa, I'm home," she called.

Her father at the sink washing dishes did not turn his gray head. Could be the water running, she thought, or he'd indeed become hard of hearing. It was another of his complaints about growing old, along with arthritis and high blood pressure. The cold was his reason to move the family from Chicago to California when he retired five years ago, working in the kitchen of a nursing home.

Raising a family of three children in a crowded tenement near Chinatown, he had allowed his sons to choose their careers but saw no other future for his daughter Rita than as a caregiver in a nursing home. The oldest son Arturo became an accountant and worked for the Internal Revenue Service. The youngest Chris became a cop.

Her father soon complained that the no-snow winter in Orange County dried his skin and gave him rash, itchy spots on his stomach and back. He used this as excuse to spend the winter months in Pangasinan. Like the moneyed New Yorkers who migrated to Florida and Canadians who spent their winter in Palm Springs, her father had become a snowbird living on a shoestring. Rita's mother had gone back to stay. Converted to pesos, her monthly Social Security check of four hundred dollars was more than the salary of a school superintendent. When she walked to the church and market, visited neighbors and relatives, a maid sheltered her with an umbrella from the sun and sudden rain.

Rita tugged at the polyester sweater covering her father's bony frame, the sleeves rolled above the yellow latex gloves swishing in the steamy sink.

"Rita, you're home," he said, shutting the faucet. "I cooked chicken adobo, also made ampalaya salad. Let me get you a plate."

"No, Pa, I'm not hungry."

"You should taste the ampalaya. It's as good as the ones I grow in summer."

"I'm too tired to eat."

He muttered, "You don't like to eat after working this late, I know."

"I'll have tea," she said, sitting at the kitchen table cluttered with avocados, apples and a splotchy papaya. Without the spots, he once told her, the papaya sold for $2.69 at Ralphs. At the Mexican market, it cost less than a dollar. Given the ethnic mix in the Santa Ana District of Orange County, he had made a routine of his shopping every two weeks: fruits and goat cheese at the Mexican market; greens and pork bones at the

Vietnamese; bagoong, longaniza and video rentals of Tagalog movies at the Filipino market.

He heated a cup of water in the microwave oven and dropped a chamomile teabag in it.

"What time did Esme go to bed?" Rita asked.

"Not too long ago. Perhaps she's still awake. She was doing her English homework. She asked me to help."

"Did you?"

"She brought home a copy of Martin Luther King's speech "I Have a Dream." She asked me what an analogy was. How the hell should I know?"

Rita braced herself for things he'd often rattle. Spend more time with Esmeralda. Don't let her stay in the house by herself after school, especially when I'm gone. She'd taken it as a reproach even if he didn't mean to, blaming her for being a single mother.

He had turned on the water and finished washing the dishes. He said, "Well, you can take the adobo to work tomorrow. I'll put it in a plastic container."

Rita nodded. "And the ampalaya, too. I'll give it to Ofie. She's read that the Germans think ampalaya prevents heart disease."

"I heard parts of that speech on TV when King was assassinated. You were a baby then."

"Why did Esme ask about analogy?"

"The teacher brought it up. A student said racism is like hunger. It'll never go away. Does analogy mean truth?"

"Comparing hunger to racism is the analogy. Maybe it's true. There will always be haters of Blacks and Jews."

Her father shrugged. "Tell Ofelia you're not doing overtime when I'm gone."

She squelched reminding him what he once said, "Blacks aren't smart enough to be quarterbacks in the NFL." She had long decided that her father deserved more thanks than blame for cleaning the house, cooking their meals, tending a summer garden, and taking care of Esme.

At times, when her feet ached or she came home after putting in twelve hours at work, she'd wonder. If only her parents had sent her to a nursing, instead of a vocational, school, perhaps she'd have an RN and not LVN degree, a registered nurse instead of a licensed vocational nurse. She could be working at a hospital instead of a nursing home, earning as much as Ofelia who got paid $17 more per hour than she got.

"RN ako sa atin," was the familiar refrain of Filipinos who had not passed the California exams to qualify as nurses. Literally, *I was an RN at ours,* but overseas Filipinos understood *sa atin* to mean "our country."

Most graduated from nursing colleges but Rita had known a few exceptions. Lito, an LVN for four years, found a job in Michigan as an electrical engineer, his other college degree. Another vocational nurse, Jaime who recently turned 40, had confided in her that he was an optometrist in Cebu. Many Filipinos had cast their lots with employment agencies that brought them to the States and found them jobs as caregivers, collecting 60 percent of their paycheck. All fair, they agreed, since the agency provided housing and secured licenses for them. If on their own they found other jobs, like the engineer Lito who had four children in Iloilo, so much the better. They could then join the more than eight million overseas Filipinos whose dollar remittances kept the country's economy afloat.

Projected by the Central Bank of the Philippines, the figure for the year was $12.3 billion. It was $10.7 billion the previous year.

Rita read these figures in newspapers full of ads, edited by Filipino journalists and gratis at Kasaysayan, a store that sold lechon on Sundays. She did not really know what the numbers meant. She only knew that when she worked overtime she got time and half pay. She had gotten tired of filing papers to get her Mexican ex-husband to pay the four hundred dollars for child support that the divorce judge had decreed. But their 20-year-old Hugo lived with him and Javier now had a child by a Guatemalan woman.

The reproach finally came. "Esme needs you. She needs you here when the school bus drops her off. She can't be here by herself while you're at work."

"I see you've started packing," Rita said, wanting to change the topic. She had blamed herself when her son Hugo dropped out of high school, after being involved in a Latino gang. He now pumped gas at a Chevron station. How well she knew the odds. Educate Esme, let her finish college or she'd spend her life clerking at a department store or working as a bank teller. She blotted any image of Esme as a caregiver.

"I'm only taking clothes to leave behind when I return," the father said. I know they'd want money instead."

A plaint of Filipinos at the nursing home, spoken with no bitterness, "Take lots of pasalubong and treat your friends at fancy mall restaurants." Jaime talked about eating at a shabu-shabu restaurant where diners had individual cooking bowls at the table before them with seasoned and boiled slices of lamb, salmon, oysters and mushrooms to their liking.

Early the following morning, Rita knelt by her daughter's bedside and gently shook her shoulder. She has Javier's heart-shaped face, Rita thought, not oval like mine, but she has my eyes. She used to make the rounds to give patients their medications, before her promotion to head Nurse's Station 2. Patricia, a retired schoolteacher whose buck-toothed face became sharper after lying in bed for over three years, once told her, "Your eyes sparkle when you smile." Another long-time resident everyone called Bob, a lanky man from Iowa who had a stroke seven years ago, had said, "You have such beautiful eyes." She found her sense of self and worth validated by people living out the tatters of their days.

"Wake up, baby, time to go to school." Rita glanced at the framed snapshot on the bed stand, showing Esme between Javier and Mickey Mouse.

Esme's eyelids crinkled. Rita knew she was pretending sleep. She wiggled her fore and middle finger on Esme's armpit.

"Mommy, you're mean."

Rita hugged her. "Hush, baby. Grandpa is making you pancakes for breakfast."

"Miss Benson says you're coming for me after school."

"Yes, baby. Wait for me at school. Your teacher wants to talk to me."

"Miss Benson told me."

"Have you been a good girl?"

"I miss my friends at the other school."

"You'll find new friends. We'll invite them to your next birthday party."

Checking her watch, Rita helped Esme dress and led her to the kitchen table. Her father had cleared it and laid out a bowl of apples and saucer of sliced papayas and plates of pancakes and sausages.

"Listen, baby, Grandpa will walk you to the bus stop. Mommy is going to work now."

Her father came out of his room, "Don't forget the adobo and ampalaya in the refrigerator.

~

Rita was seated behind the counter of Nurse's Station 2, flipping through a clipboard of patients' charts when Ofelia walked in. The Call-Ex metal plate on the wall below the clock kept buzzing. Its array of numbered inch-square bulbs lit up when patients pressed a wired button by their bedside. To mask its sound when talking to doctors and relatives of patients, Rita cupped the phone with her other hand.

"We had two deaths last night," Ofelia said in a Tagalog undertone. Rita seldom saw her smile. Ofelia was in her 50s, her hair flecked with gray softened her square face but not a severe look that hinted pain.

"Two, really?" Rita said.

"The patient in Room 10 who'd gone into hospice care a week ago."

"Walter," Rita said, thinking of his wife Betty who visited him every day. She also did volunteer work, pushing wheelchairs and tacking flyers on bulletin boards, and got a free lunch for it. A drunk driver had hit Walter making a left hand turn at an intersection and left half his body paralyzed. He languished in the nursing home for almost ten years.

Ofelia had instructed her on the treatment of patients in hospice care given a prognosis of six months or less to live. Some refused aggressive treatment, such as open-heart surgery or another round of chemotherapy. In Walter's case, it was his body that rejected medication and food. He was put on morphine until he died.

"Bernice in Room 22 also died."

"Finally," Rita sighed with relief. She did not recall anyone visiting Bernice who had to be spoon-fed. The bulletin board in her room had a picture of her husband wearing his pilot uniform in World War II. When all her savings had been spent, Social Security put her house up for sale. Enterprising employees at the nursing home got into a bidding war. A Filipino nurse got the bid after bidding twenty thousand dollars more than the asking price.

"Can you put in four more hours today?"

"Ofie, I can't. I'm going to Esme's school."

"I forgot. She's now in a public school, isn't she?"

"Javier stopped paying her tuition at the Christian school."

"Is that why you're putting in a lot of overtime?"

She nodded. She was also thinking she could make trips to countries other than the Philippines and Mexico. Javier once took her to Guadalajara. She'd listened to Filipinos after the Sunday Mass talking about trips to Barcelona, Montreal, and Rome. Maribel, an accountant, once bragged about attending a Mass at the Vatican officiated by Pope John Paul II.

Rita and Ofelia gave a knowing look at each other when they heard a voice down the hallway. Soon Jerome in his wheelchair came into view. "Lemme out of here. Would somebody please get me out of here? I want to get me out here."

A resident physician at the nursing home once said, "Jerome must have been an English teacher. He's gone through all the possible ways of saying the same thing."

Attendants pushed medicine and cleaning carts past his wheelchair. Jerome stopped, turned his sunken and stubbled face to Rita and Ofelia, and said, "Do get me out of here."

Ofelia lifted a hand at Shaheen who was wheeling a patient he'd just bathed and pointed to Jerome. Rita had heard that Shaheen, a fair-skinned Muslim from Mindanao, was supporting three children by different wives.

Jerome kept his litany. When Shaheen began to push his chair, he said, "Will someone please scratch my back?"

Rita smiled when Shaheen freed a hand from pushing the wheelchair to rub Jerome's back. She turned to Ofelia frowning at a printout and said. "Ask Jaime to work overtime. I hear he's going to Cebu."

"Again. He just went last summer. I thought he was bringing back a wife."

"I heard that the woman, also a nurse, already has a child, as old as Esme. She'll have a harder time getting a visa."

"How old is your daughter?"

"Ten, eleven soon."

"She'll soon be bugging you for a cell phone and iPod."

Rita paused. It sounded like her father but did not have the sting of a reproach. Ophelia was telling her, it seemed, she should spend as much time with Esme as she could, talk to her, make her listen, before she tuned her out with wired plugs in her ears.

~

The students were leaving La Quinta Elementary School in family cars and yellow school busses, when Rita drove into the parking lot. She walked on the hallway to the school office, taking deep breaths of air free from the smell of antiseptics and soiled linen. She glanced at classrooms now emptied of children, saw teachers gathering books and papers. At the reception counter, she wrote her name on the Visitors List and was directed to Room 18.

Miss Benson stood up from her desk, extending a hand. "Mrs. Cardenas, so glad you can make it."

Their palms touched. Rita saw the pale complexion and prominent cheekbones, the long sleeved maroon shirt and copious black hair parted at the shoulders falling back and on her breast.

"Please take a seat. Esme is waiting for you in the Nurse's Office. I understand you're also a nurse."

Rita nodded, sitting at a student's chair.

"We have a pediatric nurse, very good with the children."

"That's nice," Rita said, thinking, I guess that makes me a geriatric nurse.

"Esme's transcript from the Baptist school shows that she got mostly A's and B's there. I'm concerned, so far she's doing D and F work."

Rita shifted in her chair, her body bracing itself like the time she got the call that Hugo had been arrested. His Latino gang got in a brawl with a Black gang.

"Esme tells me you're separated from her dad. I hope you don't mind my bringing this up."

"Not at all."

"She thinks you're getting back together again."

"We're divorced."

"I thought so. Esme seems distracted. She keeps her book open during silent reading periods, but I don't see her turn the page."

"What can I do?"

"You could enroll Esme in a tutorial program approved by the school. She'll be picked up with other kids after school and driven back home."

"How much is it going to cost?"

"Four hundred dollars a month."

Rita smiled to herself, as though she remembered a joke. Four hundred dollars, Javier's child-support he hasn't paid in months, the tuition at the religious school and my mother's monthly check from Social Security.

"Esme also tells me you often come home late from work."

"Her grandfather, my dad, babysits her."

"Esme tells me he locks himself up in his room and watches Filipino videos. Does Esme also have a TV in her room?"

"She does."

"You probably need to curtail her TV time. Get her to read more. There's something else that worries me. Is it true that sometimes she's left alone in the house?"

Rita frowned. More bad news, worse than Esme's failing grades?

"You know there's a law against keeping a latchkey child at home."

"Latchkey child?"

"A child left alone and unsupervised because the parents are at work. You could be cited and taken to court."

"My dad watches her when I'm at work." Rita winced at what she'd just said. Her father gave Esme supper, cleaned up the kitchen and slipped Filipino videos in the VCR.

"Esme is a very pretty child. Your father must enjoy having her around, as much as you do."

Rita nodded, not in assent but to show she was listening.

"Something my mother said I should keep in mind if I decide to have children. She says they grow up faster in America than in Portugal. She was born in Lisbon."

Miss Benson's voice rasped, the toll on the teacher's vocal chords at day's end. Rita wondered, was Miss Benson facing a decision young women have at the start of a career, to have a child before it's too late. Maybe, like Ofie, Miss Benson was only telling her the time she spent with Esme while still a child was precious.

"You should consider the tutorial program. Give it a try for a month or two. See if it helps Esme. She's really quite far behind in her work."

The interview ended. She told Miss Benson she'd let her know if she'd enroll Esme in the after-school tutorial.

The nurse waved and smiled when Rita appeared at the door. A genuine smile? Rita thought, perhaps the smile came easy when you dealt with children. Not tacked on to a patchwork of feelings and emotions at the nursing home.

"Mommy," Esme said, as they walked down the hallway to the parking lot, "it's the first time you're picking me up from school."

Rita reached for Esme's shoulder and drew her close, tight as a hug. Esme nudged her back and smiled. Rita began to match her step with her daughter's. Esme caught on, giggling and laughing. Soon they were walking fast, as though their legs were in a potato sack racing toward the finish line. ❧

How My Mother Flew

Dean Francis Alfar

Language for Two

A I always suspected that, like me, my mother hated going to family reunions. An outsider would never know it, not from observing her: her face was made up in the same meticulous way, both eyebrows primly dotted, her hair done up with the usual exaggerated wave that was meant to look accidental, her coordinated ensemble of beige and lilac exuding unhurried elegance.

I learned to understand my mother's silent language when I was younger, after a disastrous incident involving a cherished mirror. Before long, I could pierce the meaning behind her actions: the flicker of pursed lips, the quickening of an iris, the wiping of invisible sweat from dry palms, the deliberately misused word, the subtle variations of laughter, the underlying color theory of her selected cosmetics palette.

I knew my mother more than any other person, more than my younger sister Lexi, and definitely more than my father.

First at Eight

I'd only been to family reunions twice before, both times on my father's side because my mother's family was thin and dispersed across three continents. The first time was just after my eighth birthday. I remember my father telling me how wonderful it would be for me to finally meet family members who hadn't seen me since I was a baby. But when we arrived, I was overwhelmed by the cacophony of strangers, numbed by the countless embraces and pinches and unfair questions ("Don't you remember me, hija? I held you when you were born!"), and terrified by the way I was expected to experience familial love at first sight.

By the time lunch was served, I could not be found anywhere. Hours later, one of the hunting parties led by my disheveled mother found me curled up on the floor of the back seat of the car, semi-conscious and dehydrated. My father was furious. My mother did not scold me then, and I thought there would be a devastating tempest later, in private.

It never happened.

She sat with me at the backseat and held my hand all the way home.

Second at Ten

My father exacted a promise from me to behave before we drove off for the second reunion when I was 10. I agreed and quietly settled into my usual place, already itching in my black linen funeral attire. I did not want to upset him, who was mourning his father's loss heavily. My mother, and even Lexi, gave him wide berth, and the long trip was conducted in arduous silence. I remember wishing that day and night would pass at super speed but my desire seemed to only prolong the journey.

My mother just looked blankly ahead at the unfolding highway, unblinking despite the drying effects of the air-conditioning.

When we arrived, I was shocked to discover a range of exhibited emotions, ranging from the caterwauling of my grandmother to the raucous gambling tables headed by some of my presumed uncles. There was a reprise of the painful greetings and impossible questions that I somehow managed to endure, drawing strength from my stoic mother's firm smile. But when I realized that I was expected to kiss my dead grandfather, I reneged on my vow to behave and promptly fainted. I came to in my mother's arms and listened with my eyes closed to a thousand invasive questions and fragments of unsolicited advice. I tried to apologize to my parents, but ended up crying instead, tears that were interpreted by many as genuine grief.

On the way back, Lexi leaned over and called me a moron, which did not surprise me in the least. Lexi had a foul mouth and was a child, after all. I chose not to tell my mother about it and instead turned away from my sister and watched the coconut trees roll by.

Last at Twelve

On the road again to reunite for some unknown relative's homecoming, just days before my twelfth birthday, the last thing I expected was for my mother to speak up.

"I'd really rather not go," my mother said, the suddenness breaking the immaculate silence with the force of a gunshot.

"We talked about this already," my father said.

"Can we turn back?" my mother asked. "Or we can go somewhere else. Tagaytay, Los Baños, we know people in those places."

"Are you crazy?" my father said a little too loudly. "We're expected. We told them we're coming. What–what sort of stupid thing is this?"

"Don't call me stupid."

"Don't act stupid," my father said, increasing the SUV's speed.

I listened to the entire exchange with a sick feeling in my stomach, as if my pre-dawn breakfast had turned to worms and stones. Lexi, asleep on her side, was oblivious to the entire conversation, and I entertained the notion of waking her up for no other reason than to break the spell of discomfort that had settled on the once-again silent trip.

"Please stop," my mother said, in almost a whisper.

I watched my mother's face through the side mirror, angled away my father's. It looked to me as if my mother's eyelashes were burdened by the enforced curls of Estee Lauder's Illusionist. A tooth exhibited a smudge of Avon's First Kiss. Several strands of hair were conspicuously out of place. My mother's secret language surfaced and receded on her face.

"No," my father said, flicking the lights on and off in the early morning gloom.

"Let me out, Gerry," my mother said quietly. I saw the darkness that thrummed beneath her request and tasted the bitterness that circulated in the air. I wanted to tell my father to stop the car but could not speak.

"No," my father repeated, flooring the gas, jolting everyone.

As Lexi stirred from her disturbed sleep, my mother and I exchanged an accidental look. In that instant I felt the weight of her fatigue and drowned in its depth and immensity. Floating on the dark current was a mother's doomed love for her daughters, condemned by choice and circumstance to be swallowed by the greater force of sorrow.

Goodbye, I spoke in our secret language.

Goodbye, my mother's dead face replied.

She opened the door of the golden SUV and, with a precise and wounded economy of motion, flew into the morning. 🐾

Black Dog

Marianne Villanueva

When I think of my childhood, I imagine a series of long afternoons spent in leafy gardens and sunny rooms. The air was golden, mottled with dust. Time stretched out: most of the time I read in my room, which had a balcony facing a creek; two beds: one for me and one for my older sister; and old chests filled with letters and greeting cards.

Our house always seemed to have a lot of people coming and going.

School was death. The hours dragged until I could come home and see my mother again, and taste the hot guinataan the cook prepared for my merienda. And always there would be something different to observe: another stranger's car parked in the driveway; a new vase of flowers on the antique chest by the front door.

One day I came home from school to find an old man sitting in the sala with my mother. I had never seen him before. He sat on one of our long wooden recliners, sipping a cup of hot chocolate my mother must have asked the cook to prepare especially for him.

He sipped slowly, carefully, and talked to my mother in Ilonggo, which was the dialect of the province to the south where my mother's family came from. I thought he might be a worker from one of my mother's farms. I went up to my room and did not think of the old man anymore.

Later, I heard my mother calling to me. "Come!" she said. "Do you want to go to the Polo Club?" So I knew the visitor had left. My mother spent every afternoon in the club, playing bridge on a wide verandah that overlooked the polo fields. The other women who played there had lacquered hair and fingernails; silk dresses; perfume. Yes! I said. I loved to watch these women, so intent on what they were holding in their white hands, so languorous and free. Besides, the Polo Club had the best library, filled with American paperbacks.

While we were in the car on the way to the club, my mother sighed. I looked at her questoningly. She was shaking her head.

"A strange story," she said. She didn't speak for some minutes, while I tried to hold my tongue. Then, very slowly, she asked, "Do you know who that was?"

I shook my head, no. Such a question! It was part of a game my mother played, a kind of introduction to what I knew must be a wonderful story to follow.

"That was a friend of your lola's, your grandmother's. He'd just come from the farm. But he is really a justice. He comes from Aklan."

A justice! The man was old and stooped. He spoke in the native dialect. His clothes were worn.

My mother went on: "He told me the strangest story, about a case he had tried."

And she went on to tell me the story. The car wound slowly in and out of the leafy streets. And by the time we arrived at the Polo Club, I knew all about the case, a man tried for murder, and the black dog.

The story is really very simple: a man has a daughter who falls ill one day. He brings her to a doctor, a doctor who lives in the next municipio. It is almost a day's walk away, and the doctor prescribes this and that medicine, all of which costs a lot of money. The poor farmer spends his last savings on the medicine for his daughter, but her illness continues to advance. Finally, in desperation, the farmer consults a local mangkukulam.

Do you know what these people are, my mother asks me. "They are native healers. When people are cursed, as they so often are in the provinces outside Manila, usually by people who envy another's good fortune, the mangkukulam tells them how to get rid of the curse."

And suddenly I remembered seeing a dark man hovering over a pale woman lying naked from the waist up on a wooden table. Who was this woman? Where had I seen such a thing? The man plunged his hands into the woman's chest and rooted around there. When his hands surfaced again, I saw they were bloody. Something white and shiny clung to his fingers. He flicked the matter into a wooden bowl that a servant had brought. The woman got up, holding a towel to her chest. It seemed she had been healed.

And another time, one of my aunts, who had a huge cataract in her right eye that had nearly blinded her, was sitting in our living room while a strange man pressed and pressed on her face until her eye seemed about to bulge out of its socket. The man had pulled out a green lump. "What is it?" my aunt had cried, holding her eye and crying. "Muta," the man said. Watching from under the table (I must have been only four or five years old), I had burst out laughing. Because the man had used the word for the repulsive crust that I sometimes found rimming my eyelids when I woke up in the morning.

My mother continued, "The mangkukulam told the farmer that his daughter was under a spell. And nothing could be done for her unless the farmer were to kill the thing that had put the spell on her."

"And what was this thing?" I ask.

My mother smiles indulgently at me. "The mangkukulam didn't know. It would show up at the farmer's house at midnight, that very night. Whatever it was, the farmer must kill it. This the mangkukulam emphasized, holding the farmer's arm in a tight grip, and looking straight into his eyes." My mother, at that point, also looked straight at me. If her hands had not been on the wheel, I felt sure she would have gripped my hands hard between her own. "You must not stop until the thing is dead," said the mangkukulam, who my mother described as being an old woman, unimaginably old, with matted gray hair.

How did my mother know all these details—how the mangkukulam looked, what she looked like? Could Justice Makalintal have gone into such detail? Was my mother embellishing the story purely from her imagination? Or could one of those ancient women who I sometimes saw sitting on the lanai, having a cup of hot chocolate, could one of those possibly have been one of these creatures?

"And so," my mother told me, "the farmer went home, and he waited until midnight at the entrance to his hut. And, just after midnight, what should come along but a big black dog. The dog was huge, it was enormous. Its eyes were red, its nostrils distended, and steam emanated from its flared nostrils. Its panting was so loud it drowned out all other sounds, including the beating of the farmer's heart. It sniffed around the house for a few moments, and then casually began to make a circuit around it. The farmer's heart contracted to see how familiar the dog seemed to be with the territory, and there was a terrible purposefulness to the animal's gait. The farmer could hear his daughter thrashing around on the bed inside the hut, and crying out as though beset by demons. Suddenly he could hear the sound of her body being dragged across the floor, as though by some superhuman force.

"But the farmer was patient. He waited."

"Why did he wait?" I asked.

"Why, because he trusted the mangkukulam," my mother says. And I know, though she does not say so, because it adds to the suspense, and because she so enjoys seeing my eyes grow rounder and rounder, there is never anything like this in the Literary Reader I have to slog through in Grade 6 at the Assumption Convent, the nuns at my school have no imagination and they are nothing, nothing like my mother.

"Finally, with a fierce yell (the yell is to buck up his courage, my mother tells me) the farmer attacks the dog with his bolo."

I have seen pictures of this curved, murderous-looking blade in the storybooks that tell how Lapu-Lapu decapitated that interloper Magellan. And the laborers on our farm use it to hack the stalks of sugar cane. Right and left they hack, their arms glistening with sweat. And, looking at their brown arms, tasting the juice of the sugar cane that they hand to me and my mother, I shiver, even under the noonday sun.

"The dog lets out a scream which sounds like no other," my mother says. "And suddenly, lying bleeding at the farmer's feet is a woman. A very beautiful woman, with long black hair. She kisses the farmer's feet. She begs for her life. The farmer is of course terribly surprised but he has no choice other than to hack at the woman until he is sure she is dead."

The next day, my mother tells me, the farmer is hauled off to jail and accused of murder.

"And is this how Justice Makalintal enters the story?" I ask.

My mother nods slowly. "Well, here is the courtroom and there in front of Justice Makalintal stands the accused. And how can Justice Makalintal make head or tail of this man's story. The man keeps insisting he is innocent, even though everyone has seen him with the bloody bolo, and there was a dead body at his feet when the policemen came to take him away. He told them about the mangkukulam, and so they had to send for her, and when she came the judge had to threaten her with jail before she would open her mouth. After hemming and hawing--a lot of that--she told the judge that yes, the farmer, was a client of hers, and yes indeed his daughter was very sick, but she had never told him to kill the woman. Oh, no! What he had to kill was the THING that came at midnight.

"Justice Makalintal scratched his head. For certain, there was a dead body. But no one in the town knew who the victim was, or who to believe.

"And the strangest thing," my mother said, "was that it turned out the woman was the yaya, the nanny, of a certain rich family in Manila. And she had asked the family for leave to visit her old mother in another island, which was not the island where she happened to meet her end. So no one knew what she had been doing in Aklan.

"A few people said they had seen the woman in the marketplace, a week before the farmer's daughter fell ill.

Someone even said they saw the woman talking to the young girl, in a friendly way. Perhaps that was where the spell had been cast, in the middle of the marketplace, with all those people!"

"And what happened to the farmer then?" I wanted to know. "Was he released?"

In truth, I never found out the ending to this story. I wanted my mother to tell me that the farmer was found innocent, but she was scornful of such niceties. She said only, "It is hard to say how justice works in small towns in the Philippines." And for many many years after, even when I was a grown woman and living in California, I thought of the farmer, the woman, the daughter, the black dog. ✤

Vigan

Cecilia Manguerra Brainard

When I was ten, a year after my father died, my mother decided to return to Vigan, back to her grandmother who had raised her after her parents died. We left Manila for the sleepy town with crumbling stone houses, cobbled streets, watchtowers, and other vestiges of colonial days. Vigan boasted of having been founded in the 16th century by Juan Salcedo, the Spanish conquistador who conquered Manila. In its heyday, it was the port of entry of the Spanish galleons coming from China and headed for the Walled City of Intramuros. The ships sailed up the river and moored at the edge of Old Town, near the Cathedral and Archbishop's Palace. The merchants' houses and warehouses clustered near the river. Here, traders exchanged items such as indigo, cotton, silk, pearls, tobacco, porcelain, hemp, for silver and gold.

Our family house sat in the middle of a row of ancient merchant houses, crumbling relics of limestone blocks and wood. Our house had massive wooden double doors fronting the street, which my great-grandmother said allowed carriages in and out of the family compound during Spanish times. The lower portion of our house had a shed with two pigs, four chickens, and one mean-spirited goat. A section in the back served as the servants' quarters, but since my great-grandmother had only one servant who slept upstairs, this section was unoccupied and was in total disarray. An elaborate staircase led to the second floor, which had the kitchen, dining room, living room or sala, the music room, library, a verandah, and bedrooms. There were four bedrooms, but huge, with high-ceilings that allowed the air to circulate thus cutting the oppressive tropical heat. Except for the room occupied by my great-grandmother, the other bedrooms had several four-poster beds, lined up dormitory-style, and covered by yellowing crocheted bedspreads.

I'd only heard about this house from my mother. We had never visited it when Papa was alive. So even though I was unhappy about our move, I was impressed by the surprises the house offered. The walls of the rooms, for instance, had hand-painted murals: musical instruments were painted all around the music room, the dining room had a border of grapes on a vine with a hunting scene on the wall nearest the dining table, and the bedroom my mother and I shared had a picture of Cupid sitting on a cloud and shooting his arrow at a young woman in a forest. Although the paintings were flaking and faded, my great-grandmother, whom my mother and I called Lola, was very proud of them.

What interested me most was the coffin at the foot of the stairs. An old sheet covered it and on top were all sorts of junk: newspapers, empty glass jars, and a huge vase with dusty fake flowers. I had mistaken the coffin for a table until Lola removed the sheet to reveal a bronze casket with gold decorations. She struck the metal with her fingernail and declared it was our family coffin. Apparently old families in the area kept family coffins, which were used only for the wake. For the actual burial, the corpse was wrapped in an Ilocano woven blanket and buried directly in the family vault. The coffin was cleaned, then stored, in this case at the foot of the stairs, ready for its next temporary occupant.

The idea sent me into hysterics, considering my own father was buried in his own bronze casket—cost had been no object as far as his parents were concerned. He had been their only child.

I asked my great-grandmother what happened when two family members died, like my mother's parents for instance. She said they lay side by side.

"But what if more than two die?" I persisted.

"It's never happened," she said. By that time, she was clearly annoyed with me, and so I kept quiet. Lola had not liked my father and his family, and I suspected that dislike extended to me. People said I looked a lot like my father. He was tall and thin and had a lot of Chinese blood in him, unlike my mother's family, which had a lot of Spanish blood.

Even though Lola spoke enthusiastically of the house (this remnant of our family's glorious past), I found it depressing. There were cobwebs everywhere, and at night, I dreaded going to the bathroom because I usually ran into the sticky strands. There was dust all over the old furniture. Ceiling plaster was peeling, the wooden floors creaked, and there was one section near the kitchen with wood rot. I could peer through the holes and look down at the animals. Sometimes I would spit on the goat that had butted me once.

Before we came, Lola's solitary companion was another old woman named Manang Gloria. I was never sure who took care of whom because half the time, my grandmother was the one in the kitchen cooking bitter ampalaya to strengthen Manang Gloria's blood. There were men workers who came during the day to take care of the animals and yard, but by late afternoon, they were gone.

By six in the evening, the only sounds you heard were the two old women rattling around in the kitchen, some lonely crickets outside, and my mother sighing by the window. Times like that, I would ache for my father and my old life.

~

My mother had never worked in her entire life. After college, she'd married Papa and moved into his house. In Vigan, she spent many nights crying, cursing my father for dying, and wondering how she could support the two of us. We had left Manila in the first place because she and my father's parents did not get along. They disliked her from the start, accusing her of being pretentious. It was true that my mother carried with her an arrogance that old families from Vigan had, even if their ceilings had caved in and their floors rotted. My mother, likewise, scorned my father's family, calling them "new rich" and accusing them of having no culture. While my father was alive, he kept the two warring parties apart, but after he died, nothing stood between his parents and my mother. Like cats and dogs they went after each other; of course my mother was always on the losing end. After a year of strained silences, sharp words, doors slamming, and countless tears, my mother grew weary of the quarreling, took whatever she could, and we left.

It was Lola who suggested that she open an antique shop downstairs. "Manang Gloria knows some carpenters who can make replicas," Lola said. Have them copy our antique furniture. Price them low. City people will buy them." She was right. Antique dealers traveled far to buy Mama's bentwood chairs and love seats, drop-leaf tables, armoires, chairs, and wooden statues of the Virgin Mary and Jesus on the cross. The most popular item was the plantation chair, an enormous lounging chair made of mahogany and rattan, that harked back to days of sitting around the verandah, a leg resting on one arm of the chair and a drink in one's hand.

~

I hated school. I did not fit. I was used to the stimulating environment of my school in Manila. The school in Vigan was dull and provincial. I spent most of my time in Mama's antique shop, doing my homework on the table, reading old books from the library, rearranging the display in the showroom, or bothering the workers who were carving the reproductions in the back. "Look at that," I would say, "antiques made-to-order."

I was there the afternoon Ramon arrived. He was an antique dealer from Manila. I overheard him ordering a lot of furniture and so I was not surprised when Mama invited him for dinner. Mama's clients usually lived in one of the four hotels in town, none of which served decent food. When Mama invited clients to dinner, Manang Gloria would come to life and prepare local recipes, crispy mouth-watering bagnets, steamed prawns, fried fish, and that bitter vegetable stew that local folk loved so much.

Ramon praised Manang Gloria's food, and she giggled like an idiot. She was really quite fresh, behaving more like a peer than our servant. When I tried to put her in her place, Lola always defended her, saying she was the fourth generation to work in our house.

Lola ate and left the dining table early. When she was gone, the conversation between Mama and Ramon livened up. It seemed they had mutual friends in Manila, and they discussed them one by one, Mama gushing over the good fortune of some of them, and clucking at misfortune of others. Later (they must have forgotten I was there) Ramon talked about his wife. He had married his college sweetheart, a journalist who had gotten involved in the anti-Marcos movement. She had written many daring exposes of the oppressive dictatorship. She even wrote articles about the "disappeareds" until one night she herself disappeared. Ramon spent years looking for her until his family convinced him she had been "salvaged" so not a single trace of her body could be found. Ramon had gone into seclusion until Cory Aquino came into power. He said that after the EDSA Revolution, he discovered she was still alive after all. "I found out," he said, "that I could laugh again."

My mother grew teary at Ramon's story, then told Ramon about Papa. She described how Papa started dropping things, that we thought he'd had a stroke, but that it turned out he had brain cancer. The doctors had said he had six months to live, and that they had been right almost to the date. She did not tell Ramon of her quarrel with my paternal grandparents. When he pressed her about why we left Manila, she said Lola needed her.

It was a conversation, nothing more, but I was disturbed by it. I hated how she shared a piece of our lives with him. I hated being reminded of Papa and our old life, and I hated how happy Mama seemed with Ramon.

~

Ramon would come around every two weeks. He would talk to Mama at great length — "business" they called it. He would dine with us; and sometimes he and Mama would ride off someplace. I would interrogate Mama as to where exactly they went, and reluctantly she would confess they visited the old church and rectory in Santa Maria, or the beach of Vigan, or the Luna Museum in Ilocos Sur, or the open market to buy Ilocano blankets. She said this blithely, as if I should not care. But when I thought of the two of them in these places, I would feel a heaviness in my chest, a sorrow that lingered for days.

Ramon tried to befriend me, bringing me books, which he recognized as my weakness, but even though I hankered to read them, I would deliberately abandon them in the shop, on the same table he had set them on, so he could see, so he could understand that he could never bribe me.

Once he told me, "You are very different from your mother."

I glared at him. "I am my father's daughter," I said, thinking I sounded very smart.

My mother blushed when she heard me, and later that night she scolded me for being rude. I told her I wanted to go home.

"There is no other home," she replied softly. "This is it. Those people don't want us. They have cheated us of your father's inheritance."

She was crying now. "They are the people who killed Ramon's wife. They were cronies of Marcos; that was how they made their money. They killed her; and I suppose, we are guilty too."

Her hair was disheveled; her makeup smeared. I saw how much older she had become since Papa died. I saw how vulnerable she was, how spineless, and I told myself I would never be as weak as she was.

~

In the summer when the heat left you breathless, my great-grandmother decided she was going to die soon. She called Manang Gloria and instructed her to have new satin lining made for the family coffin. After inspecting the shiny pink lining and checking the hinges of the coffin, she went back to bed and refused to get up. In a few days her legs started cramping, and it became my job to massage her with Sloan's Liniment. I would pour the liniment into my palms, vigorously rub my hands together, and massage her spindly legs. That was when I learned about my mother's bad luck.

Lola said, "There are some people who attract bad luck, and your mother is that way. When your mother was four, her parents died in a car crash on the zigzag road to Baguio. Then of course your father died. It's just bad luck, that's all. There is no other explanation."

I felt kinder to my mother after that—until I caught her and Ramon kissing. It was afternoon, and Lola had told me to call them to the verandah for merienda. I ran down, paused by the family coffin, and lifted the sheet so I could feel the coolness of the bronze. Then I went to the door of the antique shop. I caught them locked together in a tight embrace—my own mother with this man. Ramon saw me, pushed her away, and cleared his throat. Calmly I told them Lola had hot chocolate and pastries waiting for them.

Mama closed the front door of the shop and headed for the stairs. "Are you coming, Rosario?" she asked.

I shook my head. "I have to finish something. I'll be there."

I waited awhile then I opened his briefcase and went through his things, looking for something, I was not sure what for exactly. Just when I was putting his papers back into the briefcase, a picture fluttered out. It was Ramon and Mama standing happily in front of the town plaza. I took it and stuffed it into my pocket.

~

I had heard Manang Gloria talk of Sylvia, a mangkukulam who lived on the edge of town. When Manang Gloria was twenty, Sylvia had read her cards. The witch had predicted that a man would fall in love with her, but that they would be separated. A young man did come along, and for a long time, Manang Gloria tortured herself by wondering when the man would drop her for another woman. The man, however, was steadfast and asked her to marry him. They picked a date, made preparations; Manang Gloria had her white gown made. The night before their wedding day, the man walked by a sari-sari store where two men were fighting. He tried to stop the fight, but in the scuffle, ended up dead.

Aside from reading cards, Sylvia made potions. The most popular were love potions and potions to exact revenge. She could also cured sick people by catching their illness and transferring it into a rooster whose head she would chop off. If convinced it was right to do so, she could harm people. She could even turn into a ferocious black dog at night, which was why people avoided walking around after dusk.

One Saturday in June, I went to Sylvia's house. I was afraid; I did not know what to expect. I found her planting seedlings in front of her hut. At first glance, she appeared ordinary- looking, with a simple native dress and her gray hair tied in a knot. When she looked up, I noticed her sad, sad eyes. I told her I knew Manang Gloria. She stared at me, with those sorrowful eyes, until I too felt like crying. I was about to leave when she invited me in.

She led me in front of an altar with numerous statues of saints and burning candles. She took my hand, turned it over so she could see my palm. "One day," she said, "a man will fall in love with you, but you will be separated."

This sounded like Manang Gloria's fortune; I felt disappointed.

"I'm here," I said, "for my mother."

She said nothing.

"I have to save her."

"Ah, does your mother need saving?"

I nodded.

"And whom are you saving her from?"

"From a man. A wicked man. I have a picture of him. Do you want to see?"

She glanced at the picture. Her eyes became darker and sadder still. "A handsome man. Once, I knew a handsome man..." She trailed off, but then recovered, "Handsome men ...well, what can I say? Yes, they can be dangerous. Tell me more."

"He is hurting her. He is hurting us. I want him to go away. I want him to stop seeing her."

She sighed. "Your father is dead," she said. "You miss him."

This pronouncement impressed me, and I wondered how she divined this truth.

"Everyone talks in this town. You and your mother live in the Pamintuan Mansion, with Doña Epang."

Again I felt disappointment.

She stared into my eyes until my eyes burned and I felt like blinking.

"I can give you something that will attract good. You can give this to your mother, so only good will go near her. If this man is bad, he will stay away."

"Mama's a bad-luck woman. Lola says so. Nothing you can give her will attract good. I need something so he will never come back. He is evil. He has hurt her; he has hurt me."

She turned her sorrowful eyes to her altar. "All right," she finally said, "just because of Manang Gloria I will help you." She went to a corner and returned with a bottle of Coke, only it didn't have Coca Cola in it, but some amber-colored liquid with herbs and flower petals. "The morning after the full moon, rinse with this. Then go to Mass and pray that he will no longer return. Pray hard, especially when the bells ring at the Consecration."

"Is that all?" I asked.

"That is all. Leave your money in the pot near the door."

~

Back home, I hid the bottle in my closet and left it untouched until the first storm fell. Mama was in bed staring at the Cupid painted on the wall. She whispered, "It is so cold to be alone in bed."

I found a calendar and figured when the full moon was. I bathed with Sylvia's water, went to Mass, and prayed as she had taught me. When the bells tinkled at Consecration, I stared hard at the white host and repeated: "God, keep Ramon away from Mama, keep him away from us, drive him far away, separate them, God, please, God, please. You've taken my father away, I'm asking you now, God, to keep him away from us. You owe it to me, God, because Papa's gone and not only have you taken him, you've taken me away from my house and planted me in this miserable place, the last place on earth I'd like to live in God. I have no friends, no one, except my Mother. Please God, don't let her leave me too because when she's with Ramon, that's how it feels God, like she's left me too."

On and on I rambled, venting my sorrows and miseries, and pinning them all on Ramon, blaming him for them, and wishing for him to disappear from our lives. When I left the Cathedral, my hands were shaking and I felt flushed. My mother and Lola asked me if I was all right. I kept quiet. Something had shifted in me and I knew that things would be different.

~

It did not happen right away. From the time I saw Sylvia in June until December, Ramon continued to visit Mama every two weeks. When I saw his happy face, my chest would tighten. He would smile, white teeth flashing; and he'd give Lola a box of American chocolates or bag of hot chestnuts, and he would kiss her on both cheeks. And Mama, standing by Lola's bed, would beam proudly at Ramon as if he were some genius-child who had done his homework right. He would greet me too and give me a book or puzzle. With a stony face I would thank him, then put his gift down and run off to wash my hands, scrubbing them hard until my skin hurt.

When he was around and I felt desperate, I would beg Manang Gloria to tell me the story of her dead lover once again. Other times, I would go to the family coffin, remove the things on top, open it and run my hands on the pink satin lining, feeling its coolness, imagining the dead people that had occupied this coffin, and thinking that one day it would hold Lola, Mama, and even me. Once I climbed into it and lay down as if I were dead, with my eyes closed and my palms together as if in prayer. I was drifting off to sleep when Manang Gloria happened to see me and screamed so loud, Lola ran down the stairs. "You are a strange, strange child," she said. "You must take after your father's family."

~

And so time passed in Vigan, until finally it happened, in December. Ramon arrived with Christmas gifts. By this time,

I had almost forgotten my visit to Sylvia, and I must admit, I'd gotten used to his visits. Lola's house was so dark and full of decay, and Ramon's visits added some sparkle to our lives. Manang Gloria would cook; Lola used her Sevres China and Baccarat crystal; and Mama would dress up and look happy and young.

He insisted that we open our gifts immediately: an expensive bottle of French perfume for Lola, a sweater for Manang Gloria, a pearl necklace for Mama, and an antique music box for me. We were like children, fingering our gifts, and I saw him beaming happily that he had found the right gifts for us. Lola and Mama kissed him on the cheek. Manang Gloria kissed his hand, as if he were a "patron" of colonial days. And since everyone was looking my way, I went to him and planted a kiss on his cheek. He looked surprised and stood there for a long time holding his cheek where I had kissed him.

We were happy that night. Lola walked with us to the Cathedral for Midnight Mass. Later we had the noche buena meal at home. Numerous carolers stopped by our house, singing about Christ, love, and joy. It was a clear and beautiful night. From the verandah I looked up at the stars, and I could feel my soul expanding. Since Papa died, I had not felt happiness like that.

It was almost dawn when he said he had to drive back to Manila to have Christmas dinner with his parents. After a lengthy farewell to the women, he said goodbye to me. I felt a flutter at the pit of my stomach. "Ramon..." I started, then lost my words. "Merry Christmas," I finally said.

In bed, I thought of Papa in the hospital and how he struggled to speak but could not. I thought of our big house in Manila. I thought of the malls that my friends and I used to frequent. I remembered my third grade nun who lectured once about charity being the most important virtue of all. I knew that I had done something terribly wrong. I wept silently in bed; even my mother did not hear me.

~

Years later, my mother blamed herself of Ramon's death, saying she was bad luck. His car had turned turtle on the highway, heading back to Manila. I did not tell her that in this matter, she was wrong. 🌸

Old Witch of San Jose

Jonathan Jimena Siason

"Ay, Miguel, how many gallons this time? One? Or two? Your abuelo does not usually drink at this time, ah. By the way, how is Joaquin? Still up to his naughty ways, ha? Does he still go to the Chinese cemetery?" Ñora Baby, a large woman to the point of being obese, peered at me from behind the counter of her sari-sari store. She was laughing as she asked me questions; her double chins jiggled.

Cowering, I handed her the gallon-container for the tuba and answered, "Just one, please."

I suppressed a shudder as I looked at Ñora Baby's face. Like any other 12-year-old, I was afraid of a lot of things: the wakwak that whisked away children who misbehaved, the brujo disguised as an old man who lured naughty kids away from their homes, or the sigben that feasted on the innards of kids who failed to go home before dusk. Nothing was scarier than Ñora Baby. Even though she appeared human, I knew that she was the vilest monster of them all.

She was old, perhaps as old as my grandfather was. She had white hair and her mouth was misshapen. She was also missing her front teeth. What was most frightening and which gave me nightmares were the scars on the right side of her face—red, ugly, twisted scars.

I had studied those scars ever since I started buying tuba from her for my grandfather. The scars took on horrible shapes each time I looked at them. Some days they were skeletal bats with eyes and tongues as red as ember. At times they formed an angry red whirlpool. Once, the scars took the shape of a red bulbous cat with menacing red claws and whiskers, its red eyes boring into mine.

Ñora Baby laughed a lot, but her laughter was so loud. Her shrill guffaws almost made my ears bleed. She always asked many questions about Lolo so that I sometimes wished my ears were *indeed* bleeding so I wouldn't have to listen to her.

Some people thought she was a bruja who could turn small boys into ugly frogs. Jordan, the scrawniest in our gang, swore on his dead grandmother's grave that on the eve of All Souls' Day he had seen Ñora Baby roaming the deserted, cobblestoned streets of San Jose. The hag had stopped at each door, knocked three times, after which she blew on the doors. Jerry's mother said that was black magic and one way powerful witches cursed people.

Some of the vecinos said Ñora Baby got the scars from a chemical accident in a formaldehyde factory where she had worked. But we children in the neighborhood knew better. We were convinced that her scars were from Ñor Horacio, the local albularyo, who repelled her black witchcraft whenever she attacked some hapless victim. Everyone shunned her. She too avoided being seen in the neighborhood. Whenever she needed food, she would send one of her nieces who lived with her to the tiangge. Even Babu Julpa, the Muslim crone who read palms for a scant five pesos and who could cure any ailment by using herbs from her native Jolo, kept a respectable distance from her.

"Lolo, I don't want to buy tuba anymore," I complained to my grandfather one Sunday morning as he sat in his rocking chair in the front porch. "I'm afraid of Ñora Baby and I don't want to go to her store anymore. I'd rather go fly a kite with Jordan."

Lolo, in his usual loud booming voice, snapped at me, "Ay hende se puede! When I tell you to go and buy my tuba, do it or you'll receive a good spanking from me. I want my tuba. You know that I have arthritis and I can't walk far."

I stared at him incredulously. He had never complained of arthritis before! Why couldn't he go to Ñora Baby's himself?

In my imagination, grandfather's stomach turned into a vile, black monster with a deep, bottomless maw. It always knew when it was ten in the morning, at which time it needed sustenance. Its mouth was forever open, waiting, waiting for the familiar bittersweet taste of tuba. Deprived of the drink, it could retaliate and rip through grandfather's chest, like the monster in the movie that my parents took me to see when I was 10. I could not wait for the monster inside my grandfather to do the same thing.

"It's too tiring," I whined. "Besides, Ñora Baby keeps on asking about you. It'd be better if you answer her questions yourself, Lolo." I closed my eyes and braced myself for Lolo's scathing remarks. But none came. Slowly I opened my eyes and caught him staring at the madre de cacao trees nearby. He had a tired expression on his face and he was very quiet. The rocking chair was still, and it seemed to me that everything around us suddenly stood still—the Bermuda grass, the sparrows perched atop the trees, the garden sprinkler, the barking dogs of old Toñing.

I liked to make lists in my head. Things became a lot clearer when I did that. At that moment of stillness, a list about my grandfather magically appeared in my head.

A: My grandmother left him years ago. No surprise there.

B: He had kidney problems. Bitterness could do that to you. Or so I heard.

C: He never had a son. This must have been a big disappointment.

~

It was a December night when I heard fighting downstairs.

"If you had regarded your marriage the way you were supposed to, Lola would have not left us!" Tiya Rebecca screamed, her voice echoing throughout the house.

"She wouldn't have left, Lolo. She would have stayed," my mother chimed in. "Had you not tricked her...had you not taken that dreadful woman, that—"

Grandfather cut her off, his voice full of contempt. "Sin verguenza!"

I heard the front door slam shut and my mother sobbing. I sighed and walked to the open window. The cool December breeze caressed my face. The dama de noche in the neighbor's garden was blooming, its familiar sweet scent wafting in the air. I went back to bed and lay there for a long time. I couldn't sleep. The scent of the dama de noche was cloying. It filled my nostrils and drugged me with images of smiling grandfathers. *What had Lolo done?* He had always said my grandmother left because she had another family, but my aunt and mother suggested something else—could this be true? Confusion coursed through me. After hours of tossing and turning and staring at the black ceiling, I finally drifted off to sleep.

The next Sunday Jordan and I went to the old school grounds, to the tall patches of carabao grass. We were catching some dragonflies that we planned to sell to younger kids, when out of nowhere a small kite made of blue Japanese paper with white trimmings flitted to the ground. Jordan picked it up and studied the kite's rips and holes. I snatched the kite from Jordan, smacked him on the forehead, and said, "Finders keepers, el nuhay lloron!" I laughed all the way home.

Grandfather glared at me when I arrived. He was in the yard, sweeping dead leaves. "What's that you got in your hand, Miguel?" he demanded.

"Nothing, Lolo. Just a kite," I answered curtly. He placed his right hand on his hips and looked at me gravely. "Let me see that."

I grimaced. Now what?

"Hmm..." He turned it over and inspected the frame. He was scowling. "It's not a good kite. You should throw this useless piece of junk away."

There were many awful things that I wanted to say at that moment, but I held my tongue. Then he said, "Go and find the Chinese box on my bed. Get the Japanese paper. Let's fix this kite." I wasn't sure if I heard grandfather right. *Did he say he'd fix it?* I must have stood frozen for a long time because he snapped at me. "What are you waiting for, tonto? For me to grow back my black beard? Go and get that box!"

I hurried to his room and found the box in the midst of the Legion magazines that the US Embassy kept sending him. I opened the box; it was full of trash—buttons of every kind and color, variety of patches, assortment of needles, black wax, Chinese menthol stick, Tiger Balm, Efficascent Oil, and folded sheets of Japanese paper.

I was removing the Japanese paper when I noticed, deep inside the box, plastered to the bottom, a small sepia-colored photograph of a young woman wearing a Spanish traje de debutante. I wondered if it was my grandmother, Lola Anastacia. I fished it out for a better look.

It was not Lola.

My grandmother was small in stature; the photo showed a big woman with pear-shaped face and black hair pulled back in a tight bun. She was pretty enough. Her head was covered with a white embroidered veil. She looked like she was dressed for church. But what caught my attention was the laughter in her face, frozen yet alive. Most old pictures in our family albums showed faces that were serious and severe, as if they did not want to be photographed in the first place. The woman in the picture knew her photo was being taken and she enjoyed it. I turned the photograph over and saw an inscription written in Spanish. I did not understand most of the words, but the last line I did—Yo tu amor asta para cuando, Baby. It was dated 1942.

All I could do was to stare, my face burning. Dark thoughts raced through my head. I realized something. Ñora Baby was not the worst monster in San Jose; Lolo was the real *diablo*. Together, they had committed despicable, shameful acts. So what happened was:

A: Like my mother and aunts, I stopped talking to Lolo.

B: He started spending more of his time with Capital Gregorio and others, going to RT Lim Boulevard to eat barbecue and drink hard gin.

C: On many occasions, he was locked out of the house, what with him coming home at two or three in the morning. Oh, how cursed my parents and my aunts will be for locking him out! Using an empty bottle of beer as his imaginary microphone, Lolo would sing his laments and frustrations to the moon. In the morning, we would find him huddled in a corner of the balcony, with mosquito bites all over his neck and arms. Only the youngest aunt, Tiya Sylvia, attended to him.

Every day, dark thoughts troubled me. I felt as if another person had taken control of my body. I felt anger, which frightened me. I felt like a *monster.* I did not want to grow up in a world where dark secrets could destroy lives. I felt caught between one moment and the next, pulled here and there. Everything was happening so fast around me, so fast I couldn't do anything about it. All I could do was wait.

~

My grandfather had kidney failure. He suffered for three months, writhing in agony on his bed. He finally died at the age of 65. My parents said he did not suffer much. My aunts were relieved, saying it was finally over.

The day of the funeral, the circus arrived in San Jose. It was humid and we all felt that tingling sensation at the back of the neck that meant rain was coming. The large circus boxes, cranes, tents, and other paraphernalia had been set up in the old school grounds the night before. Muscled dwarves scampered about, picking up ropes, pulling rigging, and transforming the mess into a fascinating world. Because of the heat, the workers took off their shirts. A sign propped up by sacks of cement announced: ON THIS SITE WILL RISE A MINI MART.

The driver of the funeral car, a black Mustang, was late. Overcome with fatigue and grief my mother, who was standing near the coffin, fainted. Tiya Becky caught her in time or else she would have conked her head on the edge of the coffin. I was in the kitchen helping Tiya Sylvia with the sandwiches and Kool-lip juice. All around us, people laughed and talked. Babu Julpa set herself up near the entrance to our house just in case someone needed his or her palm read.

I was there when Ñora Baby showed up.

She arrived with one of her nieces, Sunshine, who was a few years older than me and who attended my school. Ñora Baby wore a white cotton shirt and faded black pants. She looked very plain, very fat, and very old. She came in hesitantly, her head bowed down, arms close to her side. Near the coffin, she suddenly paused and turned to my mother and aunts.

The entire room became silent. Everyone was tense, especially my mother and aunts. Some guests stared at Ñora Baby; others stared at my mother and my aunts.

I focused my attention at the chiaroscuro portrait of my grandparents hanging on the wall. No one said a word. Even Old Toñing's dogs remained doleful and sleepy under one of the long benches in the sala. Babu broke the silence by letting out a loud *"Aheeem!"*

Fortunately the funeral driver arrived and we forgot Ñora Baby. A flurry of activity happened. Everyone took their places behind the funeral car. I sat beside the driver but before getting in, I scanned the crowd for that familiar scarred face, but Ñora Baby was gone.

The funeral procession headed to the parish church for the Mass. Along the way we passed by Ñora Baby's store, and that was when I felt it—no, I heard it. It sounded like the ruffling of bat wings, or the rustling of dry leaves. I was wondering where the sound came from when I realized I was hearing it *inside* me. I felt a huge, black blob of anger, of hate, deflate. I felt it floating inside me—now lifeless, useless. The monster was gone.

Sure enough, Ñora Baby was already behind the counter. She had removed her veil and was now sitting on a stool that was too small for her. She had left my grandfather's funeral quickly. She was alone. She looked old. I held my gaze. She stared right back. In my head the words appeared: She is just a lonely old woman.

And in that brief moment, as we drove past her, I could have sworn I saw the scars on her face reshaping, transforming, one final time. They became what they really were—just normal, ordinary scars. Perhaps even ugly reminders of a sad past. For the first time, what I saw did not repulse me. 🌸

A Season of Ten Thousand Noses

Charlson Ong

I had gone with him to see the noses. A big ship full of noses. Ah Beng said there were more noses there than anywhere on earth, and Ah Beng should know, he had been everywhere aboard his Uncle Lim Pay's sampan.

You see, many years ago, after the angry typhoon made the Pasig River rise, flooding Tundo and Binundok, a many-legged insect bit the nose of the rich Kastila Don Camilo de la Serna and made him very ill. The old people say Don Camilo's long nose grew even longer and turned red. The doctor could not find a cure, and when the herbularyo from Tundo pasted brown leaves over the Kastila's red nose, the roaches and rats swarmed all over him at night. Don Camilo's sickness grew worse everyday, and his long nose began to fall off piece by piece.

At last, said Tiya Nenita, the Kastila was so angry he took his sword and sliced off his own nose. Don Camilo fell to his knees at once, regretting what he had done and praying fervently, but it was too late. He covered his face in shame and had to put on a mask. His beautiful wife Doña Lisandra was very angry and threatened to leave Don Camilo. She said he was no longer a real hombre without his long nose.

One day while Doña Lisandra was in church to pray her novena, a miracle happened. Behind the sacristy, she saw the Christian Sanglay, Andres Yang Liong, carving the statue of the Nazareno. Doña Lisandra almost fainted when she saw the face of the statue. It looked so real she thought God had come to console her in her deep sadness. The eyes were so bright and blue they seemed to see into her soul, and the nose was so sharp and strong she could almost feel it breathing. And suddenly she knew what had happened.

"Make my husband a nose, Andres," she said, "and I will give you more silver coins than a horse can carry."

"But I only make wooden noses, Doña. Only God can create a real one. I cannot do as you wish; it is not right," Andres said in the sing-song way the Sanglays do when speaking Tagalog or Kastila.

"You will make my husband a nose or I will tell the Zura and Gobernador that the face of your Nazareno is in fact the face of a pagan god you worship," Doña Lisandra shouted. "You will be flogged and sent home to your country a beggar!"

Andres bowed and tied his pigtail around his neck. He cried and pleaded with Doña Lisandra, but that night, he went home to make a wooden nose for Don Camilo.

Don Camilo's joy was boundless when the wooden nose fit the hole on his face. It looked so real that everyone thought the Kastila had been cured and had grown a new nose. Don Camilo gave Andres two bilaos filled with silver but ordered him to return home to Amoy—the land of the Sanglay across the sea—so that no one in Maynila would ever find out about his wooden nose.

Andres rode home in Lim Pay's sampan with his load of silver. But on the way, he too was bitten by a two-headed insect and fell ill. When Andres died, the sailors threw his body overboard so that they would not catch any sickness and they divided his silver among themselves. Lim Pay saved a few coins for Andres' wife Sio Bee, and when they reached Amoy, he gave these to her and told her the whole story.

Sio Bee wept when she heard the tale and she burnt some spirit money for her dead husband. But she soon stopped crying and said: "I will make more noses."

"What did you say?" Lim Pay asked the woman who seemed to have been possessed by a powerful spirit.

"If Yang Liong could make so much money with one piece of nose, think of how much we will earn with a whole sack of wooden noses," she said, her eyes shining.

Lim Pay could not believe his ears, he tried to stop Sio Bee from doing anything foolish, but she had already gone out to tell her neighbors the story about Yang Liong's nose. Everyone agreed with Sio Bee that they would become rich making wooden noses for the huanna and the white people in Lu song and Mexico who loved long, strong noses. Someone said that many of the white people's noses where falling off because of a strange sickness.

All of Sio Bee's relatives and neighbors sat down to carve noses. Farmers stopped working their fields, fishers no longer went out to sea, and the children gathered wood for the carvers. When they ran out of trees and twigs, some of the people even took down their own homes to use the wood for carving noses.

Soon, the people of the village did not have any food left to eat, and when the snow fell, they were cold for there was no more wood to burn but only coal which they could not buy. They only had sacks and sacks of wooden noses which they begged Lim Pay to load aboard his sampan and bring with him to Maynila to trade for silver coins.

Lim Pay could not refuse seeing how his friends and their children were hungry and cold. But as his sampan neared Maynila, Lim Pay's heart grew heavy, knowing that he was carrying a worthless load of wooden noses.

Ah Beng said his Uncle Lim Pay went to the gobernador to sell him the wooden noses, but the Kastila only laughed at the Sanglay. The gobernador laughed so hard he started coughing. He coughed until his heart came out of his mouth in pieces, then he became very angry. The gobernador said Lim Pay was planning to do something bad. He said the Sanglays were thinking of hurting the Kastila and stealing their silver to bring back to Amoy. He said Sanglay boats with many warriors were coming to attack Maynila and ordered Lim Pay to surrender his wooden noses. Lim Pay was so angry he shouted at the gobernador and ran out of the palacio.

Lim Pay went to the Parian—the Pueblo of the Sanglays, where Father, Mother, and I often go after Sunday Mass to eat at the panciteria—to tell his friends that the gobernador was sending soldiers to take away their goods and close down their stores. Ah Beng said the Sanglays were very scared and some became angry. They thought of taking their knives and attacking the palacio but Lim Pay told them not to.

I remember how afraid everyone was inside Intramuros. From our window, we could see the guardia civil running and marching and the comandante shouting. Mother told me not to leave the walled city and brought me to church to hear Mass. Prayle Sebastian said the Sanglays had been possessed by a demon because they danced with a colored dragon and set off fireworks during the feast of Our Lady of Sorrows. He said the wooden noses were really crucifixes of the devil that Lim Pay had brought with him to capture the souls of Indios. Don Camilo also remembered that the insect which bit his nose years ago had small eyes and a pigtail and must have been from Amoy.

Father did not believe Prayle Sebastian or Don Camilo. He said the Sanglays did not care for anyone's soul but only for their silver. Father did not like the Sanglays because they worked too hard and took away everyone's rice. Father made wooden shoes—just like Grandfather— and before many Sanglays came to Maynila to sell things to the galleons from Nueva Esapaña, he had sold many shoes and we had much to eat. Then, he said, everyone started buying everything from the Sanglays, and the Tagalogs became poor. Father wanted me to become a guardia civil.

I saw Ah Beng hiding behind the large stone when we came out from church. I told mother I was going to buy panutsa and ran off to meet Ah Beng. He had with him the red kite with green and yellow wings shaped liked a butterfly's. Ah Beng had promised to bring me a kite when he came back from Amoy. It was the most beautiful kite in the world, and I wanted to hold it, but Ah Beng pulled it away as I reached out.

"Where is the yo-yo you promised me?" he asked in his funny-sounding Tagalog which made me laugh as he frowned. Ah Beng did not like people laughing at the way he spoke.

The first time we met at the Parian, he asked me over to play checkers. "Oy, huanna, I will give you this gold medallion of the Emperor of Cathay if you beat me," he said. "And you give me your pañolito if I win."

I agreed to play with him as I had beaten all my friends before, but Ah Beng's fingers were quick as lightning, and before I could make a move, he had eaten all my pawns. I knew he had cheated and refused to give up my pañolito. We almost fought, but he agreed to teach me his checkers tricks if I would bring him around Tundo and Intramuros. Since then, we became very good friends, and he would bring me small toys and strange fruits from the many places he visited as a servant boy aboard his uncle's sampan. He told me stories of horses with horns and pigs bigger than our church and dark-skinned people with earlobes reaching their bellies.

Mother did not like me being friends with a Sanglay orphan who was not baptized and sometimes looked dirty. But she often allowed me to fly kites with Ah Beng at the marshes beside the river and to catch fishlings. She said I should teach him about Jesus, and I did, but Ah Beng said the Sanglay gods were stronger and did not allow demons to crucify them. I knew he was only fooling but I did not care too much for Church stories myself.

"I have your yo-yo at home," I said.

"You're lying," he shouted.

"No I'm not!" I said. "We Tagalogs don't lie; only pagan Sanglays do that!"

Ah Beng stared at me with eyes that reminded me of those of the colored dragon the Sanglays dance with. He picked up a stone, and just as I thought he would hurl it at me, Ah Beng turned and marched away. I ran after him.

"I'm sorry, Ah Beng," I said, and I truly was. I also wanted so much to get my hands on the butterfly kite. I had never wanted anything more. "I'm sorry," I repeated. "I'll get you your yo-yo. I promise."

"All right," he said, tossing the kite to me. "Take it. I have three more back at the boat." I handled the kite carefully as I would a newly-born chick, afraid of injuring it however slightly. Then Ah Beng told me about the many sacks of noses aboard Lim Pay's sampan and how the gobernador was angry with the Sanglays and that people were sharpening their knives. I understood then what the older people were so scared about, and without telling Mother, we ran off to look at Lim Pay's wooden noses.

We were halfway to the Parian when we heard the loud explosions and people shouting. We could see smoke rising to the skies and the clouds turn reddish and gold.

"What's going on, Ah Beng?" I asked, at once fearful.

"I don't know," he whispered, and I could see that he was just as scared.

"I think we should go back to Intramuros," I said. "It may be safer inside."

I could see tears in his eyes, and I realized for the first time that Ah Beng was not as tough as I thought, that he was just a boy like me. "I must go to our sampan," he said, swallowing his tears. "I must go to my uncle."

"Come home with me," I shouted, trying to drag him with me. And then a heavy hand gripped my shoulder. It was Father, his face pale as the moonlight on a cloudless night.

"What are you doing here, Manolo?!" he screamed. "All of Maynila is going mad!"

"What is happening, Father?"

"The Sanglays have killed the cura," he said. "The guardia civil and many men are marching to the Parian to find the culprits. Come. We must hurry back to the walled city before the fighting erupts!"

I looked at Ah Beng who seemed rooted to the earth like a young tree whose branches had been cut. His face was blank. "What about him?" I asked Father.

Father stared at Ah Beng a while and turned away. "He is one of them," Father said. "He must go where he belongs."

"He is my friend!" I shouted. "I won't let anyone hurt him!"

"We must save ourselves, Manolo!" Father yelled and dragged me away. But a number of men bearing torches were suddenly upon us. "Here, Carlos," one of them said, handing Father a torch. "Let us go punish the pagans!"

I looked at Father and saw the beads of sweat running down his face. He turned to me slightly, and his hands were shaking as he took hold of the torch. One of the men collared Ah Beng.

"Go home, boys!" Father shouted us. "Go! Manolo, Roberto...go!" But the man held to Ah Beng's pigtail. "They are my sons," Father said.

"This one too?" the man called Procopio asked, pointing at Ah Beng.

"Yes," Father whispered, and I think he brought the torch closer to the other man's face. "He is a binyagan—a baptized Christian— a mestizo Sanglay, an orphan I have adopted," Father said, his voice no longer shaking but strong and hard.

The man looked at us and pulled at Ah Beng's pigtail. "Then, what need does he have for this?" he said and brought his knife to Ah Beng's head. Ah Beng screamed, and Father pulled out his own balisong. "Leave him alone, Procopio," Father shouted. "I will take care of that myself."

The man let go of Ah Beng, and Father pushed us both away so hard we almost fell to the ground. "Go back to the city," he screamed at us. "Take care of your mother!"

I ran like the wind, like there were a hundred hungry hounds chasing us, like there were horses with horns behind us and pigs the size of churches as I dragged along a weeping Ah Beng.

Ah Beng stayed with us for many days. Father forbade him to leave the house. Father said that if the men found out that he had lied about Ah Beng, we would all be in trouble. When the fire at the Parian at last died out and the older people stopped shouting and acting like crazy, Mother allowed us to leave Intramuros. All I wanted was to run to the marshes and fly my butterfly kite, but I knew Ah Beng would go back to the Parian.

Father had told us not to go there and I was afraid of what we might see. No houses were left standing and everywhere were ashes and burnt wood. The Sanglays had been taken away and were to be sent home in a boat. Someone told Ah Beng his uncle Lim Pay had died in the fire that burned their sampan.

I thought Ah Beng would burst into tears, but he just stood at the dock looking at the remains of his uncle's boat— the beloved sampan that had taken him to many shores and brought home to me countless toys and tales. I knew he would not have anymore stories to tell.

I told Ah Beng he could say with us, that my parents wanted to adopt him. But when the boat came to take away the Sanglays, Ah Beng went with them. He said he would find another sailor to serve. Ah Beng took with him the yo-yo and promised to fly a giant kite someday from Amoy that would bring me toys and fruits. To this day, whenever I see a large kite sailing across the sky, I think of my old friend Ah Beng and wonder where in the world he has sailed to. Perhaps soon my kapitan will allow me to navigate our ship, and we shall sail to the land of the dark-skinned people with long ears where Ah Beng may have gone to catch blue and yellow butterflies.

Not long after the burning of the Parian, the older people began to complain about the lack of rice, sugar, sweets, shoes, clothes, and other stuff that they used to buy from the Sanglays. Some of them were angry at the gobernador for having sent home all of the Sanglays and said that some should be asked to come back. Slowly, some of the Sanglays started returning to Maynila, and by the time I became a sacristan, they had built up another pueblo beside the Pasig.

Few people remember the story that I have just recalled; some say that none of this really happened or that no one found out what Lim Pays's sampan really contained. Still, some years after the Ingles went away, a fisherman in the island of Cebu named Alon-alon brought ashore a sack of old wooden noses that he took to the cura. There was at that time an epidemic sweeping Cebu, and many were sick. The santos in the churches, my grandmother said, were all sad and weeping and their noses had began to fall off. The cura, knowing God had sent him an omen, asked the Sanglay artisans to repaint the old noses from the sea and replace them on the disfigured santos. The old people say that all the santos suddenly looked so real and became miraculous so that the sick were healed and sickness went away.

I often tell Father, who is now a printer of books, that many strange things happened that year when the Parian burned down because it was the year of the monkey. The *Sanglays* say that the naughty monkey loves to create confusion and make people angry. "Don't be silly," he answers. "There are no such things; times do not behave like animals. It was 1766."

And so it was. But sometimes I like to remember it too as a season of ten thousand noses. 🐒

Old Man

Brian Ascalon Roley

Late last year my father, a man whom I had not seen in many years, slit his wrists in an unfurnished apartment on the dry dusty foothills of San Bernardino County. A nurse from the hospital called to inform me that my father was recovering and under suicide watch and suggested I come over.

He looked so gaunt there, in his hospital bed, his knobby knees visible beneath the thin sheets. He looked so different than the young handsome man I remembered, who'd left us for a mistress and filed for divorce right after running up a credit card debt and filing for bankruptcy. He'd just bought matching Saabs for himself and his girlfriend, an Iranian dentist whose snooty exiled family lived in Beverly Hills. His wavy Italian hair, his dimples that charmed so many women, the soldier's hardened arms—none of it here now on the man before me. His skin had become ashen gray, his hairline receded to show a freckled sallow scalp, his arms scrawny and biceps gone to flab. His eyes seemed larger now, vulnerable in their sockets, as they looked needily up at me.

Hey Tomas, thanks for showing up, he said. How'd you know I was here?

The nurse called.

I didn't tell her how to reach you, didn't want to subject you to this, he said.

I know, I said, not calling him on his lie.

He glanced away, then back again.

You look good, he said. His smile caused his face to wrinkle, like piecrust that took effort to move.

Why'd you do it?

I'm sorry.

He looked away to stop himself from crying. I worried that I would irritate him that way and changed the subject. What you been up to? I asked. You living in Southern California again?

Yeah. For the last two years.

You didn't like New York?

It didn't work out.

The nurse said you'll be fine. You'll be able to leave here in no time.

Yeah, they wanted to release me into your care. I refused to let them do that. They just don't want the responsibility.

What about Ramita?

She left me. A year ago.

I nodded. What have you been up to work wise?

I'm an optometrist.

No shit.

Yeah, it's true. Can you believe it? He reached over

to his bedside table and took up a pair of reading glasses from their case. He placed them on his face. They looked expensive with wire rims and a contemporary design but their youthfulness made his skin look haggard.

I got these at a discount, he said.

Do you need anything?

He hesitated.

What?

Is Gabe around? he asked.

No.

Where does he live?

He still lives with Mom. With his girlfriend and daughter in the main house. I live in a bungalow cottage—a shed really—I built out back. We're all together.

My father's face changed. Gabe didn't want to come here, I said.

But you did.

I came.

That's what I meant, he said. Thanks.

I gave no reply.

Gabe is the one I'd thought would have come, he said.

I know it.

He nodded. He pushed his wire rimmed glasses, which seemed too large for his gaunt formerly handsome face, up on his nose. This made him squint and I noticed a permanent vertical furrow dividing his forehead. He said, You'll come back tomorrow?

~

On my drive back to Venice, on Los Angeles freeways that bottlenecked near the glistening skyscrapers of downtown, beneath an azure sky wind-scoured from last night's Pacific Ocean storm, I was thinking about this man I called my father. And I happened to hear an old Neil Young song on the radio, "Old Man." I had loved the melancholy banjo and slide guitar and feeble voice, but never paid attention to the lyrics before. But I caught them now, and the hair stood on the back of my neck.

Old Man take a look at my life
I'm a lot like you
I need someone to love me the whole day through
Old man take a look at my eyes and you can tell that's true

Hands on the wheel, I froze. Gripped tight. Images arrested me of my son hugging my leg, tightly pushing his face against my side, saying, Please don't go, Daddy, stay and play with me.

I've got to go, Em. I have to work.

He clung. Please.

The desperateness of his voice, the wide eyes. He could read me. He'd see my hesitation, my weakness, and his charming smile came in for the kill, with the lower lip threatening to push out into a cry. And I'd reach down and hug him. I had to go to work, but I'd stay and play his game of Candyland, help finish assembling the Lego castle, push Percy around the Thomas the Train set.

You would not think I was like him by looking at my life, my lonely bungalow, its empty bed, all my nights alone.

But my father. You could look at his life, when I was a kid, and see the old man in the song with that thirsty need. I recalled an image of Dad in bed, wearing his robe, face haggard from a bad hangover, as I stood in the door with my backpack.

Don't go, he said.

I have school.

You don't need what those idiot teachers tell you in those stupid books. You think they have something to share with you, some knowledge to pass on that I don't? How many of them have PhDs? Not that my doctorate is good for shit, but you got to wonder about a person like that why they didn't go for one.

Really, I have to go.

Don't leave me here. Come on. We'll hit the boardwalk, have ice cream, walk down to the ocean.

I nervously clutched my bag straps. I'll get in trouble if I cut class.

I'll write them a note.

We've done this too many times already this year. I've hit my limit.

All right, then. Don't come if you don't want to.

He turned away from me, lips pursed angrily. He faced the wall. He touched his jaw as if someone had punched it with a sledgehammer.

We can go to the boardwalk after I get out of school, I said. I'll skip basketball practice.

Don't bother. I know you don't want to.

I do want to.

Maybe Gabe will want to come with me. We'll go fishing.

We ended up going on a deep sea fishing trip off Marina Del Rey. I was suspended for truancy, but I'd caught ten fish with my father. He taught me how to bait the hooks, reel them in, put the flopping creatures out of their misery by holding them still against the deck in their rucksacks and hammering their heads. He seemed alive now, no sign of his morning funk, his face boyishly smiling, his blue eyes large as Easter eggs, full of contagious spark.

And then, after the divorce, he often came by to take me fishing. He would leave Gabe behind. My brother would sit on the couch with his hands on his lap, muscles tensed, shoulders hunched forward, staring at the carpet, as I got the gear ready and stacked by the front door. Waiting for Dad to arrive. I looked eagerly out the window, at the grainy predawn light, the ghostly outlines of the street. When he pulled up in his black convertible Saab, I gathered up the gear and hurried out the front door so he wouldn't have to come in and rub it in Gabe's face.

You could go for years like this, as a kid, and be thankful for a few days a month or summer. To drink in your time with your father. But I got older and began to see things different, began to unforgive him for what he had done to our mother, how he made her cry, how she couldn't face her extended family for months and avoided the fiestas and barbeques. How we could not even rent movies at the Odyssey because we could not get a credit card because the man had filed for bankruptcy right before the divorce. How our house took on a mildewy odor because his old fish tanks broke one night, splaying algae-ridden water and baby octopus and sea urchin and shark over the blue carpet, along with bright flopping tropical fish, carpet we could not afford to replace. Mom stayed up all night trying to shampoo and scrub the smell away, but gave up near dawn, crying over the orange bucket, and entered a funk she did not get out of again; I latched the door to his old hobby room and plastered the gap along the floor, but the stink still seeped out to the rest of the house. I'd wake up from dreams thinking I could feel the residue of seawater on my skin, which was sticky to the touch.

I stopped returning his calls, and right away he began taking Gabe on our old outings. He took him fishing and camping up into the Sierra Mountains. They surfed together. They went on road trips to Mexico, Santa Fe, a visit to family out in New York. Me, I would not even talk to family on his side. They were all NY Italians; I spent all my family time with the West Coast Filipinas eating sizzling adobo spooned onto steaming rice, crisp lumpia, and empanadas baked with sugar on their brown crusts.

On my brother's eighth birthday, my mother threw Gabe a party. She invited all the kids at his school, made the invitation cards herself using parchment paper, colored inks, shapes of cakes and candles cut delicately out of colored tissue paper. She dressed up our house with confetti, bright streamers, hung a piñata in the yard which she had splurged to buy on Alvarado Street. She bought little gifts for the kids, candies and toys wrapped in small plastic pumpkins. She made the cake herself, yellow with purple ube frosting—my brother's favorite, a sweet Filipino root.

The kids were to arrive at noon. Mom hurried about the house making last minute preparations, fretting because she wanted everything to be perfect for the kids, and because she worried about what the white American mothers would think of our little house, the ube frosting, the gift packs, the lunch she'd made. Nobody likes Filipino food, she fretted.

You don't know that, I said.

All our restaurants go out of business, she insisted. You can find Thai, Chinese, Japanese, Korean everywhere—everything but Filipino! She wrung her hands and shook her head. Maybe I shouldn't have made lumpia and adobo. Maybe I should have made BLT sandwiches instead.

I reassured her it would be okay.

At ten the doorbell rang. Someone's early! my mother panicked.

I set my hand on her shoulder, squeezed it reassuringly, and went to answer it. I opened the door and was shocked to see my father standing there. He wore a tailored black blazer, ink blue designer jeans, maroon silk shirt, and wing tip shoes, which I noticed looked expensive. Yet his hair had grown out, and he had a scruffy beard that pressed uncomfortably against his expensive collar as if it felt confined.

What are you doing here? I said.

Nice to see you too, son, he said. Can you get Gabe?

My mother came up behind me. Russ?

I'm here to bring my son to his birthday lunch. I made reservations at The Ivy.

He can't come, I said.

It's his birthday. I'm his father. You had him for breakfast and will have him for dinner. It's a Saturday.

We talked about this, Russ, my mother said. He's having a party.

You didn't invite me.

It's a kids' party.

Well, I can see I'm not welcome.

Don't be like this. Please.

He pursed his lips and turned aside, fingering his shirt button as if to keep up his dignity. Just get Gabe so I can talk to him, wish him a happy birthday.

My mother hesitated, sensing ulterior intentions. She looked at me warily.

He's getting ready, I said. Why don't you come back later?

I live an hour away.

Dad, you didn't come by last week. You were supposed to take him fishing.

Not last week I wasn't.

Yes you were, I insisted. He was waiting for you all morning. He sat there on the couch, with his rod assembled and his tackle box at his feet. He refused to eat Mom's eggs, because he said you and him always stopped by McDonald's for breakfast. He didn't eat or put his rod away until two.

Well, then he got his facts wrong, my father said: Why didn't he call me? Why didn't you call me?

Russ, my mother said.

He should have called rather than sitting around worrying everybody. Get him here so I can have a talk with him.

Russ, please. Mommy was chewing on her knuckles; she glanced at the front lawn through the window, then at her watch. The other children and their mothers will soon be here, she said.

He stared at her harshly. You don't want them to meet me?

I don't want Gabe to get upset before the party. You know how long it takes him to recover.

My father nodded as if in agreement. Then he fumbled with his shirt button again, deep in thought, and shook his head. You're embarrassed of me.

No, Russ.

Listen here. You aren't married to me anymore. And I am the boy's father. You have no right to be *embarrassed* of me. That's not your role anymore. Not your *right*.

He was pacing now, scratching his overgrown beard. It had really gone shaggy, with white ends.

Dad, why don't you get out of here, please?

He turned on me with a gaze that burned. My cheeks caught fire. He kept his eyes on me for an excruciating moment, then, with the manner of the insulted, he turned down the hall to find Gabe. And I did not go after him. He'd always done demonstrative little gestures when he got drunk and felt Mommy was afraid he'd embarrass her; on a trip out to Manila for my cousin's debut, at the Makati Polo Club he had had too much to drink and tried dancing up her teenage friend, only to stumble over a banquet table and spill punch and liquor over a dozen dresses and white barongs.

I turned to my mother, worried that she'd be crying. But she seemed too busy worrying, glancing back and forth between the front window and then around the room at the party's preparations. The table laid out with festive shimmering purple table cloth and sparkling gold center pieces, the colorful streamers hanging from the walls, the yellow HAPPY BIRTHDAY GABE! banner, the balloon clusters pressing up against the ceiling, their strings dangling ready to be taken as a party favor by the little guests.

Against the opposite wall, we'd placed a portable banquet table, covered it in the festive tablecloth, and set dish upon dish of Filipino foods, covered in foil and condensation-beaded cellophane wrap. All cooked for the parents.

To be honest, I felt a little embarrassed that the other mothers would see how much effort she put into this, given how few mothers would probably be here. Usually at these parties, several fathers would drop off their kids and disappear to run errands until the ending time. Mom had fretted over this party for weeks, because she knew Gabe was quiet and had few friends. He had seen a speech therapist and there'd been talk of keeping him back a year, and some professional debate among his therapists and teachers over whether he was developmentally delayed or simply exposed to too much Tagalog (Mom's sister, brother, and mother often ate with us and always talked in Taglish). It was decided that the family should try speaking only English. Now, Gabe and I could no longer speak the language, though we could understand it, though less well each year, like memories of old friends and places that were fading no matter how hard you try to cling to them by going over them in your mind.

Look, Tomas, it's Kayla and her mother!

She was at the window, but I nudged her to back away so that the approaching pair would not see her looking out.

We waited by the front door for them to knock. She was clenching her elbows tight.

Relax, Mom. Everything looks great.

I hope everyone shows up.

They RSVP'd.

I know. But there's been so many birthday parties already this fall. Maybe people will change their mind.

Why don't you open the door? I suggested.

Let's let them knock first, she said.

So we waited. Maybe we should get Gabe, she said. But she made no move to go back there.

Dad would come out, I said. Maybe we should let him say what he wants to say, and then I'll go back and try to get him to go out the back door.

You think he will?

Sure, I said uncertainly.

She looked at me doubtfully, then jumped at the sound of the door knocking. But she put on her best social face and greeted Kayla and her mother, a South Asian woman in completely western clothes. My mother, unlike most Filipinas I know, was not a gregarious person and you could see the effort in her anxious smiles, as she led the girl to the play area she'd set up. She chatted with Kayla's mother for a moment, but seemed to struggle with small talk, and glanced at me with pleading eyes, asking me to go back and check on Gabe.

As I went into the hallway, I heard the doorbell ring and the voices of more kids and parents entering.

Our house is rather narrow and long, because the rear was originally a screened porch and you have to access it through a separate hallway closed by two doors. The party voices became muted behind me and I could hear my brother and father talking, as I stood outside Gabe's door. My father sounded unhappy with him, but also a bit eager to please. I knew that tone. It meant that he did not want to be alone.

Stiffening, I forced myself to knock. Father's voice hushed, a needling silence, followed by an irritated, Yes?

I nudged the door open. They looked at me: Gabe was standing and my father sat on the edge of my brother's bed.

We're having a talk, Tomas, father said.

Your friends are beginning to arrive, I told my brother.

We'll be out in a few minutes, our father said.

Gabe was avoiding our eyes, staring at the ground.

Actually, if you don't mind using the back exit, I think that would be best.

You think that would be best.

Yeah.

You're a twelve-year-old boy. Twelve-year-old boys don't talk like that, he said. He made no move.

Mom put a lot of effort into this party. You're not going to ruin it, I said. My voice was trembling. My hands at my sides shook too.

Fine. He suddenly stood. Come on, Gabe. We'll go out the backdoor. We'll skip this clam bake. After the Ivy, we'll head down to San Clemente and do some shore fishing. Get your rod and tackle box.

He started for the backdoor, and looked back for my brother to follow him. Gabe hesitated. But my brother noticed our father's face begin to crumble and he went over to his closet and got out his rod and tackle box.

Gabe, I said. What are you doing?

He avoided my eyes, both of our eyes, as he began to fit the pieces of his rod together. He was kneeling to screw them tight, keeping his face away from us, and I thought he was crying. He finished assembling the rod, but stopped there. I thought he was deciding to stay. We were all quiet. We could all hear the muffled party noise coming in, the laughing kids and gossiping mothers, even the lower sound of somebody's father telling some boisterous joke. I had told my mother to buy a case of beer for the parents, and maybe that was working.

My brother needed a nudge. I approached my brother to put the rod back in the closet. I got my hand on the thin spry surface. It was an expensive rod our father had bought me several years ago, with money that he was not supposed to have, but I no longer used it. I began to lift it.

Don't let him take it, my father snapped.

His voice had changed now, to that angry tone, and Gabe held the rod from me. I froze, then proceeded to peel his fingers off one by one. He did not resist. I took the pole back to my closet, my back turned to our father's face, because I did not want to see his reaction—whether it be anger or hurt.

Then I returned to my brother, who himself was keeping his eyes rigidly focused on his shirt sleeve button as he fingered it; I took his hand and led him towards the inner door, the muted sounds of the waiting party. He tried to look back at our father, but I touched his cheek to redirect his eyes.

My own eyes did, however, catch a glimpse of his feet. His polished shoes were awkwardly pigeon-toed, touching at the fronts, nervously tapping, and his hands drooped beneath his knees almost down to his calves.

I expected our father to call out to us, or even to set his hand on my back. But he did not. However, as we left the room I could hear his heavy breathing.

We did not look back, as we made our way to Gabe's party: I held my brother's elbow and pulled him against me tight. 🌼

My Father's Tattoo

Veronica Montes

*A*long time ago, before he was my father, my father was 19 years old. On a drunken dare, the complete facts of which have never been known, he stumbled into Chinatown with a couple of buddies determined to prove his devotion to a 17-year-old girl with dark eyes named Rosario. In the tattoo parlor, a bald and toothless Chinese man observed as his teenage prodigy delicately etched "Rosario" in perfect script on my father's left bicep. In awe of his own talent, the young artist surrounded it with elegant curlicues at no extra charge.

But two weeks later, Rosario was seen all over town in the passenger seat of Romy Bautista's racing green convertible sports car. My humiliated father explained to anyone who would listen that Rosario was the name of his long-deceased mother.

Two years later while my father sat nursing a vodka tonic in a San Francisco nightclub called Bimbo's, he saw my mother for the first time. Her skin was the color of cream-filled coffee and her straight black hair fell halfway down her back like a perfectly draped sheet. When he asked her to dance, she made him smile by saying, "No, thank you." Her friend, an unusually tall and badly dressed girl, invited him to sit down. My mother shrugged her shoulders. She liked that my father's shirt was white and starched and didn't sit square on his shoulders, but drooped a little. The two of them talked until the tall girl, irritated by neglect, began to tap her fingers on the table. My mother refused to write her phone number on a matchbook, so my father learned it by heart while he walked them to their car.

On their fourth date—a trip to Stinson Beach—my mother saw the Rosario tattoo for the first time. She spent the afternoon with her fists clenched, digging her nails into her palms. My father napped in the sun, mistaking their mutual silence for the comfortable kind that exists between two people who have been in love for a long time. He was encouraged. When he brought her home and she stepped out of the car without saying anything, he reached over and touched her arm.

"Rosario," said my dramatic mother.

~

A continuous sore spot in an otherwise ideal courtship, the tattoo almost prevented their marriage. "I want to meet her," my mother would say. Choked with jealousy, she imagined face-to-face confrontation the only way to exorcise the threat of Rosario and to be certain that her own beauty was superior.

"I don't even know where she is, Isabel," my father would say. "I don't even remember her last name." This was true. In fact, except for her eyes, he remembered very little about Rosario. He tried over and over again to remind my mother that the entire short and uneventful romance had ended two years before they had met that foggy night at Bimbo's, but it was useless.

"I don't care, Raymond. I want to see her. Ask Benny. Benny will know."

Tito Benny is my father's older brother and his partner in the two-generation-old family business—"R & B Tailors: A Shop for the Discerning Gentleman." He wore a thin moustache and slicked back his hair, secure in his good looks and beautiful clothes. He dreamed of becoming a movie star and attended drama classes in secret so that his eventual stardom would appear accidental, unrehearsed. His handsome face and false sense of modesty were inherited from my grandfather, who cautioned his children against self-promotion, but coaxed compliments out of unsuspecting people at every opportunity. Tito Benny was blessed with humor enough to look in the mirror every morning, pinch his own cheek, and say, "Don't you ever die." My mother was right. Tito Benny knew.

"She's dead. Last year. Didn't you know? Got hit by a bus on her way to City College. It was right after she was crowned queen of the May Festival," he said.

My father put his head in his hands. A dead Rosario was much worse than a live one. A dead one would remain forever young in my father's memory, a martyred beauty queen struck down on a quest for knowledge.

It was almost more than my mother could stand. A year passed before she was calm enough to say, "Alright," when my father proposed. They staged an elaborate private ceremony a month before the wedding in which she agreed to go through with the wedding as long as he promised never to wear short sleeve shirts and to never, ever attempt to make love to her with the lights on. For her part, my mother promised not to mention the tattoo again.

During the first few months of their marriage, they shut themselves up at home, politely refusing invitations from friends and relatives. They shared secrets and talked about the way their life would be. "I" changed to "we" or "us," and soon they were saying the same thing at the same time, finishing each other's sentences, and waking up having dreamed the same dream, like twins. She brought lunch to the shop every day and fed my father with a long silver spoon they'd received as a wedding gift.

I was born two months after their first anniversary and instantly demanded the kind of attention they wanted only to give to each other. I interrupted them at inopportune moments, oblivious to the importance of privacy for two people so in love. I remember them together, always. I wanted to walk down the street between them, holding hands. And when we came to a puddle I wanted them to swing me high in the air.

Once, when I was very small, I sat on the living room floor tracing patterns in the carpet and pretending not to watch them. They shared the big chair in the corner, tucked neatly into each other and talking in low, singsong voices. My father caught me looking and his smile flew across the room and landed like a kiss on my eyelids. He suggested a game of hide-and-seek. Just the two of us. I flushed red with panic. I thought I was being tested and that if I passed the test I could sit in the chair with them.

I scampered around the house, hiding first in one place and then switching to another. My father counted out loud slowly, and I felt that my whole life hinged on where I was when he finished. Out of time, I hid in their bedroom closet, leaving the door open just a little. I surrendered to my failure and sat on the floor with my legs tucked under. After awhile, the two of them stumbled into the bedroom, whispering and hushing each other. My father put a hand over my mother's mouth for a moment before they fell onto the bed. She lay perfectly still until he removed it, and then reared up as if to bite him. When he started to undress her, I closed the closet door quietly and lay down next to their neatly lined up shoes. I fell asleep.

Months later on an otherwise forgettable day, my mother collided with my shirtless father in the hallway. *Shirtless*. I was playing in my room when I heard my mother's disappointed whimper. I stuck my head out of my bedroom door to watch. It happened in slow motion. They froze. My father looked down at his arm and then back up at my mother. She ran out of the house and I stood staring, open-mouthed, at my father's beautiful tattoo. He covered it with his hand and walked into their bedroom. He closed the door behind him.

She returned hours later, unforgiving. "Never, Raymond," she said. "I was never supposed to see that thing again." Her jealousy bordered on the maniacal, complete with hair pulling (her own) and illogical complaints about the order of the universe. "I wish you'd never met her. I wish you were never 19. Why did you ever have to be 19? God! You make me sick, okay? You make me sick. Get away. Just get away." She pounded her fists on her thighs. My father tried to hold her like in the movies when a beautiful woman becomes hysterical, but she punched at his chest and in the end, he had to leave. He took enough clothing to last three days and walked the four blocks to Tito Benny's small apartment. He was back home by the end of the week, but things were different between my parents.

By the time I was seven years old, fights about Rosario could be counted on, just like dentist appointments and birthdays. I spent my time running from our house to Tito Benny's and back again, observing the behavior of my lovesick parents. I did it for myself, enjoying what it felt like to be near one of them without having the other around. But even apart, they were too wrapped up in each other to notice me, neither one deceptive enough to use me to their advantage. I wanted them to, though. I thought the whole thing could be a family project.

I spent the mornings with my mother, who was always crying and puffy-eyed and sorry. I watched her from the bedroom doorway while she sat on the edge of their bed, her pretty hands folded in her lap. She stared at a spot on the wall and repeated Rosario's name for minutes at a time. Then she would get a terrible look on her face, like she'd eaten something rotten, and she would shake her head from side to side quickly, her black hair flying all around.

After school, I went straight to my uncle's apartment and tried to keep my father company. But we were never alone. Tito Benny always had girls at his place. White girls with blonde hair, noses that ended in a tip, big earrings. He met them in drama class, where his slight accent and long, elegant Spanish cigarettes made an impression. The women had curvy, full figures and bright, defiant mouths and teetered around the place on high heels, smoking cigarettes and humming. This seemed wrong to me. It seemed that Tito Benny should be just as in love with my mother as my father was. Or at least be attracted to approximations of her— women of approximately the same height and build, women who dressed the way she did, wore their hair the same way, walked the same way, and who wore shoes that she might have picked out for herself. But he gravitated towards her garish opposite and I felt sorry for him.

"How 'bout the tits on that one, Raymond? Huh? Great tits."

My father sulked on the couch, ignoring his brother. I sulked with him, leaning my head awkwardly on his arm.

~

When my mother became pregnant, she grew more sensitive than ever to reminders, real or imagined, of Rosario. Soon, women named "Rose," or the announcement of the new May Festival Queen, or tattoos, or Chinatown, or the sight of my father's buddies teasing him into one more beer or one last card game was enough to drive my mother into a relentless tirade about her life's misfortune.

"I deserve more than this, Raymond. I am no one's second choice. Do you understand me? Queen of the goddamn May Festival. So what? Are you listening to me? Raymond? Raymond!" She went on and on while my father sat on the couch, staring at her.

Just as my mother's body began to grow heavy, my father moved to Tito Benny's permanently. A few weeks later, I came home from school to find Tito Benny waiting. My mother, he said, had left to stay with her cousin in Sacramento. I can't remember if I cried—I suppose I must have—but I do know that I expected to stay in our house by myself and, in fact, had been preparing for it for quite some time. I knew how to make macaroni and cheese, soup from a can, cinnamon toast, orange juice, hot dogs. I knew how to vacuum, make my own bed, and dust.

But my father came home to me.

~

I was nine years old that summer, homely and clumsy, with a tangled, half-hearted ponytail and small spaces between all of my teeth. Still, my father taught me to dance. He kept his eyes closed and gave a tiny kick when he stepped back, a little flit of the ankle, very cool and smooth. He wore a white shirt buttoned to the top, baggy brown trousers, shiny brown shoes. I kept my shoulders still, like he said, and moved from the waist down, like he said. Tito Benny sat in a corner smoking and counting out loud for us: one, two, one-two-three.

When I learned how to pivot, it was the triumph of my childhood. "Yes, yes, yes!" my father said, laughing and spinning me around. Tito Benny tossed his cigarette into his beer can so he could whistle and clap. Dizzy and exhausted from my effort I fell to the floor, smiling.

~

On sunny days my father and Tito Benny sometimes closed the shop, complaining that they'd been working too hard. "Don't you think so?" they'd ask me. We took drives along the coast, sometimes just the two of us, sometimes all three. The Cadillac was a gift from a happy customer—a stocky, pockmarked, Irish gangster whose wardrobe my father had tailored extraordinarily well.

We drove for hours at a time, occasionally stopping for lunch in Santa Cruz or Monterey. I liked to sit between them playing with the buttons on the radio while my father whistled and Tito Benny tapped his long fingers on the dashboard. I fell asleep to their music and woke up groggy, squinting at the sparkling ocean. More than once, I opened my eyes to find that we'd made it as far as Santa Barbara, where we feasted on Mexican food and checked in to a motel so close to the beach I could hear the sound of the waves as they hit the shore.

~

"Daddy, my lips hurt."

"You're eating too much mango, that's why."

"Who says?"

"I says, that's who," he answered, playing our private "incorrect English" game. We liked to play when Tito Benny was around because he never quite understood what we were doing, and so we shared secret laughs and crossed our eyes at each other. Tito Benny always said, "Ano ba? What's going on?"

"Will my lips shrink when I get older?"

"Do you want them to?"

"No. Because then I'll look like Alice Tipler."

"She has no lips?"

"Just skinny ones. Itty bitty skinny lippies." I sucked on a mango seed. "And short hair. Awful yellow hair." My father cut a mango into thirds from top to bottom, cupped an outside section in his hand and scored it. He handed it to me, and I pushed on its belly. It bloomed like a flower.

"That one's for me," he said. "You're getting sticky." He took the mango from my hands and kissed my palms.

"But I love mangoes. Love, love, love, love them." He handed it back to me.

"Why don't you call your mom today?"

"Why don't I don't?" I said, trying to play our game.

"See how she's doing."

"Why doesn't you?" I said.

We left it at that.

~

Sometimes when I napped in the afternoon, I stayed asleep until dinnertime. My father and Tito Benny would come to wake me up, sitting on either side of my bed like two old ladies.

"Are you dreaming" Tito Benny would ask in a whisper so exaggerated it was louder than his speaking voice. I kept my eyes closed, but could never stop myself from smiling.

"It must be a good dream, Benny. She's smiling," my father said.

"Smiling? I think she's laughing," Tito Benny said. And by then, I was.

"Well? Good dreams?" my father asked, lifting me so that I sat up against the headboard.

"Yes."

"Are you going to tell us?"

I shook my head.

"A secret, huh?" my father asked.

"Yes."

~

On a Sunday morning at the end of that summer, my father and I were slicing onions and smashing garlic for the corned beef hash while Tito Benny read the comics out loud. We laughed together at the funny things and looked at each other skeptically when we didn't understand the jokes. Then we had a "skeptical look" contest which Tito Benny, with his drama school training, easily won. He arched his left eyebrow way up and curled his lips to one side. My father and I laughed so hard we had to hold on to each other to keep from falling down. Then a key turned in the lock and the door opened and my mother was standing there beside her suitcase with a baby in her arms, looking beautiful.

We stopped laughing and my father let me go, gently. Tito Benny was the first to greet her. He kissed her on the cheek. "Kumusta ka, Isabel? Everything fine with you?" he said. He pulled aside the receiving blanket to peek at my baby sister. Then he left.

My father stood beside me, perfectly still. In the space between us, I could feel his desire to do exactly the right thing. He walked towards her, and for a moment I thought maybe he would keep walking, that he would brush past her, and walk straight through the door and down the street without looking back.

But he didn't.

Of course he didn't. 🌸

Clothesline

Edgar Poma

Robby's mom was planning a September wedding to a guy who was a famous jockey, as in horses, not radio. The problem was that Robby, who was 11 years old, had gotten used to just him and his mom living on their own. Their house was spread far apart from their neighbors: it was surrounded on three sides by hayfields and orchards, and bordered on one side by a levee and the Sacramento River. There was not much excitement where they lived, though the clothesline in their backyard seemed to move just inches out of the reach of the shade tree that sprawled outward with the passing of each year.

It didn't impress Robby that his future stepdad, Sebastien, nicknamed Seb, was a rich, good-looking celebrity who had a huge home in Northern Kentucky that he had bought from his earnings as a very successful jockey. Robby didn't have anything against thoroughbred horses; jockeys were another matter. If he had to have a dad, he would have liked one who relied on his own power, and not some animal's, to make a living. He also wasn't impressed that Seb was moving his new family to a gated farm called Peppermint just a mile from where he and his mom lived now. The farm sat on 92 acres, with an 8-bedroom brick house, guesthouse, pond, stables, track, and grazing cows and horses.

Seb purchased the farm after the three of them had looked at some stately Victorians with multiple turrets and wraparound porches that stood proudly on the levee, but the adults decided that they needed a quiet and secure place that wasn't exposed to his fans, stalkers and the just plain curious.

One thing that bugged Robby was that his future stepdad was like a garden gnome come to life. Seb was under 5 feet 4 and 110 pounds, age 38. When Robby stood next to him, they looked almost like twins. Robby, though, had darker skin. Seb was Filipino on his mom's side and French-Canadian on his dad's, while Robby was Filipino on his mom and dad's side. Robby's dad left his girlfriend, Robby's mom, while she was carrying their child, and was never heard from again.

Early in the summer, Seb asked Robby to be his Best Man. Robby was silent at first, but accepted reluctantly, after his mom gave him the "look" from across the room. When they were alone, she said, "It won't be so bad, honey. Being someone's Best Man is an honor. You're the important guy with the rings."

Robby's eyes suddenly lit up. "Hey, isn't the Best Man also supposed to take care of the bachelor party with strippers? I can do that."

His mom said, "Keep dreaming."

He theatrically rubbed his hands hard like he was scheming, and said, "OK, but at least I get to toast him at the reception."

"Yes, but we'll make sure that your glass is filled with sparkling cider."

Robby had accompanied his mom while she was doing her volunteer work and this gave them the opportunity to chat. For a while now, every week, she prepared and delivered baskets of hot homemade food wrapped in foil to seniors who lived on their own.

~

In the car, Robby was distracted by the wonderful smells from the backseat. His mom seemed to read his mind, and said, "Oh, I made you a snack pack." She reached into the space beside the driver's seat and brought out an ice cold Coke and a rectangular Tupperware filled with hot rice and slices of juicy roast pork.

Robby gobbled that down, and for a while he was content helping his mom. But after the third basket delivery, he got antsy. The old people were lonely and tended to delay his mom with chatter. By the 11th delivery, he'd had enough. He was bored and tired. But his mom said they had only one more delivery to make—it was to a Filipino man, a manong, which technically meant older brother but could refer to an older male relative or acquaintance. Roberto Labrado lived in a dilapidated two-story bunkhouse in a pear orchard outside town. He was infirmed, and confined to his room all day long.

"Why does this Robert dude live so far out of town anyway?" Robby asked.

"Call him Uncle Robert," his mom said, reminding him that he had to show respect. And gratitude. She said that Uncle Robert, like her own late father as well as Robby's dad's dad, was one of many young Filipino men who left the Philippines to travel overseas to the United States in the 1920s to find work and send money to their families back home. They did back-breaking work in the sugar cane and pineapple fields throughout the Hawaiian Islands, before moving on to California for more back-breaking work picking crops.

Uncle Robert settled in the Sacramento Valley where he was hired to run the pear orchard for a Danish family that had owned the land for several generations since the 1890s. When he was 75, the family he worked for moved from their one-story house that was next door to the bunkhouse after hiring a company to run the orchard for them. But they made it clear that Uncle Robert could remain in the bunkhouse, or their old house if he wanted, for as long as he lived. Now, at the age of 100, he was approaching the end of his life. He chose to remain in the bunkhouse.

When Robby said he wanted to stay in the car, his mom said, "No, you're coming with me. Besides, he has the same name as you do."

"That doesn't mean anything. I'm a junior already, remember? Just because I had the same name as my dad didn't make him stay. He didn't even wait until after I was born." His annoyance was made worse by the thought of Seb. "By the way, with all the dudes there are in the world, couldn't you hook up with one who was tall?"

"Quit talking, get out of the car, and help me deliver the damn basket."

Robby gave in, but slammed the car door. He removed his T-shirt because it was hot outside, but it was cool inside the dark, gloomy bunkhouse. He carried the basket. She brought some medical supplies, since she was a registered nurse. Side by side they went up the creaking stairs to Uncle Robert's room. There wasn't anyone else living in the bunkhouse. Previously, it had been the home of numerous workers, depending on the season. But now workers were bussed in from other places, so there was no need for them to live onsite. The company hired to be the caretaker of the orchard looked after many orchards, not just one. Unfortunately, they didn't care for the land as closely as the Filipino men they replaced, old-timers like Uncle Robert.

The room was warm. They found him in his bed, under the covers. He was awake, and welcomed them with a smile, though he looked weak. While his mom checked his heartbeat and blood pressure, Robby looked around the room. A fan and portable heater stood on the floor next to his bed. There was a large trunk at the foot of the bed. Nearby was a dresser, with a hotplate on it, a small microwave oven, soup packets, crackers, bottles of water. In the corner was a small table and chair, pressed up against the bottom edge of the room's only window, which was open and looked out at the empty house next door and its grassy back yard. The house had a weather-beaten roof. An old wire clothesline stood firm in the yard, despite its rusting posts, away from shade trees it had deftly sidestepped to remain dutifully in the sun.

His mom proceeded to feed Uncle Robert. During this time, Robby stayed near the door. The place gave him the creeps. The room disgusted him: it smelled like urine. He couldn't wait to leave.

As his mom was hugging the old man goodbye, Robby happened to see three large boxes on the floor next to the dresser. Two-foot poles with pointy tops stuck out from the boxes. He moved closer and realized that they were tall clusters of pleated white cone cups, like those used for snow cones, hundreds of them stacked one on top of another, pointy tails up. They were layered with dust.

The snow cone cups fascinated Robby. At home, he went on the Internet to find out anything he could about the ranch and orchard where Uncle Robert lived. When he came up with nothing, he went to the library in town and went through files of old photos and clippings. When he got to the bottom of the last stack, he found a yellowing newspaper photo of a Filipino worker who made extra money on weekends by making and selling snow cones in the town plaza and assorted carnivals. He recognized the vendor as Uncle Robert. He was younger then, with his jet black hair slicked back, but he had the same gentle eyes.

According to the caption, he shaved his ice with an implement that fitted neatly in his hand. He made his own syrups, with sugar and fresh fruit. He mail-ordered the paper for cones, which he formed and glued together himself, and he found a supplier for the ice blocks. He drove a beat-up old car that kept threatening to break down but never did completely.

In the weeks that followed, Robby became more comfortable around Uncle Robert. He no longer hung back near the door. Eventually his mom made Uncle Robert's her first stop, and Robby stayed behind with him until she returned to pick him up. It was now Robby who sat by his bedside to feed him. They hardly said a word, but Robby felt like they were getting to know one another.

In late August, Robby bought a machine-made snow cone from a store in town for Uncle Robert. When Robby presented it to him, the old man smiled, but after a few small bites he lost interest. Robby sulked and complained later to his mom who simply said, "Maybe the ice made his teeth hurt, maybe it wasn't powdery enough like he made them, maybe he thought the strawberry syrup sucked, maybe he liked making those things but not necessarily eating them, or maybe he just didn't have the strength today. Honey, you always have to go beyond the surface to understand something."

The following week, Robby tried to get Uncle Robert to play cards with him, but was unsuccessful. "You don't like cards?" Robby joked. "Are you sure you're Filipino?" When Uncle Robert let his cards fall out of his hands, Robby looked at him, as if to plead, "What can I do for you? Do you want me to read to you? What is it that will make you happy?"

Uncle Robert pointed to the trunk at the foot of the bed, motioning for Robby to open it. When Robby lifted the lid, he found rubber-banded stacks of thousands of unrolled, splayed snow cone cups, all unused. Each of them contained a detailed colored pencil drawing of the same scene: the Danish family's clothesline below, as seen from the window, weighted down with clothes and sheets and pillow cases and aprons and even favorite stuffed toys, week-in and week-out, for at least the past 60 years. They were done so meticulously that Robby could see the design of the buttons on a blouse hanging on the line. The items on the line changed over time, but the scene overall remained the same: it brimmed with more color and life than Robby had ever known.

"You drew these?" Robby asked.

Uncle Robert said nothing but Robby understood that the old man had documented what he'd seen out his window. He probably did it every weekend without fail. It probably relaxed him. It probably pulled him out of any darkness, despair or pain.

It occurred to Robby that perhaps Uncle Robert was trying to convey to him that he wanted to see the panels again, so he sat at his bedside and showed him batches of his creations. But Uncle Robert looked indifferent to them. When he fell asleep, Robby looked at the panels one more time, packed them carefully into the trunk, and then caught his breath. He would tell his mom about the drawings, but he doubted that he could describe how magnificent they were.

There was nothing he looked forward to more than visiting Uncle Robert once a week after school on his mom's days off, sometimes even more than once, even after the family moved to Peppermint Farm and was busy adjusting to its awkward enormity, even for a kid who caught episodes of *Cribs* on MTV now and then. He only missed a visit during the week of the wedding of his mom and Seb, which was held in Sacramento at the Cathedral and a fancy downtown hotel.

At the reception, Robby gave the toast to the groom and said all the right things, but he knew that Seb would be traveling most of the year to ride in big races and make commercials and whatever else he did, and therefore would be clueless about what was happening in Robby's life.

In early October, on a Saturday morning, Seb came home from his travels unexpectedly, and proceeded to unload dirty clothes from his luggage into the washing machine. Robby's mom wasn't home; she had gone to a nursing conference in Tahoe for the weekend. As Robby ate breakfast over the sink in the kitchen, Seb said from the adjacent laundry room, "How do you turn the machine on, Rob?"

Robby sighed. "Is this your way of telling me you want me to do the wash?"

"No, I'm doing it, I just forgot how it works. I know the housekeeper usually does this, but the calendar says it's her weekend off."

Robby went to the laundry room, where he wiped his muffin-oily hands on a shirt because it was going to be washed anyway. Anyway, it was his shirt. Or maybe it was Seb's, he couldn't tell. After he showed Seb the rocket science of turning on the washing machine, and how to measure the soap and put it in, Seb said, "This idea came to me while I was on the road. I couldn't wait to get home this morning to see you and do this."

"What idea? You couldn't wait to come home to do your laundry?" Robby didn't get it.

Before Robby could leave the laundry room, Seb asked him how school was going. Robby wanted to say, "I know this is the first time you've been home in weeks, but you don't have to act like you're so interested in me," but he bit his tongue. When the wash was done, he helped Seb stack the wet clothing in a basket. He was confused, though, when Seb gave him his car keys and told him to load the basket in his car instead of loading the clothes into the dryer. "Let me get a jacket, I'll meet you in the driveway," he told Robby.

Robby wasn't sure what Seb was up to, and was shocked when they drove to Uncle Robert's. He watched Seb carry the basket of wet clothes to the back yard of the one-story house, which Uncle Robert's window overlooked. After searching around, Seb found some old clothespins in a canvas sack. He shook them free of dirt and cobwebs and used them to pin the wet laundry securely on the clothesline. Robby went over to him and said, "How did you know about this? Why do you even care?"

"Aren't I supposed to know what's important to you?" Seb said. "Besides, shouldn't you see if this could possibly be what he wanted all this time?"

Robby raced up to Uncle Robert's room, sat at his bedside, and kissed him hello. He opened the window and motioned toward it. Uncle Robert looked puzzled but allowed Robby to help him out of his bed. By this time, Seb had found his way to the room and helped Robby lead the old man to the window. At the sight of the filled clothesline, Uncle Robert's face brightened with joy.

After they helped Uncle Robert sit down at the table, Robby took a clean snow cone cup from the closest tower and put it on the table. Uncle Robert took the cup apart and pressed it flat. He opened the drawer of the table and took out colored pencils. He set to work, studying the scene and drawing it, while Robby and Seb watched in amazement as he captured the quiet perfection of the moment: their boys' department clothes swaying and dancing in the breeze, their colors turning in the changing light of the sun and clouds, their soft flapping sounding like the beating of wings.

Robby couldn't help lean against his dad, and in doing so, felt, for the first time, the warmth of his presence. 🏵

Son of a Janitor

Tony Robles

*T*he house of a janitor is supposed to be clean. One would assume this to be true because the janitor performs his duties with the sacred mop, broom and toilet brush. My father was a janitor for some 20 odd years at the San Francisco Opera House. It would be 10 years before he'd realize his dream and start the "Filipino Building Maintenance Company" and go into business on his own. At the dinner table he'd ask me questions such as, "What did you learn in school today?" I've always been somewhat of a bad listener. "Nothing" I'd reply—I always replied nothing—not that I was indifferent to school—even at a very young age. Yes, I was very aware of the things they were doing to me in school and after the bell rang I'd let it fall from my mind like some brown, withered old leaf falling off a tree—destined to be stepped on by some kid on their way home. I always liked the sounds those leaves made. My father always told me if I didn't do well in school, I'd end up cleaning toilets all my life. My father didn't graduate from high school and I guess he carried that with him. Somehow he felt that the high school diploma was a key—some kind of rocket fuel which would kick start you into the realm of possibilities. Somehow that slice of paper with whatever burned into it would bring you closer to your dream. It was an access pass of sorts.

"Do you know how to clean?" Dad would, on occasion, talk shop with me--an 11 or 12-year-old kid with no work experience.

"Yeah, I know how to clean," I'd reply.

"Ok," he'd say, "how do you remove chewing gum from a carpet?" Dad would slip in the hypothetical in this manner. I was supposed to use logic and deduction in finding the correct answer.

"I would take a pair of scissors and cut the gum off..."

At this point my father would belch or fart, or perform both simultaneously.

Shaking his head he'd say, "It's very apparent and clearly evident that you don't know anything about cleaning. The way to remove gum from a carpet is to take an ice cube and place it on the gum. Wait 'til it hardens, then remove it with a putty knife." I never asked him what to do if you didn't have an ice cube—perhaps I should have. My father would proudly demonstrate his expertise—explaining how to remove wine stains from a carpet or the correct way to vacuum a rug. "You have to use nice long strokes in the direction of the nap of the carpet. Nice long strokes until it makes you feel good..." By the end of his speech, my food would be cold but my father would urge me to "eat all that food on your plate or I'm gonna knock you upside your head." He had a great sense of humor.

~

The one thing I was fairly proficient at was cleaning the toilet. It was one of a couple of chores assigned to me. The other chores were drying the dishes and vacuuming. My father didn't clean at home—he left that duty to my step mom and me. Why would he want to bring his business home? I remember once during the Christmas season my father worked during the showing of the Nutcracker. This meant lots of kids. Dad not only had to mop floors and empty trashcans, but he had to get on his hands and knees and pick up hundreds, perhaps thousands of sunflower seed shells. He came home exhausted, complaining that those kids made him "sweat his butt off" that day. At home, my father took to gardening, which proved therapeutic. He would take a spray bottle and sprinkle water on his plants— large and unique cacti, whose spines climbed the walls. He'd sometimes shoot me in the head or ass with a narrow stream, intended for nobody but me. I'd hide behind a cactus or palm plant but he had good aim.

~

Toilet duty, for me, was a peaceful duty. It was a simple thing—take some cleaning solution, pour it in the bowl, take your toilet brush and start scrubbing. I had a certain finesse or technique to my bowl cleaning system. Depending on my mood, I'd employ several different methods. There was the "Around the world in a day" method, in which I'd use wide, circular motions with my toilet brush in order to bring out the luster and shine of the pot. It was almost like stirring a bowl of soup. I also called this method, "Stirring a bowl of soup." I also employed the "splish splash" method, in which I'd very rigorously scrub the toilet all over, creating a small puddle at the base of the bowl. Again, it was a good system—although a bit messy. I was a quick learner. My father only had to show me how to clean toilets once—after that, I was on my own. My favorite method was "The Beethoven." I coined this particular method, "The Beethoven" because it could be both graceful and rigorous, depending on my state of mind. I would use the toilet brush like the conductor of an orchestra; slow and graceful with a calm rippling effect—etching an invisible melody, which seemed to outshine the other porcelain in the bathroom. Then I'd get more rigorous, splashing and creating waves—a crescendo and the finale—the flush. Those remain to this day some of the most creative moments of my life.

~

My father continued after me about things over the years. I can't blame him really. I wasn't particularly talented but I managed to get out of high school and out of college. The getting out was the most rewarding part. When we eat dinner these days, he doesn't ask me about what I learned in school, which is good because I remember nothing. But the one thing I do remember was cleaning those toilets. And believe me, it's helped me a lot more. 🕸

The Price

Oscar Peñaranda

Every time my fragile Uncle Andres came to the house, someone would always end up arguing with him about the ideas he had concerning his land. This someone would almost always be my father. And because it was my father's house he would always leave before the argument got too hot and the name-calling started. He would exit respectfully with a bow, smoothing his curled-up moustache. Everyone knew my uncle's stand was hopeless. He himself must have had glimpses of it.

First of all the land was too close to the provincial capital city of Tacloban, where lately only cement seemed to grow. Secondly, the Community Board was bent on building a road through this land that ran along San Juanico Bay, and our town Santander was blossoming into urban stature and it— our town— was beginning to feel its muscles. The president of the country himself had built a bridge (dedicated to the first lady) across this bay joining the two islands of Samar and Leyte, his wife's birthplace.

They didn't look like brothers at all, my uncle and father. My father was stout, clean-shaven, well-dressed, and streaks of gray hair spread abundantly over his light-brown yellowish round face. My uncle had a curled-up moustache, always shabbily dressed, with a thin, delicate face covered with scaly skin, and, though several years older than my father, still had his full jet-black hair.

The fact that he always turned around and left just before the argument was on its peak, even though he did it humbly, enraged my father. It somehow offended his integrity, as if my uncle's over-formal bow patronized, or condescended to his opposing.

"He knew that I would prove him wrong, that is why he left; that is why he always leaves. He knew he had no show, so he did not want to stay and hear it," my father would say.

But it seemed to me at the time that every time my uncle spoke he always had a show. He was that kind of character, my uncle. But then I had not seen his land yet. I did not yet know the conditions, nor the tremendous odds my uncle was up against.

Once, however, my uncle was caught in the middle of an argument. It was the time the party was thrown in our house by the parents for their children who were graduating from elementary school, two weeks before final examinations. I was one of them and my father was the host. My uncle had come from his farm near Magellan's Landing by Carigara Bay on the other side of the island. I suppose partly to congratulate me and partly because we had not seen each other for some time, and I think he had heard the strong rumors that we might be leaving for America.

When I saw that karomata, that one horse cart, I knew it was he. When he arrived, he paid his respects to everyone and then we went to the patio on the back of the house, sitting down on a bench canopied by giant trees of kamagong and narra.

"And how are you, my nephew?" He waved his hat downwards to me. "Sit down."

Smiling, I sat on a rattan chair opposite him. "Well," I said not knowing what else to say.

"I have no gift to bring you —" said he.

"You are here," I said.

"Well, yes, but isn't customary to... however, since I have no gifts, could we have a talk instead?"

"About what?"

"Oh, about things — perhaps of importance to you, since you are now graduating."

"Oh," I said, a bit disappointed.

"No, no. It is not advice, my nephew," he laughed. "I know you are filled with it by now."

"What then?" I looked up at him. "What is it?"

I could see he was in agony trying to tell me something. Sitting back, I let him take his time.

"My nephew," he began, "you know you have always had this, how shall I say it, this heart of a poet..."

I heard the clatter of feet from inside, the sound of laughter, and soon, as I half-dreaded, I heard them call my name. The patio door suddenly opened and my father had my hand in his and was dragging me inside.

"The guests have arrived, Amador." And then I had to mix with the other people because I was supposed to be Salutatorian.

Leaving my uncle to meet the guests, I seemed to have lost all sense of the familiar. I had just begun to feel comfortable with my uncle when my father came in. I passed before a mirror and saw a monster. It seemed that I was looking too close at everything. I saw dead bones in living skin; the love-bird had the snake's eyes, and shadows were walking people...

Before we parted my uncle told me that this time, no matter how heated any argument with my father or anyone else became, he would not leave until he was sure I had some notion of that thing he was trying to tell me earlier when we were interrupted. Both of us knew that when once parted that afternoon, we would not easily get the chance of talking alone again in the house. So we watched for each other's eyes.

A little later in the festivities, my father was asking my uncle Andres to stop delaying to sell his land. "In business," he said, "timing is of the essence."

"I refuse," my uncle kept saying. They spoke to each other from a distance; they always did.

"But why? What good is that land of yours? It is barren, Mano. It is fungus-ridden, it is craggy and rocky. It is lifeless and grows nothing and yields nothing. Everyone in the Board already ridicules me about it."

My father spoke very fluent Tagalog, the national language then, even though they originally spoke a provincial tongue, Visayan Waray. He had already lost the provincial dialect accent. My uncle was the other way. He spoke the national tongue with a thick provincial accent. And I, born in the barrio and raised in the cities Manila and Tacloban, was more familiar with the national tongue. I understood both, however. So did my father and uncle. We simply had to feel for words when talking to my uncle, that was all.

My father had a better idea, "Why do you not sell it to the community, Andres? They are going to get it sooner or later. So you can at least have a financial hold and stop being... living a wasted life, a vagabond...sayang!"

"I do not beg," said my uncle, "nor do I sell."

"I know you do not beg; but at least invest in something that stands fast. Your land is nothing."

"Nothing stands faster than land."

"But your land is nothing."

"It does not have to be anything. It is everlasting," my uncle said, and lowering his voice he added, "and I refuse to sell it."

"What is wrong? They offer a high enough price for it," my father said. He was also a member of the Board.

"Price indeed is too high"

"Then why not take it?"

"I talk of the price of accepting their offer."

I could tell my father was already getting excited and pikon—touchy. He had begun punching the tip of his cigarette filter with his thumbnail, pressing crisscross lines of all sorts. "Did you know," he said, pointing at my uncle with the two fingers that held his cigarette, "did you know that people like you have no place in the world? No place whatsoever."

My uncle struck a match against his teeth and lit his pipe. "I never made it that way."

"I think you're in love with being a bum. Why can you not live like other people?" My father shouted that time.

"The price. It is the price, brother," my uncle whispered, looking at me. I felt his eyes; they were the eyes I had watched for. He faced my father but his eyes were speaking to me.

Right after the argument Uncle Andres took me for a ride in his old buggy-cart to his place that the community could not buy. The ride felt very fresh. We, that is, my father, owned a jeep. As we left, we saw my father standing in the middle of the dirt road getting smaller and smaller, for the horse was now in full gallop.

"He is a good man," I said, "but he has not much faith, Uncle."

"Faith in me, you mean?"

"Well...just faith. He has not much of it."

"It is not a question of faith, Amador. But still you are right. He is truly a good man. A man of prudence."

"But so are you, in a way. You are a man of vision."

"It is my bad luck," he smiled. I thought his face, so brittle-looking and scaly, would fall to pieces.

"Why is it Father always talks to you like that?" I asked him. "I mean, you are older, are you not? He never lets me talk to Antonio like that." Antonio was my older brother.

I did not think he heard me, for he said nothing. Then he suddenly released the reins and stopped the cart. "Hey did I ever tell you the story of the guitar and how it all came about?"

He had told me about three times before, but I could see from his face that he had forgotten. He looked so eager to tell it, so I said, No, he had not.

And he told me again. About how a certain young lad a long time ago was banished from his village in Spain because he had leprosy. This young man used to sing love-songs in the market place. Sang them one after the other; wanted to sing them all, for he knew he did not have much time left and the people would ostracize him sooner or later.

And they did; for the lady in his songs felt very insulted. She and her parents, for they were aristocrats, organized a board of some sort and ordered the leper out, who refused, until the lady herself confronted him (from a distance, of course) in front of the marketplace and told him how disgusting and revolting he looked, and how dare he even think of her existence. The leper turned around, left town and was never seen by any of them again.

But he hid himself in the hills of the Sierra Nevada and lived in a cave there. He carved out a hollow tree in the shape of a woman's body. He made her neck long and slender so that he can stroke it and caress it as his hand glided over it. And every time he held the thing he would imagine his arm embracing her tender waist. Finally he bored a hole where the heart should be and connected strings from there to her lips. Her lips he manipulated with his fingertips, and as he plucked he imagined the strings to be of her heart as if their destiny depended on the singing of his song and the playing of his guitar.

Of course I did not believe him. But it is strange, because while he told it, I did. But only while he was telling it. Right after, once I started thinking about it, I could not believe it anymore. It was not logical and just could not be. But I believed him, knowing it was a lie. It was so pretty, the way he told it.

My uncle started the karomata again. "I will show you the land, Amador. And I will tell you what we will make of it."

"How do you mean we? I know nothing of the land." I was only in the sixth grade.

"I will teach you," he said. "I realize it is not much but we will make it bloom just the same."

When we got to his place I was somewhat horrified at the sight. There was not even a slight breeze to at least move the carpeting dust. Where there was no dust, there were rocks already cracked by the tropical heat. From where I stood I could see no water nor any sign of it. There were only rocks and dust and parched scales of cracked earth; Father was right about it.

"Why do you pick such a time of all times, the dry season, to plant, my Uncle? Why not wait till the rainy season; at least you will have a chance then?" I was more and more convinced I knew more of farming than he did.

"Because they are after me, my boy, by then they will surely have taken this land and built apartments on it or used it as a garbage dump or golf course. But I will show them. They just do not see the beauty of it... and you will help me, won't you?"

"Sure," I heard myself say. My lips said it; I did not say it at all. "Father said they will get it sooner or later."

I looked once more at the stretched-out, thin-layered, scale-cracked earth. "Father says it yields nothing. Everybody else says it is lifeless."

He looked at me limply and said, "I refuse to believe that. This is the land of our ancestors, Amador. It is not ours to sell. It is only ours to wonder at and to witness all its marvels. This land is very alive, my nephew,"

"They say that the land is nothing."

"The land does not have to be anything. It is already something. It's the land. It doesn't have to be anything. It will give of itself."

He squinted his eyes to the setting sun without shading them with his hand, and without moving he said, "So," with a smile, "America, eh?"

"That's what they say." I really did not want to talk about it. They had planned so many things before, hardly any of them had materialized that I was beginning to learn not to worry or waste any emotions about something you were not sure of to begin with, so I really did not want to talk about it.

"Where in America?" Uncle Andres asked again.

"I can't recall. Are you going to be all right here?"

"Oh, of course," he said. "Where in America?" he insisted.

"I don't know," I finally said. He was not going to get off it. "Over some big bank or something. Sounds like that anyway."

He paused for a while and said, "So it is true, then."

"I don't know," I said. I remembered in Manila while we were rummaging through garbage cans looking for bits and pieces to make toys with, my friends and I had found three stamps from a torn envelope. They were soft purplish and each had a picture of a lady's face and they smelled from far away. Each said Canada.

"My nephew, I grow old and silly," he continued, "for I am childless... and wifeless... and homeless. I grow old. Things left to hang on to are getting fewer and fewer...."

His words ran shrieking through me; a chalk had squealed along the blackboard and the sound flashed like lightning down my spine. I wondered if his arm felt that. A moth fur had entered my eye and, too self-conscious to move before, I had just now taken it out.

"I will therefore clear everything with your father and the board tomorrow," he smiled. It was then that I noticed the fat red sun had disappeared, leaving only the surrounding pieces of sky and clouds stained with its blood.

~

He was still smiling at the board office the next afternoon. He shook his hands with everyone, and everyone smiled back. But I could feel them all eyeing Father.

"Why did you bring the boy?" my father asked my uncle.

"I wanted him along."

"Did you go to school today?"

"Yes, I've finished, Father," I said rising.

"Did you know this is his last two weeks? He has examinations, you know." He turned to my uncle.

"He did not mention it." He looked at me; I turned quickly away.

"Hmm," my father glanced at his watch. "Well, you are finally handing it over to us?"

"No," my uncle said. "I am going to cultivate it. I've bought all the equipment. All I need are your signatures." He looked around at the board members, "Giving me at least till the end of the rainy season, that's about a month from now, to grow something on it."

The usual argument broke out again. My father got redder and redder, and he begun punching the crisscross lines on the cigarette filter with his thumbnail. While my uncle's words got fewer and fewer until at last they were down to two again; "I refuse," shaking his scaly-skinned head, "I refuse." Until they gave my uncle at his last show. Until the end of the rainy season then, if still nothing grew, then my uncle's land would be sold to my father and the board.

My uncle went his way and we, my father and I, went ours. It was a very quiet ride home. The pressing silence deafened me. But my father with some restraint broke it.

"So, you are going to help him," he said.

"I do not know."

"What do you mean 'do not know'? I can tell you are, my son. You *want* to help him, let us put it that way."

"Yes," I answered.

"What about your schoolwork? I mean, how will you study? The examinations are only two weeks away. You simply do not have the time, you know.

I said I knew.

"But how are you going to manage? You and your uncle do not know it yet, but it is going to take the devil's zeal to work it. You are very good in school. I hate to see your marks drop just when you are going to graduate."

"They will not drop very much"

"You have seen the land, have you not?" My father laughed dryly.

I said, yes; I had seen the land.

"You fools! You really think you have a chance?" He raised his voice and knitted his brow. I could feel something coming—for he was looking at me more than he was looking at the road. The lights from the lamp posts filtered through the trees and flashed now on his face, now on his profile and at times the trees completely hid the lights and we were in darkness. "Listen," he said, and for a moment I thought he almost implored me, the flickering lights seemed to have distorted his face. I had never seen him like that before. He tilted his head and squinted his eyes, as if he were having great difficulty in speaking, in letting the words fall from his lips.

"You are my only hope, my son," he said. He was looking straight at me for such a long time that I thought he had forgotten about the road. "Antonio has quit school. He said he wants to take a break. Don't tell me you will, too." My father began to shift restlessly on his seat and his voice had broken now. "Amador, I know you are quite fond of your uncle... I envy him at times. No, no, no, don't apologize for that, my son. We are different, your uncle and I; no need to apologize for that." And the intensity of his voice began to disappear. His voice was no longer broken, but whole again. "That is why," he continued, "for you, I will help him, too."

"How?"

"I will purchase him some other piece of land, a much, better piece, at a much better price, from the money he gets from this one. I know some people, and I will personally see to it that—"

"I do not think he will allow it, my father."

"Of course, he will. He must!"

"You know him. It is not his way."

"Then we will make it his way!" He flicked his cigarette out the window. "I do not care whether it is your uncle or the Community Board who gets the land or not, the devil take them both. They are nothing to me. But you are my son. And you are my pride. And I know as well as you that you will not graduate if you plow the fields with your Uncle Andres."

"He will be destroyed," I pleaded.

"He will be crushed whether you help him or not," he answered quickly. "He hasn't a chance, the old fool. Tell him to dream another dream. Do you really think he has a chance?"

I said I did not think so.

"Then why help him?"

I said I still do not know if I should help him, but I wanted to just the same.

"Why? Why do you want to just the same?"

I tried to say something, to answer, but nothing came out. "I do not know," I said.

The jeep stopped. My father opened his door, shut it then opened mine. "Come out. We're home," I heard him say.

Snapping out of my thoughts, I jumped out. His hand was waiting outside to take mine. He pushed the gate open and walked along the cement path towards the door. I gently released my hand from his.

"Are you not coming in, my son?" He forced a smile that made me feel very cruel. He tries very hard, I thought.

"The night wind is chilly. Hadn't you better fetch a jacket first?" he asked,

"I will be all right. I'll just be around here."

"Very well then. Listen for supper call."

He turned around and walked towards the door, kicking stray pebbles and dry leaves that were strewn along the cement path.

I walked towards my right and then down towards where the winding river-film was being covered by falling leaves and water lilies. The night sky was exceptionally clear and very quiet, save for the occasional cry of the sparrow and the muffled voices of squatter-dwellers below on the muddy banks... They were not supposed to live there, these squatters. Someday soon they would be evicted by city officials and they would again roam around with their six or seven children, looking for a place to stay. Totoy is one of them. I hope they do not get him. I will miss him, and Budyong, his water buffalo...

Across the silent sky, a wisp of cloud had suddenly sailed past the broken moon whose frowning crescent pulled the veil of clouds over as if it had wanted to bury its face and cry. And then I heard again the forlorn crying of the sparrow, and soon I heard my parents calling me in for supper.

I ate my supper hurriedly and went straight to my room. I do not know whether I spoke at supper or not, or whether I said good-night. Sprawled upon the bed, I lay thinking for a moment, and then I sprang right back again and stood up, staring at my bed.

I could hear children from a sari-sari store crying like damp winds, rising and dying like a moan. I opened my window wide and sat by the sill for a while, looking outside. Across the street, bedsprings squeaked between a woman's sobbing. I saw one of our wet socks hanging on the backyard's clothes line drop, and it made a sound of kissing.

I went to my bed and lay down again, my ankles crossed and both hands under my head.

Why betray my own father? Judas. Yes, I would be betraying Father if I helped him plow. Father thought only of me, and thought ... well, what is wrong with having a decent life like his, anyway? He is not bad just because he is a success. Is that not everyone's goal? He has enough problems just being riled and harassed and bullied by that damned Community Board, and I am his son. The look on his face when we were driving home, when I told him that I would help *him*. He looked so resigned and defeated, my father. He tried to hide it, but still I could detect it. But yet—

I took both hands under my head and propped myself up. Yet... *he* is growing old. And my father has a wife, has a home and other children. He has nothing. How will I feel when I get old and paltry, with the world closing in on me, and with no one, with no one standing by when I am going down? I could not bear it. Too heavy then for my shoulders.

I turned to the window once more, for I had heard a pitter-patter on the roof. Raindrops on glass. Where did the rain come from? It was such a clear night. I walked towards the window and stuck my arm out, my palm turned upwards. It was beginning to rain. I shut the window a little and looked through the drops on the pane. Clear on clear.

The next day my uncle, still smiling, came to the house to get me. He was so sure I would go. I would be gone about four weeks and go the remaining days of school from there. Paying his respects to all, he looked up at me as I came down the stairs with my luggage.

"Got everything, eh? Don't forget your books now." He laughed and turned to my father who was quietly looking at me. I nodded I had them. "You look like you're going to America already," he smiled.

My father and I did not speak a word. There was a solemn air between him and me, and both of us knew, I think, the weight of our silence. He had felt it last night when I left him to walk, just before supper. And when I heard him downstairs this morning listening to me pack, I knew he would not go to work that day.

With one hand on the balustrade, my father stood at the bottom of the stairs, motionless, expressionless. He looked very tired. Uncle Andres waved goodbye to everyone and he was already in the one-horse cart when I got to the door. Opening it and putting my luggage across the threshold, I eyed my father goodbye; he did not move.

The rains had already begun in scatterings. Uncle Andres drove me to school every day and picked me up afterwards. After school, I studied awhile then worked with my uncle for four or six hours.

Well, my father was right. It was a lot of work. But my uncle and I stayed with it for the whole two weeks just the same. My grades dropped more than I had expected. I did not make salutatorian, of course, nor anywhere near it. I did not graduate that year. And if my uncle was a poor farmer, with a thin delicate body, he made up for it with his diligence. He checked and rechecked and replaced every seedling and changed its coverings all through the winds and rains and mud.

I lived in my uncle's shack and watched with him for three more weeks before the preliminary rains were over. When the winds have finally died, and the sky started to clear, he dressed in his finest suit. He was running up and down the old shack getting ready "to greet the flowering fields."

"Hey, don't just stand there! Where's your suit?"

"In my suitcase, where it's supposed to be." I smiled, "Don't tell me—"

"That's right. Go put it on, boy. You're in the parade, too. You and I worked this land, remember?"

"How can I forget."

"Come, my nephew. Do not try to hide emotions from me. It is only me. I know you feel it, too." He fixed a buttonhole. "I feel like a whale lifting the sea!" he puffed. "Or a bird moving the wind. Or the mountains rising with the morning!" He turned and caught me smiling. "That's it. Laugh! Don't hold back that smile. I know you feel it, too."

He was right, I felt it, too.

We hopped on the karomata and whipped the old mare. "To the flowering fields!" he shouted.

When we got there, however, we saw nothing.

Nothing. Not even a single seedling had pierced through the covering. They were all blown by the winds or suffocated by the thick mud that had already begun to harden and crack anew in the sun. We walked some more, a little slower this time, my uncle's face sunken and haggard, but still found nothing. The earth was beginning to form thin layers of scales again.

"I think it's time that I go," he whimpered. "I must leave, leave."

I started feeling desperately for words, but nothing came. My uncle looked and appeared like a stranger already. So I said nothing. There were too many kinds of goodbyes crowding my brain and I felt the difference in language growing thicker than ever. I felt like we were two minstrels who had sung all the songs and played every tune in the world only to realize afterwards that no one was listening. ❧

Uncle Gil

Max Gutierrez

Uncle Gil was bad. Uncle Gil was nothing. Uncle Gil's teeth were falling out. He had no money and he had no sense. That's what everybody said. Watch him when he comes to your house—he might steal something. I stood next to the window of our house on Eddy Street. I looked at the cars floating by. They reminded me of fish with big fins darting in all directions. The church down the block with its crumbling cupola stood alongside a liquor store. Eight or nine men stood laughing and drinking in front of it as the church stood in silence. I saw one of the men walk away from the group. He wore a gray suit with creases in the pants that were razor sharp. A black tie hung from his neck over a shirt that was whiter than fresh milk. He walked with a certain rhythm or cadence—as if music that only he could hear were being piped into his ears. The man's face came into clear view. I opened the window.

"Uncle Gil! Uncle Gil!" I cried out.

The air was warm and sticky. I ran through the living

room and down the stairs. I opened the door. I looked in both directions. Where was Uncle Gil? I walked out onto the sidewalk. The cars continued to pass and the trees waved gently in abrupt spurts. Where was my uncle? Maybe he went to church. He was dressed for it. Yes, that was it—he was at church saying a prayer. When he's through with his prayer, he'll come to our house and stay. He'll tell me his stories and make funny sounds with his lips and cheeks. I sat on the stoop in front of our house. The neighborhood kids began passing by. They rode bikes and cruised by on roller skates.

"Go get your bike and ride with us," one of them called out.

"I'm waiting for my uncle Gil," I replied.

The church bell rang and the men in front of the liquor store scattered away like flies. Maybe I should go back into the house, maybe uncle Gil is playing a joke; maybe I didn't see him at all. Maybe it was a guy that looked like him. I sat and heard the faint sound of footsteps that became louder. It reminded me of the sound of a small horse. My father walked like a horse and worked like one. That's what he always said.

"What are you doing?" he asked, looming over me.

"I'm waiting for Uncle Gil."

My father spit on the ground. His trousers were stained with dirt and paint. He reached towards his shoulder and kneaded relief into it with nubby fingers.

"Uncle Gil" my father laughed, "He's not gonna show up. He's only good for two things...*drinking and not showing up.*"

My father looked down at me and laughed

"Your uncle Gil never worked a day in his life."

I thought about what my father said. I never worked a day in my life either. I liked Uncle Gil. My father always talked about work and how his body ached all over. Uncle Gil never had aches and pains and wore nice clothes. My father walked to our front door.

"You're gonna be waiting forever. That no-good uncle of yours is out blowing his money, kid."

Dad disappeared into the house. I sat thinking about his words. Maybe I was going to wait forever. I began to wonder how long forever was. The sky darkened a bit when I saw a figure a half block away. As the figure got closer, I recognized the slacks with the razor sharp creases.

"Uncle Gil!" I cried, springing to my feet.

Uncle Gil reached out and ran his hand over my full head of black hair, tossing it out of place.

"How ya doin' kid?"

I looked at Uncle Gil's tie. It was black. He smiled.

"Uncle Gil," I said, "You have teeth!"

Uncle Gil smiled wide, wide enough to cover the sky.

"Yes...you have to smile to survive," said Uncle Gil.

We sat down and watched the cars pass by.

"Survive what?" I asked.

"Never mind," Uncle Gil replied.

We sat for a while saying nothing.

"How are you doing in school?" Uncle Gil asked, yawning.

"I'm doing OK."

Uncle Gil ran his hand over his pants, making sure the creases were still there.

"Just study hard, kid. Get your education. They can never take that away from you".

"Who's *they*, Uncle Gil?" I asked.

Uncle Gil looked at me. He reached into his jacket pocket.

"I got something for you."

Uncle Gil put his two fists out towards me.

"Pick one," he said.

I looked at both fists. I pointed to the left one. Uncle Gil opened his fist. In it sat a silver dollar.

"Wow!" I said.

"Buy yourself an ice cream."

I looked at the silver dollar. It looked new. I didn't want to spend it.

"What's in your other hand, Uncle Gil?"

He opened his right fist. In it was a candy, a sucker wrapped in bright cellophane.

"Who's that for?" I asked.

"For your father," Uncle Gil answered, sticking the sucker into my shirt pocket above my heart. We sat and he laughed with bright teeth that covered the sky. 🐝

Hammer Lounge

Geronimo G. Tagatac

S ix of us stood at the edge of the curb, in front of Jessie and Celia's house, and passed around a bottle of brandy that went down like gravel. Jessie had taken the brandy out of the trunk of his gray Monte Carlo. It was November and chilly, but Jessie's wife who was a recent convert to the Church of Christ, no longer allowed smoking or drinking in the house.

"What you doing tonight?" Jessie asked me.

"Not much," I replied, knowing the question was an invitation.

"I've got this place I think you'd like," he said in a drawl that he'd picked up from 12 years in the army.

"That thing running?" I said, nodding at the Monte Carlo.

"On two cylinders," my brother shot back, handing the brandy to my brother-in-law, Walter, who put the bottle to his mouth, tipped it up, swallowed, and passed it to me, saying, "You drinking anymore, Tony?"

I took three full swallows and handed the bottle off to my sister, Jasmine. Brandy fumes filled my throat and nose, but I suppressed the urge to cough. I waited a second, until my sister had the bottle to her mouth. Then in my most deadpan voice, I said, "I'm trying to taper off." My sister choked once and blew an amber spray of liquor from her lips. Everyone backed away quickly, laughing. Jasmine doubled over, her narrow shoulders shaking. Then she stood up straight and yelled, "Shit, Tony!"—which brought on another burst of hilarity. It felt good to be back, among all of those dark, familiar faces after a two-year absence. I wondered what my Portland officemates would think had they seen me standing with that gang, on the edge of a broken-down street, passing around a bottle of convenience store booze.

A late model, blue BMW came up the street, its wheel rims flashing in the cold sunlight. Neither the driver nor his brunette girlfriend made eye contact with any of us. The car got to the end of the cul-de-sac, made a quick U-turn, and sped past us going the other way. I wondered what the driver and his girlfriend thought of me, the only person in the group wearing an Irish knit sweater instead of black leather, a seagull in a flock of crows. Cousin Jessie had on his black motorcycle jacket, its sleeve ends white from wear. It had a patch over the right elbow.

I stood silent for a moment in the wind and watched the brandy bleach some of the brown out of Jessie's face. It had been a bad couple of years for him. His daughters, both in their early 20s, were living at home with their infant daughters. Home was a 40-year-old, 2-bedroom house that must have been built of lumber mill seconds by a blind Boy Scout troop. One good rain would strip what remained of the paint off the house's outer walls and what passed for a lawn, too. Jessie held down a nighttime security guard's job that paid fifteen hundred a month. Celia worked for a housecleaning company that paid even less. Neither job came with enough medical benefits to treat a headache.

If I turned my head and squinted a little I could see a flash of the guy Jessie had been 19 years before. In those days he was six-feet-three-inches of broad shouldered craziness. Back then he was like someone who knew that he was hiding a set of wings under his jacket.

I stood across from Jessie, feeling the alcohol weaken the muscles of my legs, and I took in the heaviness of his face which held a hint of sadness mingled with the resentment in his brown eyes. I wondered if it might be anger over what the years had taken from him. There was a downward bend in his upper spine that wasn't there the last time I'd been home. My mother had told me that he and Celia were barely on speaking terms. Compared to him I had it pretty good. In the morning I'd fly home to my northeast Portland apartment with its neighborhood cafés and specialty grocery shops where an unsliced loaf of ciabata went for nearly $4 and a 16-ounce cup of coffee cost 2 bucks and no free refills.

"I'll come by around seven," Jessie told me as we broke up.

Darkness had fallen by the time I heard the rumble of Jessie's car coming down the street in front of my parent's place where I'd been staying for the week. A part of me didn't want to go. I knew that Jessie would want to pay for my drinks and it was money that he and Celia needed. The car's exterior looked like it had been through a weeklong sand storm. He waited for me to come out, not wanting to face my mother's accusing stare. I grabbed my jacket and went down the front walk. I pulled the passenger side door open, climbed in and sat down.

The interior was surprisingly clean. When Jessie cranked the engine over it caught and ran smoothly all the way up Highway 280. I shouldn't have been surprised. Jessie had always done all of his own work on the car until a few weeks before my visit. Someone had broken into his and Celia's house and taken his tools along with his 45-caliber service automatic. "My father-in-law lets me use his tools, but I have to work on the car at his place," he told me. After a few miles, he said, "You see anything of Angie any more?"

"She re-married and moved to Salem a year ago," I replied.

"How come you guys never had kids?"

"I don't know," I said, not wanting to get into any long explanations. I listened to the sound of the big V-8 and felt the vibration of the car's tires on the concrete through the seat. It took me back to that Saturday morning, early in the summer of '89, when Jessie came home from his second enlistment in the army. I was a junior at San Jose State then and 21-years old. He'd driven up Seventh Street and parked the new Monte Carlo in front of the wood framed building where I rented the upstairs flat. Jessie hadn't bothered to ring the downstairs bell, which wasn't working anyway. He just stood beside the car and bellowed, "Tony!" He'd wanted me to come to the window and to see the car, which was the first he'd ever owned. He'd driven us south on Highway 17, to Santa Cruz. The air blasting into the open passenger-side window was warm and smelled of pine. I knew with more certainty than I'd known anything else in my 21-year life that there was nowhere else I'd rather have been than sitting in that car on the way to Santa Cruz.

Tonight, I knew I was about to break new ground from the moment that I saw The Hammer Lounge. It was one of those low, badly painted cinderblock-and-metal-roof places. The Hammer was one of those bars that attracted police cars with flashing lights after midnight. No cop would go near the place without lots of backup. It was the kind of booze hole that had a blood stained parking lot, a place where you don't walk through the metal-covered door unless you know somebody, a couple of big some bodies. Even then you might wind up being part of the collateral damage from an argument between a guy and his best friend, or his wife, his girlfriend, or all three. In The Hammer there were no innocent bystanders. But I wasn't about to refuse Jessie's hospitality. He was my cousin and he'd once saved me from a week in the San Jose City jail.

He led the way in through a steel-covered door that looked like it had taken a pounding from a gorilla with a crowbar. No one in the place was paying any mind to the state's no-smoking ordinance. I followed Jessie past the four pool tables and across a dark brown, linoleum tile floor that would've forgiven anything but a drunken fall. He took me up to the bar and introduced me to a brown-haired woman bartender who looked to be in her mid-30s. "Marti, my cousin Tony. From Oregon," he shouted over the rock music. "Treat him good, he's got an office job." She shook my hand in a strong grip and I saw that she was an inch taller than me. She smiled with the lower half of her face while her pale blue eyes gave me a going over that let me know that she knew, to the nearest dime, how much money I had on me. She could probably have told me what the expiration date was on my library card. "He's killing everybody," she said, nodding toward a stout, thin-haired guy at the nearest pool table. The middle-aged man at the table wore a green bowling shirt with the name "Pat" embroidered in gold thread, above the breast pocket.

"What're you drinking? I said to Jessie.

"Seven-seven. You?" he asked, reaching for his wallet.

"I got it," I told Marti, handing her a twenty.

"What about you, Oregon?" she asked.

"Double Tequila Gold," said my cousin snatching the twenty out of her hand and replacing it with his own.

"On the rocks? Water back?" she asked,

I shook my head.

"Hard core," she said to Jessie.

The truth was that I'd probably drink more with Jessie in this one night than I would in a year back in Portland, though I wasn't about to tell anyone. I tried not to think about how beat up I'd feel the next morning on the eight a.m. flight home.

I looked around the bar. Other than Pat there wasn't another white face in the place, though it didn't seem to bother him. He was running the table, snapping one striped ball after another into the side and corner pockets. And every time he did it the cue ball wound up where he wanted it for his next shot. The other guy at the table, a tall dark brown, gaunt man with black hair pulled into a tight rat's tail at the back of his head, watched him with a look of reverence in his black eyes.

When Pat had sunk all of the striped balls he looked up at Rat Tail and said, "Eight ball in the corner," pointing with his cue.

"You're gonna' scratch," yelled Jessie, laughing.

Pat hit the cue ball low and hard. It tapped the eight, sending it five inches, into the corner pocket. Then the back spinning white ball slowed until it stopped, two inches from where the eight ball had vanished. Rat Tail shook his head, put his cue up, and walked over to where we stood at the bar. "Mamacita," he said softly, and took a long swallow of his drink.

"You're up, Tony," Jessie said.

"The hell I am."

Jessie smiled down at me. "Go on. You can take him, cuz."

"What's it going to cost me?"

"Nada. It's all in fun."

"Yeah? For who?"

"Go on, honey. It won't hurt much," Mardi said from behind me. I could feel her sneer against the back of my head. "Try the third cue from the left," she said.

I swallowed half of my double gold and turned toward the waiting Pat. "Sure, why not," I said and walked over to the cue rack. I pulled out the first stick and looked down its length. It reminded me of a snake with a bad case of cramps. I went through two more cues, deliberately skipping over the third from the left. Finally, I gave Mardi's recommendation a try. It was an all-black number, straight as six o'clock. I walked over to the table and chalked its tip.

Pat broke the racked balls with a shot that sounded like a nine-millimeter pistol going off. It sent balls spinning all over the place, bouncing off the table's green cushions. A few ricocheted four times before coming to rest. Astonishingly, he didn't sink a single one. It was an open table. The cue ball lay in the "kitchen," the left quadrant of table's head. The way Pat had blasted it I was surprised that it was still in one piece.

I walked to the head of the table, to where I could eyeball the line between the cue ball and the possible shots. There were two. The three and seven balls lay in easy alignment with two of the far corner pockets. I tapped the seven, sinking it in the right corner, leaving the cue where I needed it for the next shot. I sank the three in the left pocket. Then I went for the five in the left kitchen area and sent it into the corner pocket. The white ball bounced off the cushion and came back within a foot on the far outside of the four ball that lay six inches from the right side pocket. "Whoa! Look out, Pat, the kid's playing his hundred-dollar game!" yelled Jessie. I flashed a sidelong glance at Pat's face as I walked to the far side of the table. His blue eyes were as cool as the ice in his rum-and-Coke. But it was not the hard look of restrained rage that I'd seen a few times in the eyes of my once-upon-a-time wife. It was that of a man who makes allowances for luck and the occasional run-in with a ringer. I took as a good sign the smile that softened the line of his mouth.

As I walked to the table's far corner I noticed Jessie and Mardi watching me, smiling as though they knew something I didn't. I lined up on the cue ball, aiming for the spot on its right side and took the shot. I heard it tap the four, knowing that I'd sink it. I looked over at Jessie and Mardi without bothering to watch the four ball vanish into the pocket. It was as though I knew the future as surely as I had known it on that perfect morning, decades before, when Jessie had turned up unannounced at my place driving the Monte Carlo. We were in our 20s and our futures were a couple of fat checks waiting to be cashed. I was going to get the office job that was the fast track to a car and a great apartment. I'd have fine clothes that women wouldn't be able to keep their hands off of. And Jessie would go on being the wild man, the life of every party with the fast car, and a 12-gallon tank full of comebacks. It was going to be that way forever.

Now I turned to look at my cousin and I saw that his eyes were shining and he had that crooked come-and-get-it smile that I remembered. Beneath the bar light the leather of his jacket shone like the skin of a black snake. He said something to Mardi and they both threw back their heads and laughed.

The tequila had loosened my muscles and turned the trumpet and the bass notes pouring out of the sound system into a warm wind. It no longer mattered to me that Jessie and I were both a step away from middle age, and that his marriage was failing and mine was five-year-old history. There was nothing but those notes rattling the billiard balls and blowing soft spaces between the shouts. The way Jessie stood and leaned in and over toward Mardi behind the bar brought back the way we had walked into a party, that night in Santa Cruz, in the fall of 1979, where we didn't know a soul. We'd changed the taste of the air in that place. Maybe it was the way the straps of Jessie's leather jacket hung like unfinished sentences or that loose way he had of moving that was something between a walk and a slow dance. But it worked because, before even I knew what had happened, the music had changed and the room's energy went through the ceiling. Suddenly we were dancing with a couple of women, throwing out enough heat and light to strip the paint off of the walls. Then everyone in the place was on their feet and shaking like wet dogs until three in the morning. What a night. On the way home the next morning, we talked about scrounging up enough money to make it to Europe for a few months. That was late July. By September he was getting serious about Celia and she was pregnant. They married in October and went to Mazatlan for a week.

I left for Europe the following June. Jessie drove me to the airport in the Monte Carlo and went with me to my gate. When they called my flight he took off his leather jacket and held it out to me. "Hang on to this, 'cuz, but don't fall in love with it. I want it back so take care of it." He looked down at the jacket and back at me. "It's the closest I'm going to get to Europe."

My first two nights in Paris, all the hostels were full and I didn't have the money for a real hotel room. I slept under Jessie's jacket, beneath a bridge alongside four other backpackers from Australia and New Zealand, who were headed for the festival of San Fermin, in Pamplona. I fell in with them and was probably the only person in a leather jacket to run with the bulls that year. I drifted through San Sebastian, Santander, Madrid, Milan, Florence and Rome, and back up to Paris. I spent three months of wandering, drinking, basement club dancing, and sleeping with women whose names or faces I can no longer remember. Yet I never experienced quite the same crazy energy that I'd known on that summer day and night that Jessie and I had spent in Santa Cruz. In September, I hopped the train from Banyuls sur Mer to Paris and caught my return flight to the States.

On an unseasonably cool, September morning, I drove out to Jessie and Celia's place to return the jacket. I hadn't seen them in over a year. Their small house had a new coat of bright blue paint. Celia was nursing their first daughter, Marianne. Jessie made potatoes and eggs, bacon, and poured strong cups of coffee. His voice filled their small kitchen as he told me about the warehouse job he'd just landed with a big sound equipment company. "Eighteen bucks an hour," he said, his smile radiating the lines at the corners of his eyes and mouth. When he walked me out to my car, I noticed that the Monte Carlo was up on blocks in the driveway. "Threw a rod. Soon as I'm ahead a little I'm going get it fixed and repainted," he told me. As I'd driven off that morning, I felt as though my life had outrun Jessie's. It felt sad and triumphant at the same time.

"Sweet," Pat said.

Now I turned back to the green-faced table. The cue ball had bounced off the end cushion and stopped a few inches from the one and six balls that lay, one behind the other, in a perfect line with the corner pocket. I had to stretch out over the table to line the cue up right. I gave the cue ball a solid enough strike to send both balls into the pocket. But I made sure to hit it low enough to keep it from scratching. The two ball lay a foot-and-a-half from the opposite corner pocket. Without thinking, I had set the cue ball up in just the right spot. I took the shot. Nothing but the eight ball remained, but it lay across the expanse of green felt, six inches from the corner pocket, on the far side of the table. Between the eight and me lay the ten and fifteen balls that belonged to Pat.

Pat walked to the bar and took a two of swallows out of his glass, set it down empty and nodded to Mardi who brought him another. He picked Jessie's pack of Camels off of the bar, shook one out, put it in his mouth, lit it, took a drag and blew it out of the side of his mouth. Then he smiled over at Jessie and shook his head. "Thanks for bringing him in, asshole," he said loud enough for me to hear him. Mentally I drew lines down the table and pretended not to hear Pat or Jessie's answering laughter. I could try a bank shot off of the right cushion and graze the eight on its near side enough to send it into the corner pocket. It would spin the eight clockwise enough to pull it off to the right. That would be tricky. I could shoot left but the angle was wrong. I considered a soft right hand shot, enough to tap the eight from behind leaving the cue ball bottled up so that Pat wouldn't have anything to go on. I had a quick vision of his blue eyes doing a hard freeze and the muscles of his jaw tightening. I could almost hear the swooshing sound of the thick end of his cue making for the left side of my head. Oh sure, Jessie would be on him like a tight suit but I'd wind up playing stripes and solids with God.

I looked down at the lines I'd traced with my mind on the pool table and thought about the last time I'd seen my ex-wife, Angie. It was on a Saturday morning, three years ago and I was sitting just inside the window of The Café Lena, browsing the op-ed section of the paper when she'd walked by less than three feet from where I sat. She'd cut her hair short and was wearing dark slacks that complemented her legs. I watched her cross the street, mid-block and vanish into the shadows beyond the Motown Bakery's front door. Now I wondered what would have happened had I followed the line of her passage into the bakery. What if I'd pretended that our meeting was coincidence and suggested a cup of coffee? Instead, I'd paid my bill and walked off down Hawthorne in the opposite direction from the one Angie had taken, leaving a half full cup of coffee cooling on the café table. I'd played it safe. Had I been Jessie, I would have followed her into the bakery and greeted her in a booming voice as if months of silence had not passed between us. Screw the coffee. I would have invited Angie down the block to The Havana, poured a couple of mojitos down her and taken her dancing. But I wasn't my cousin that morning. I never would be.

I took my shot and watched the cue ball bounce off of the cushion to the right of the eight ball, graze its near side and send it straight toward the corner. I could feel every eye at the bar watching the eight. Even the music held its breath. The black eight slowed and stopped, at the very brink of the pocket. The people at the bar erupted in a chorus of howls. "Somebody's lookin' out for you, Pat," said Jessie.

Pat walked up to the table, lined up on the ten ball and sent it rocketing into the side pocket. The cue ball bounced off of the far cushion, nicked the fifteen ball on the return, and sent it straight at the eight ball. "Ah shit!" Pat said, as the fifteen tapped the eight into the corner pocket.

"Bad luck," I said.

"Screwed shot," Pat replied.

Suddenly I felt as though I'd been wearing a lead suit and playing with a 21-pound cue. Jessie walked over to me and handed me the rest of my drink. "You better knock this one down fast. You're a long ways behind me." Mardi slid two fresh Double Tequila Golds onto the bar and gave me a wicked smile. I swallowed the other half of my drink and put the empty glass on the bar.

"Way to go, ace," said Mardi as she walked off to tend to another customer.

I picked up the double gold on the left, swallowed and felt it walk its way down my chest.

"You play just like your Dad." Jessie said.

"Hey, you remember that day you showed up at my place?"

"The man was a razor. Never lost his cool."

"It was the day you brought the Monte Carlo over to my place on Seventh."

He took a swallow of his drink. "I never saw the man lose a game, not to anybody."

"We went over the hills that morning."

"You've got focus, Tony. I always liked that about you."

"You know that morning was one of the best of my life,"

I said, seeing again the cast of the morning light on the hills.

"When was that?"

"June 16th, the summer of '89," I said.

"Where'd we go?"

"Santa Cruz," I replied, feeling as though I'd swallowed a handful of lead sinkers. For a moment I hated Jessie. That morning hadn't meant a thing to him. It wasn't even background noise. I might as well have asked him what color socks he'd worn on his twelfth birthday. And maybe that was the secret of Jessie's charm. There was no past for him. His only mistake had been to stop moving, to age. And now he was chained to that faded house on a dead-end street. I drained my Double Gold to take the edge off of my disappointment and reached for the third drink.

Sometime after two in the morning, when we walked across The Hammer Lounge parking lot to Jessie's car, my legs felt like rotten wood. Under the glare of the streetlight the Monte Carlo gleamed as it had on that July morning over twenty years before. I would have liked for Jessie to blast by the McKee Road off ramp, through the tangled interchange that straddled 101, and out to Highway 17, then southwest into the folds of the coast range. By the time we topped the pass over the coast range the sun would be at our backs and the Pacific would be a gleaming shard against the horizon's line.

"You need a ride to the airport tomorrow?"

"My mom's taking me," I said, hoping he wouldn't be hurt.

"That's good, 'cause I'm gonna be in a world of hurt and Celia's going to have case of the jaws," he said.

"Thanks for the drinks and all. I hope you don't get too much grief out of it," I said.

"I look at it this way," he said. "She's only pissed because she loves me. And hey, you're only young once."

I began to laugh, and Jessie's laughter joined mine, until we were howling like a couple of stoners all the way to the McKee Road off ramp. Right then, I envied him as I had in the years past. 🌸

Be Safe

Kannika Claudine D. Peña

For a while it was all about the arm sling. Our oldest brother, Kuya Maki had it, and it was about the coolest thing ever. It was all that Kuya Mon and I talked about a few minutes after they got home. Then after the two of us had exhausted most of the details of the accident, Kuya Maki went into the bedroom the three of us shared and ruined the excitement. You'd think that for someone who just had a near-death experience, he would tell tales of seeing his whole life flash before his eyes or the gore that the whole accident, however minor, involved. But all he would talk about was how the hospital people put on his arm sling.

"They splinted it and —"

"What? They split it?" Kuya Mon sat up, looking shocked and intrigued.

"No, dummy, splint, as in—"

"Oh, come on!" Kuya Mon rolled his eyes and made gagging noises but Kuya Maki continued regaling us with mind-numbing accounts of all the medical procedures that he went through earlier. I thought that if it had been me in the accident, I would've at least embellished the whole thing with blood and visions of, I don't know, death things or something equally scary. Listening to him yak about his blood type and such was like listening to a person describing the seat belts in a moving roller coaster instead of the thrill of being on the brink of danger while riding it.

"Did you feel your soul moving away from your body while they were operating on you?" I said right in the middle of Kuya Maki's meditation on the wonders of a hospital hallway or something. I wasn't really paying that much attention to him.

"What?" The glazed look on his face disappeared and he tilted his head at me. Kuya Mon, who had begun to arrange his cassette tape collection out of boredom, stopped and smirked at me.

I repeated my question and Kuya Mon snorted. Kuya Maki made a face and said, "Of course not. I wasn't dying."

"You could have," I pointed out.

And after I did, it wasn't about the arm sling anymore. A few seconds earlier, it was as if Kuya Maki purposefully got into an accident to get an arm sling, and not the other way around. The arm sling didn't represent anything.

Actually, a few hours earlier, I hadn't even thought of the possibility that Kuya Maki, or anyone I knew for that matter, could get into an accident. How did this day turn into the day that Kuya Maki got into an accident from one that didn't even have a label?

~

Some days start out ominously. Years after this incident I would hear a song called "Lonely Day" and would remember this particular day for no direct reason. It goes like, "I could tell from the minute I woke up, it was gonna be a lonely, lonely, lonely, lonely day." Well, some days are like that. You wake up and you know it's just going to be generally lonely, or you're just not going to hear a particularly good joke that day. The day Kuya Maki got the arm sling wasn't one of those days. It wasn't as if I could've written a song where I go, "I could tell from the minute I woke up, my brother's gonna be in an acci-acci-acci-accident." I had no idea, he had no idea, Kuya Mon had no idea, Nanay and Tatay had no idea, the whole world had no idea. I suppose that's why it's called an accident.

Could I have seen it coming? I dunno. So I relived the whole day in my mind, just to see if I may have overlooked some sign that this day wasn't going to be just one of those days, but a day that we would perhaps remember for a couple of years, maybe our whole lives.

There was nothing special about the day, just that we got our exams back and I did pretty well, and that Lisa finally talked to me (she asked me if I had an extra red pen and I didn't, so I guess it wouldn't exactly qualify as a conversation), and that Carlo, one of my best friends, gave me a mixed tape labeled Nirvana vs. Foo Fighters. Then when Carlo, Greg (the 1/3 of our unit) and I biked home from school in the afternoon, we sang "Big Me" at the top of our lungs and then talked and laughed about the video of the song until we got to my street. They went straight ahead, and so did I, and when I got to our house, I realized I was locked out again.

I suppose I should have taken that as a warning. But really, this was nothing new. I'd been locked out of our house many times before, ever since my brothers started high school. How was I supposed to know that getting locked out this time was something different?

The first thing that came to mind when I saw our gate locked and our carinderia closed was the video of "Big Me," maybe because it was the last thing I talked about. The video mocked those popular Mentos commercials wherein people get into a fix and then, just by popping a Mentos into their mouths, they think of something to get themselves out of the mess and all is happy. I wished I could pop a candy into my mouth and somehow think of something brilliant.

I propped my bike against the gate, sat down on one of the plant boxes in front of our yard and stared at the thin cow tied to a post on the empty lot in front of our house. We'd been waiting for the cow to die for a few years now, but it managed to outlive most of the old people in our neighborhood which was mostly made up of old people anyway. I counted up to a hundred under my breath and when I reached forty, I grumbled and stomped my feet uselessly. All I could think of was where were they and what time will they come back home. It wasn't really a question of whether they would actually come back or not, or what state they'd be in when they did. I was pretty sure they were coming back, because how could they not, right?

I remembered my walkman after I calmed down and stopped grumbling impatiently. I put on my headphones and pressed play but the tape wouldn't wind. So I got up and went to the sari-sari store and asked Aling Concia if she could just add to our IOU list a pair of double-A batteries. She gave me two red EVEREADY's and I complained. They were puny excuses for energy generating metal tubes. One wind of the tape and they would probably die out. She didn't have anything else, so I had to settle for them.

Lily, this girl I had biked to school with since the third grade, walked by as I sat on the plant box, putting the two batteries into the battery slot of the walkman. She said hi but went on walking towards Aling Concia's. When she came back, I already had my headphones on. She did a double-take when she saw me and stopped to ask a question I didn't hear.

"What?"

I didn't have the quick sense to take off my headphones and when I did, she was already halfway repeating her question.

"Again. Rewind," I said.

"Why are you out here? You don't have a key? Where is everybody?" I bet that was verbatim repetition.

"Nope, no key. I have no idea where they are," I said. I noticed the bottle of Betadine she was clutching. "What's that for?"

"Oh, this." She raised the hem of one leg of her shorts and revealed a skinned knee. "I fell off my bike earlier."

I had the urge to blow on it because I could feel the sting myself. Good thing she covered it up again with the hem of her shorts. Then she showed me her elbow and it was dotted with blood as well.

"Um, I'd invite you in, but Lola's having her general cleaning day, so." She pursed her lips.

"Er, that's okay. I'd invite you in, too, you know, except that, well, I'm locked out, so." She stared blankly at me. "Ha-ha," I said for effect.

She was nice and all, but she wasn't really quick, or I wasn't really funny.

"I have to go." She ran back to their house as soon as she said this. She might not be very quick-witted but she sure ran fast.

I suppose I sat there for a few more minutes doing nothing but bopping my head to the music. I imagined myself putting Betadine on my imaginary skinned knee and the sting felt so real I winced. That was about the height of danger that I knew then. My imaginary skinned knee was more real to me than what was really happening elsewhere: Kuya Maki's ride slamming against another vehicle.

I kept checking my watch and looking at the backstreet to see if my parents were getting off a jeepney at that moment. But the minutes kept ticking and no one even walked down our street, no one resembling my parents or my siblings anyway.

I thought about where they were most likely at that moment. This wasn't new, so I had options. Kuya Maki must be in a club meeting, or several club meetings, or maybe in an extended review session for a quiz bee. Kuya Mon must be in some friend's house, playing video games or he could be playing billiards. Nanay and Tatay must be together, 'losing track of time,' as Nanay would say, in a movie house. I remembered this one time I got locked out of the house and when they came back, Nanay told me they'd seen the film I had wanted to see and then she spoiled the ending. I frowned at the thought of them possibly in a movie house again watching a film I'd wanted to see over and over again just to spite me.

Why did it not occur to me that they were probably gone that long because they, or at least one of them had to be rushed to the hospital? Because they *couldn't* possibly be in an accident. As far as I was concerned, accidents involving moving vehicles bumping into each other didn't happen to people I knew, much less people I was related to. This was about my only explanation why our baranggay was made up of mostly old people—they never ran the risk of dying in an accident, that's why they had the chance to live that long.

~

I got bored after an hour of staring at an immortal cow that did nothing but turn sideways at me and look at me with its beady eye as it chewed. So I decided to bike off somewhere just to pass the time. I jammed my walkman into my bag and strapped my bag behind me and got on my bike. I rode towards the next village that had slopes, and on my way there, there was a procession with a long funeral car that I thought was as close as one could get to a limousine in our place. I tried to get a glimpse of the coffin inside the funeral car which had a glass window.

I was surprised to see a miniature coffin inside it. I wondered whether the family of the deceased was perhaps trying to save money by stuffing the corpse into a miniature one; I heard coffins were expensive, and cemetery lots worth a lot more. It didn't immediately occur to me that a small kid, or a baby, could be inside that coffin. When it did, I found myself muttering, "But that's not possible." The thought creeped me out, so I biked faster.

I couldn't help but catch the irony of hearing the song, though. "Maalaala mo kaya," the song went. Sure, it was the quintessential song for funerals, up there with "Di kita malilimutan." But the possibility that a child was in there made the song somehow inappropriate. Was the child old enough to remember? Do dead people remember, anyway? Or was the song supposed to be sung by the dead people, asking their live loved ones if they would remember? Do dead people sing anyway, and can they carry a tune better than those who were alive? Etc.

It depressed me so much I biked even faster than I already was until I reached the sloping village. I biked up and down repeatedly until my legs almost cramped. I even had the guts to take my hands off the handle of the bike as I biked down, but this lasted for about a few seconds before I grabbed the handle again. I was glad I was alone and not with Carlo or Greg, who loved showing off on their bikes and riding with their hands off the handle.

But riding the slopes without anyone to joke with got boring, and at any rate, I was tired of hearing the dogs barking at me whenever I would bike in front of the houses. Okay, I wasn't tired; I was scared. I imagined the dog owners to be vicious killers who would set their dogs loose on an unknowing kid for fun. Though I had to admit that my fear had no basis; the dogs who were fiercely barking at me were a beagle with bowed legs and an askal with a bald tale. But they had teeth, right? Yes, dribbling with saliva. So I biked down and went home.

~

When I got home, our gate was unlocked. I brought my bike to the back yard and chained it there. Nanay probably heard the tinkling of chain or my footsteps so she hurried out of the back door with Tatay behind her. I frowned at her to show that I had spent an hour waiting and I didn't particularly like it.

"Where have you been?" she demanded. I wanted to say that I should be the one asking the question, but she seemed mad for some reason.

"Uh, nowhere," I said as I went past her and got into the back door. I saw Kuya Mon raiding our refrigerator. He turned around when he heard the screen door shut and grinned at me. "Have you seen the arm sling? It's so cool," he said.

"What arm sling?" I'd never seen anyone with an arm sling in person before, so that should probably explain my excitement about it.

"Stop it, Mon," Nanay said behind me. Kuya Mon stalked off with a jar of peanut butter and four slices of bread. I was about to follow him but Nanay stopped me.

"Your brother was in an accident," Tatay said. As if on cue, Kuya Maki, with his glorious arm sling, appeared in the dining room. I wanted to inspect it, but I had the decency not to.

"Your brother was in an accident and then we get home after dark and find you nowhere," Nanay said. "What do you think immediately came to our minds?"

I didn't know what to answer to this except what was painfully obvious in my head: that I was biking somewhere. So I just said, "It's still early," but I knew this was not the point.

"You could have been in an accident! You could've broken your arm, or something else. You could have been in an accident," she repeated. "That could have happened to you!" She pointed to Kuya Maki, but his restrained grin didn't help to scare me much about what could have happened to me. "If that happened in daylight, what more could have happened to you in the dark?"

"Well, I'm here now, right? I'm okay," I said as I walked off towards our bedroom.

"Well, sorry to let you know we were worried about you," Nanay said as I closed the door behind me. I felt a little something like guilt when she said that, because I knew that they were only doing their job of being parents and worrying about me, etc. But then when I entered our room, Kuya Mon started telling me about the accident in the same tone of voice that he would use if he were describing a Lois and Clark episode. It was only when I pointed out to Kuya Maki that he could have died that I knew my parents were being more than just parents.

All they were really saying was, "We know that you will die eventually, but we want to put that off for as long as we can." It was their parent-like way of saying that they were afraid of death, just like a normal human being.

~

Yes, Kuya Maki could have died, even if it were just a minor accident. He could have died just as I was grumbling there in front of the house about being locked out again. But I couldn't have known, really.

After the dead air that followed my little offhand statement, Kuya Mon snorted. "But Miong, there was no way he could have," he said with a grin.

"Shut up, Mon," Kuya Maki said, grimacing as he tried to move.

"Because Kuya Maki is not of this world," Kuya Mon continued. "He belongs to another universe where the beings always try to get into earthly accidents. When they do, they go straight to the hospital and then afterwards, they kill earthly beings with boredom by telling accounts of hospital procedures," he said with a laugh. "Death by boredom," he added.

Kuya Maki rolled his eyes.

"Don't expect him to up things, Miong," Kuya Mon said as he stood up. "This is about as exciting as it gets."

I was a little thankful for the interlude because all I could think of then was, I wasn't looking forward to another afternoon of getting locked out the house again. Because I knew that it wouldn't be all about waiting. It could involve another set of arm slings, and I was not sure about how I feel about them anymore. ❀

The Music Teacher

Dean Francis Alfar

I will never forget how Mr. Rosales, my music teacher in second year, vanished. My parents, convinced at that time that I had a degree of hidden musical brilliance, engaged him as my tutor every Tuesday and Thursday night, in addition to my regular class under him on Fridays.

Mr. Rosales came from a small town in Negros, from one of those places whose names the mind finds impossible to recall, the ones where moths, wings tipped in poisonous dust, trail after and would-be suicides. He was a peculiar man who talked about his life to anyone who would listen. After private lessons at my house one evening, he told me how much he loved music but felt that his entire life was a failure. I remained quiet, out of respect. But it was true.

Against his lips, the flute acquired an altogether different aspect, lilting, rising, falling, persuading, leading all who heard it almost but not quite to the precipice of utter joy, like a sad Pied Piper. Consistently, at the precise moment when the next note would transport his audience of students to an unearthly paradise, he'd falter, reversing in mere moments the experience of delight and replacing it with a cacophony that could only rouse an exasperated sense of regret, enveloping those of us within earshot with the fading echoes of his desperate longing.

One Friday afternoon in class, right after another truncated recital that ended in the manner all his performances did, Mr. Rosales walked out of the music room, in tears. My fellow students and I followed him at a cautious distance down the corridors, past the classrooms where voices expounded on genes and peas, down the stairs past the glass-enclosed trophies that proudly attested to the school's victories in volleyball, origami and spelling, and out into the pristine and uniform-length grass of the quad. It was there that he turned to us and said, "I'm done with this—and with all of you."

The whirlwind that engulfed him appeared out of nowhere. It came as an inverted cone, swirling with the tip on top, ten meters tall, colored mostly green and smelling strongly of crushed leaves. It just covered him, like a cup in a shell game, and was simply not there the next moment. The fascinating thing about it, in fact the very last thing that everyone who witnessed Mr. Rosales' leave-taking remembered, was that the entire event took place in silence. There was none of the expected sounds associated with a whirlwind, even a completely unexpected one. It just came, upside down, covered him completely, and vanished, all in silence.

Mrs. Flores, the teacher who replaced him, was less memorable.

I think she taught piano. 🏵

Period Mark

Aileen Suzara

*F*orget love. Love was Nick Hernandez. He was Chicano and beautiful, with slicked-back hair, brown eyes, and a perverted sense of humor. He was the first cute boy to show any interest in book-wormy, straight-A, shy and short me (Peter and Ben, my only real friends, were even weirder than I was because they liked anime and weren't in an AYSO soccer league; therefore to the other girls, they did not count as boys). I met Nick when he came to Sacred Heart in the beginning of sixth grade, and that fall, I melted to puddles in the cool halls of our tiny Catholic elementary school. We would laugh together in class, and all the girls, noticing this unheard of situation—a *boy* likes *Lili!*—teased me while we waited in single file line after recess. He was the reason why I, the class prude, joined the other girls (all cheerleaders) in rolling up our pleated, plaid uniform skirts and pinning the hem with pilfered safety pins; why I left two, not one, buttons undone on our prim, many-buttoned, white Peter Pan collared blouse.

Besides getting reprimanded by the teacher, I didn't understand what all this would accomplish, but all the other girls did it (also, I hated always being *that* girl whose oversized, second-hand skirt hung past her knees). There's a picture of Nick and I slow-dancing: I wore a new, shiny blue dress with my mother's old elasticized sandals; the flash glared off the thick, round-rimmed glass I wore, before I had contacts. Like everyone else in the room, our arms were stick-straight, bodies apart, yet he smiled, looking down at me, while I grinned wildly at the camera. I couldn't believe my luck. We never "dated" but always talked.

Then in seventh grade, Stephanie Kniefl, a blonde girl with the highest rolled skirt, a woman's body, and too-big eyes, walked off—strutted off, actually—with him.

One day I jokingly asked him as he passed, "Hey Nick, why don't we talk anymore?"

"You're too young."

What? We were the same age. Was he making jabs at my height?

"It's not my fault I'm all little!"

He didn't even look as he muttered, "No, *that's* not what I mean."

Nick kept walking and I looked down at my flat chest and the worn black sneakers thick with Mojave dust. His arms had thickened over the summer and I just noticed how tall he had grown. He walked over to his girl waiting by the new red lockers and never said hello again.

I realized it wasn't love that I wanted. That could wait. No, what I wanted was something for myself, something better, something I could *keep*. Besides, a few weeks after Stephanie, Nick was already moving on to my then best friend Angela Cachero, the very popular, very busty Filipina newcomer. Angela wore low cut spaghetti-strap tank tops, was perpetually scented with Calvin Klein knockoff perfume, and always curled her bangs to a perfect curl. She even had the beginnings of teenage acne. I knew I couldn't be her, and I didn't want to be her.

No, what I had always wanted and now, in the seventh grade, constantly fretted over, was having a period. Every other girl had hers, and as one year after another passed, it was some sort of trend that I was increasingly excluded from. Periods weren't some mystery. I know exactly what happened, down to the very last detail, thanks to my advanced peers, the college novels I sneaked from my sister's shelf, my father's medical anatomy books, and the glossy, colorful, and very visual "Family Life" workbooks the class faithfully laughed at ever since sex-ed started in the fourth grade and we all learned to correctly spell "vagina."

With periods came everything: height, hips, breasts. You would get cramps, but I knew how to deal with those—you took a hot water bottle and placed it on your belly, or you lay in the yoga "baby pose." If you were caught without a pad you could use anything available: a clean sock, spare cloth, paper napkins. I knew all the tricks and had been saving them for a rainy day that never seemed to come. I committed my sister's 1987 edition of *Girltalk* to heart and formulated backup plans in case I was caught while wearing white pants (I didn't even own white pants, but this was useful information nonetheless).

With periods you would look like grown-up women. Not only would my body change, but I *knew* that my period would change *me* from being nerdy to being something else. It would set everything in its logical order. It was the first, necessary step in a series of steps. First, your period.

Then the first kiss. Then a boyfriend. You would fall in love, and either sex or marriage came next, probably marriage. Somewhere along the way came lifelong friends and a career. I hadn't figured out the details yet, but in the end, everything would make sense. I didn't know just then how out of order these things could actually occur in real life.

By the end of seventh grade I was getting upset. I had already passed a self-scheduled period deadline. All the girls, except for Lauren Galvez and myself, had had theirs already. In the fourth grade, Lauren and I had been called "twins" because of our dark-haired, dark-skinned looks. This physical similarity did nothing to cement any sort of close friendship. Lauren spent her time being as un-nerdy as possible, cheering with the cheering squad, kicking up gangly legs and red polyester skirts to reveal vivid red bloomers, screaming "we've got SPIRIT!" She also spent her time trying to keep Angela from staying friends with me. This was a slow process, which took nearly the entire year to accomplish. In the meantime, the three of us pretended to be friends. As Lauren plotted the destruction of our friendship, I was hoping that, at the very least, my body could beat Lauren to my period. Yet womanly curves did not appear on my body, and she was undoubtedly growing an edge.

The only physical change that spring was my hair. On my 13th birthday the two girls cut my waist length hair up to my shoulders. My lola in the Philippines had insisted to my mother that lengthy hair "takes away her nutrients! That's why she's so skinny and malnourished-looking!" For Lauren and Angela, with their superior fashion sense, this was the perfect opportunity for them to cut off my hair to mimic their own short bobs. I finally consented, and sat blind-folded, listening to the harsh snip-snip of the scissors. Afterwards it was if a great weight had been lifted from my shoulders. I ran my hands through my hair, surprised by the sudden, sharp end to the strands. Looking into the mirror I surprised myself, running into the closet to cry for half an hour. Before, I had been a "skinny and malnourished" girl with long hair and no period. Now I was a skinny and malnourished girl with short hair and no period. I could hear the two outside chatting, giggling a little with some concern; in a few minutes the talk turned to Brett and Nick and the other boys. Sighing, I slid out of the closet, and ignored the long dark strands on the floor.

The summer between seventh and eighth grade I was nearly frantic. I pushed the period deadline to eighth grade for sure. I gave up on Angela and Lauren, who were busy shopping at the mall and cheering. That summer, while the Mojave temperatures soared to the 90's, I buried myself in books and in the cool, dark kitchen to bake new types of bread. I read about menstrual rituals in distant cultures, planned the schedule for student council, committed a new Chopin piece to memory, nursed my re-growing hair, and steeped cast-off roses from the garden just to watch the color to seep from petal to water and turn it glistening, ruby-red. There was still no period, and I was alone. My body was still unchanging, except that my feet, already disproportionately large, were now casting off shoes every few months.

"This means you're going to be very tall!" my mother would tell me, smiling smugly. She had *hers* at 11 and was unprepared. For all the new height, I was still short; there was still no softening, no curves, and no period. I checked under my arms searching for a few tell-tale strands, which in the books signaled the impending period. Every time I felt a stomach cramp, I became hopeful.

"Don't worry," Aimee, my older, wiser, and taller sister told me in her visits back from college. "I had it when I was nine. It was terrible. At least you'll be ready!" This was no comfort. I had been prepared for years, and my body wasn't giving me the chance.

When fall came, everything was a mess. Lauren and Angela had become clones over the summer, the best way of showing one's friendship in junior high. They wore matching friendship necklaces, curled their bangs in the same curl, and came to school on free dress days wearing identical clothing bought from the outlet store. The desert was burning cold, and all the girls sat out on the sloppily painted wooden lunch tables, shivering in plaid jumpers, smoothing on pink gloss, some of them eyeing the boys. A ball came flying out from the playing fields and hit me near the chest. I reacted to it more than I needed to—the pain wasn't that bad—but I acted as though it had hurt. Angela, eager to seize the spotlight, loudly joked, "Now we know why Lili's chest will never grow!" Everyone laughed, and I forced myself to laugh with them, but felt my cheeks burn with shame. My body was not my own.

I still waited for my period, with lessening hope—what if, in all the history of females, some never had theirs? I gave myself new, extended deadlines, anticipating. I told myself not to worry, that it would be very, very soon. I wanted change. I was eager to leave.

That winter my family moved away from the Mojave Desert of California to the Big Island of Hawai'i. Suddenly, there was beach sand and the cool forest; there was hula class and rough children, fragrant ginger instead of roses, the thick smell of burning pakalolo, pregnant classmates and uncensored cuss words. There was eighth grade public school and then high school. Everything, everyone, was brand new. Everywhere I looked were brown faces like mine. I learned real quick that local people only knew I wasn't a born-and-raised local too when I opened my mouth and talked like a "mainlander." There was no more Angela and Lauren, but girls with names like Hi'ilei and Sam, Sheena and Stormy. There was no more Nick Hernandez, but bronzed boys who roamed in packs, who ran crashing out of waves, boys with names like Kaimana, Keoki, and Kalei. My hair grew long, fed by saltwater. There was no period, but now, I didn't care.

In the ninth grade I was walking with a new friend, Brooke, and her then-boyfriend Ken (her third boyfriend that fall) when I suddenly ducked into the restroom between classes. Oh, my God. I squinted in the dim yellow light, trying be certain if this was it. I decided it was. I ran out again, only somewhat elated, and tagged Brooke down. I asked her for a pad (a line I had been practicing for years), which she didn't have.

"What should I do?" I asked her, feigning helplessness. I wanted this moment to feel dramatic and played the necessary role.

"Come on. Every woman knows her cycle. It's really not a big deal. See you after class!" she quickly smiled. Still clutching Ken, she ducked off to her building.

I ran off, almost late for afternoon biology lab. As the teacher droned on about epithelial cells and genetic codes, my mind was lost in the strange new world of my own changing physiology, the invisible, internal changes that had dropped in, unannounced. And I suddenly dreaded the moment when I would have to tell my mother—I knew she'd pull some corny stunt and exclaim tearfully, "Now you're a woman!" or something like that. I tried to think of a very commonplace way to drop it into a conversation, wincing at her imagined reaction.

The moment came, and went. 🐾

Outward Journey

Jaime An Lim

That December, shortly after my 16th birthday, I received a card from Rich (bright seagulls and sailboats in Maine), something which I thought was symbolic of that time of my life, a time of fullness in the protective embrace of my home and family, which consisted of Auntie Tita and Uncle Kee Chuan, and my sister Lu.

Lu and I were orphaned when our parents died in a car accident, a tragedy which did not register on us, young as we were then. We were taken under the wing of Auntie Tita, father's younger sister, who had no children of her own. It was inevitable that she should lavish on us the love and care she was unable to give to her unborn children. (The family story had it that Uncle Kee Chuan took so long learning Cebuano that by the time he could manage "gihigugma ko ikaw," Auntie was already 39 and past safe child-bearing).

So you might say that ours was a case of a happy misfortune. In our comfortable home, and within the fenced backyard, among the many star-apple and avocado trees, stalwart giants that bore generous fruits in their season, love engulfed me so warmly I felt forever safe from harm, from any pain.

That day I got the card, along with a chocolate cake from auntie, I thought the cheery greetings in light italics summed up my life.

Happy Birthday!
I wish you all the pleasant things
That mean the most to you
Good luck, good health and happiness
For now and always too!

At the bottom of the card, Rich scrawled a postscript with a playful pen: "How are you, old man? Better do double time, gypsy's coming and the next day, you're 60!"

I imagined his blue eyes crinkling at this, the way his eyes crumpled pleasantly in that snapshot where he stood before their white colonial-style house in Inglewood, California: pressed khakis, merit badges, neckerchief, and all. He was named after his father who himself was named after his father, so that Rich became Richard Knight III, a name which evoked medieval adventure to a confirmed romantic like me. It was a name you didn't encounter just anywhere, much less in the ancient library of the Misamis Oriental High School. But that was where I found Rich.

Mrs. Renes, our history teacher, had sent me there indirectly when she had shrilled indignantly in class, "What, nobody knows where the Mediterranean is? All right, assignment for next meeting then..."

And so that visit to the dusty reference section where I came upon an obscure magazine in Boy Scouting (aha, a classic illustrated, I had thought), which featured an international friendship club ("Building youth is better than mending men," its motto said), and there was his evocative name. In the picture he enclosed in his first reply, I saw a blond, blue-eyed youth, already 19.

I had thought that the name was all that mattered when I wrote to Rich, but I realized now that my writing him had been impelled by two fears: first, my abject poverty when it came to intimate friendships; and second, my frantic need for a confidante, because even then I was already beginning to be troubled by certain things. Most of them things I didn't understand.

I understood though that I was a catastrophe. My legs were rough, knotty sticks; my frame the ruined figure of a basketball star; my hair, instead of falling rakishly over my forehead like Elvis Presley's, bristled like mad; I stumbled on stairways and stammered in front of stupid giggling girls; I suffered from B.O., halitosis, and every other evil-sounding disease; pimples had a malicious way of flourishing in the shiny flares of my nose. O God, I thought aloud, what would people think of me?

I unburdened all this to Rich, who wrote back: "What a crazy thing to say. You think people notice your pimples and thin legs so much? Well, they don't. And why should you care anyway? So why don't you just cut out all this melodrama. Really, it's so mushy. Nobody has died of adolescence, did you know that?"

I did not like that. My agonies were real enough, and if he thought I would sit back and enjoy the show, he was out of his mind. But then I realized at the same time that if I chucked Rich for a Japanese friend, for instance, he might not understand half of what I'd be talking about. I'd have to live with Rich even if he made such profound and crazy pronouncements as "Himmler had only one small ball" or "A man has to face his destiny bravely."

Still, my agonies deepened while Rich, in the sharpness of his wit and wisdom, tried to soothe my anxieties. He told me about his friend Ed, whom he met in a hospital ward. Ed, he wrote, had been to the Philippines, taught somewhere in a place called Surigao ("How far is that from Cagayan de Oro"), and came down with an exotic gastrointestinal disease. He said Ed was forlorn, not because of the worm, but because his girl who "promised to wait out the Peace Corps time" did not wait. He said that this was just another hazard of falling in love with very beautiful girls who were apt to be flighty, "as you very well know."

It was then that, with an impossible ache, I confided to him that I had never fallen in love with a girl in my whole life and could not see the connection between beauty and flightiness.

His quick retort was a startled, "What? And you're 16 now you said?"

"To Rich," I wrote, hurt at what seemed to me a careless insult, "what do you expect me to do?"

"To David," he answered. "Find a girl."

~

It was shortly after this that I noticed Shirley. She was Lu's classmate at Xavier U where they were taking BSEEd or some other equally idiotic course. She had been to the house before but I never bothered to be sociable. I had such prejudice against fat oysters and Lu's skirted coterie: neither appealed to my taste. But this time around I looked, and she was pretty.

"Boy," my sister sweetly called to me where I stood in the doorway waiting to be invited. That sweetness was suspect. She had something cooking in the back of her mind, I was sure. But I lingered. "Boy, come here, meet my friend Shirley," she beckoned graciously. "And by the way," she added, "would you mind getting us some more Cokes and roasted peanuts?"

I had prided myself in defying feminine caprices, but this time I happily hurried down to do Lu's bidding. I even brought up thick slices of cake and some ice.

"Well," said Lu, "if this is not something!"

"Thanks a lot," Shirley beamed at me, and her eyes were the softest brown I ever saw.

"That's okay," I stammered, quickly looking away from her. "Would you care for some more ice? I could bring you some more ice."

I blushed like a virgin bride. They giggled. Confusedly fingering my nose, which was swollen with lurid pimples, I stumbled down the stairs.

That night I sat in the study and wrote: "You would probably be surprised but I already found one. She is slender and shimmering, her small breasts tremble a little whenever she giggles, which she does a lot with my sister over their secret conspiracies, I think..."

And stopped. In the other room, I could hear Lu cooing *Moon River*. Ordinarily she had a thin, astringent voice, but this time it was surprisingly not bad at all.

I went back to the unfinished sentence, adding: "... something wonderful is going to happen soon. I'm happy, but strangely I'm also afraid."

"I'm also afraid of something," Rich said when he wrote back. "I'm very much afraid of death."

I thought of Rich as one who had learned to come to terms with all that the world had to offer, gallantly and gracefully, so it baffled me, this fear he expressed, for it was so unlike him.

At this time, in our literature class, we practiced a lot of empathizing, a pretty heavy word for the simple business of "standing in other people's shoes," as Miss Loyola put it. So I did it with Rich. I knew that if I could only stand in his place, even for a moment, I would learn something, a piece of wisdom, a truth, so that in my own dark time I would not be so afraid.

I conjured up a fearful vision: *It is night, I am alone, a loose board rattles in the teeth of the wind, a shroud billows darkly, death stalks like a cageful of bones, a sickle whistles toward the back of my neck...*

Try hard I did. But I just couldn't be frightened enough. I was 16 and I held my youth like a shield. I felt certain death could never, never touch me. So, failing to understand his fear, I could only reply with a taste of his own exasperating logic: "Oh, Rich, come on. You're getting melodramatic. Do you know that?"

In the weeks that followed, he never mentioned the topic again. If he was hurt, he did not show it in his letters. They became bantering again, the familiar lightness recaptured.

In February I wrote: "We had a competitive scholarship exam last weekend, the whole of Saturday. It was for nuts. It had stupid questions like 'A farmer had 15 goats. All but 9 died. How many did he have left?' Naturally I answered: 6. What else, unless you're a blockhead?"

In early March he replied: "It's nearly spring now in these parts. You don't feel the difference in Inglewood so much, though. This part of California has a more or less uniform temperate climate. But in the Midwest or on the East Coast where I had been, you can smell the changing season sharply. It is everywhere, in the sudden bright air, in the warmish sun during the thaw. Spring comes and the rich green sap rises, flushing through the veins, making things grow big. P.S. It's nine goats, wise guy. *Nine!*"

There too was a change of season in me. I felt it like a fever. My days were now touched with a sort of mistiness, in which enchanted birds twittered feverishly. I smiled to myself at the oddest times, saying foolish things, and I even spoke to the dog, Toffee, quite seriously, and to chairs and pictures—to whatever was handy at the moment.

"What's the matter, hijo?" Auntie Tita fretted, feeling my forehead for symptoms.

"You look pale, no good," Uncle Kee Chuan decided, then looked into his medicine box, fishing for dried Chinese herbs and roots to boil.

"Na. I know why, uncle!" Lu snickered.

I glared at the witch and chopped her, chopped her, into tiny shapeless pieces.

~

But she was right, of course. Before the long mirror, after my morning bath, I looked at my legs, not quite as knotty as before. My fingers sought my body with a new sensitivity, touching the hardening mound of my chest, slid down the flatness of my stomach. There, O Shirley! As if pierced by a vicious sting, the slumbering joys and anguish in me stirred and moaned, crying out for strange needs, overwhelming me, for although this was a land that I knew, it trembled so in new awareness, trembled furiously as if on the brink of a thousand glories.

On the altar in my room, a plaster cast of the Immaculate Conception watched all, saw all. My cheeks burned and my fists clenched with a guilt I could not understand.

"Rich. Is it such a terrible thing to touch oneself? Why does it leave me so depressed afterward? Why this wretchedness always? Everytime? Everytime?" I waited but my question remained unanswered.

No such guilt troubled my moments with Shirley. There was only this sense of well-being, this trust in the rightness of whatever I felt for her. It was as if I walked, in light, among angels and kings.

"I like you," she told me one time.

"Well," I stammered, as usual. "You must like an awful lot of people."

"No. That's not true. I don't like Freddy, for one."

"Freddy who? Freddy next door?"

"Yes."

"Why?"

"Because he has such wild hair and he stoops. And, also he's a big snob. I hate snobs."

"Well, he's supposed to be bright. He's taking engineering."

"I don't care. I don't like him. Really, I don't like him one small bit. Honest."

"I believe you," I said happily. Then: "Shirley?"

"Yes?"

"Will you be my partner for the seniors prom? That's in April yet, but—"

"David! You know I'd be happy to, yes!"

I felt so tall it seemed I could touch the sky. I leaped in the sparkling air and caught a dipping branch of the star apple tree. Swinging there, I sang, amazed at the sun that danced and flashed through the lace of golden leaves and smiled out of a burnished sky. Everything was, oh, so beautiful!

I wrote: "Hi Rich. Do answer me now. Today! This minute! You procrastinator. I have so much to tell you! Life is happening to me!"

I had not long to wait after his letter. The following week, I received two letters. The first, an official-looking letter, was from the state university in Marawi.

"You flunked the exam?" Lu grinned, a devilish light in her eyes as she peered over my shoulder.

"Na, scram, will you?" I said.

"My condolence," she said solemnly. "It does happen, you know, despite our best efforts."

"Thank you, my dear Queen of May, but as it is, I have to disappoint you. The registrar says here to notify him if I decide to accept the scholarship. And do you know what this is?" I waved a check in her face. "My travel allowance."

"Oh, really?" she said, but I could see she was impressed and happy for me. "You'll go, of course."

"Go?" My eyes brightened, for just then an idea began to beat in my mind. "Who said I'm going? Who said I'm going anywhere at all?"

Expectedly, the other letter was from the States. The unfamiliar handwriting said he regretted letting me know that his son died last March 20. His son, he wrote, had had an operation, his second this year, they had hoped... I stopped, puzzled. What was this? I examined the handwriting again. I noticed it was a little too heavy and formal. I looked at the signature at the bottom. It said: Richard Knight, Jr. His son, the man had written. His son. Rich.

I stood transfixed in disbelief. My mind refused to accept the message. Rich dead? I sank into a chair.

A slight wind came, stirring the curtains, bringing shadows into the room. Although it was a cloudless day, I was suddenly afraid. Afraid, not sad. Now, I thought, I saw the dark apparition Rich had talked about. I thought of Father and Mother, the car skidding over the cliff, their faces in the faded photograph tucked neatly underneath the glass top of Auntie Tita's dresser. I thought of Rich caught up in his one mortal fear. And I, who had not given him one word of comfort when he needed it, gave one to myself.

"Courage," I said, not knowing why I said it, but knowing that from now on I must grapple with my own ghosts alone. Tomorrow morning, I promised myself, tomorrow morning, I would go to Charlie Beach. The water would be very cool...

Escape was useless. I turned to go upstairs, but Lu was in the hallway. She was bound to notice something was wrong and say something like, "Unsa, your girlfriend busted you or something?" So I decided to go someplace else. But she had already spotted me. "Unsa?" she called.

I scurried away to the back of the *bodega* where they piled all the empty shirt boxes and the empty sock boxes, high against the wall. I sat down behind the door, and Toffee came to me, perhaps knowing how I felt, dragging his long ears. He lifted round moist eyes as I patted his head, and from his throat a thin plaintive whining keened. I held him tightly to me.

I pressed my cheek against the door and for the first time numbly mourned all my dead.

~

By the second week of April, we began practicing our graduation song in earnest. In the library our dim voices could be heard after all the other students had gone home. *"For Misamis Oriental our alma mater dear...so come and join us to sing to victoryyy."* Passing by the Xavier U campus after one such later rehearsal, I thought I saw Shirley talking with someone who looked very much like Freddy—the thick hair, the stopping stance. But already the tartanilla was clip-clopping past, so I was not sure.

That afternoon I saw her to check on our final plans for the seniors prom.

"Sorry. Something came up. I can't make it," she said.

I stared at her. The soft brown in her eyes was suddenly not there any more.

"My gown's too tight now," she said. "I mean, it's really out of fashion—old-looking, you know?" She looked down, kicking a stone.

I stood numb, my hands thrust deeply into my pockets. So it was Freddy, after all.

"I'm really sorry about this," she said, sounding really sorry.

I was silent, wondering at my own calm, wondering when it would break.

"I hope you understand. There are things we—"

"Oh, I understand," I said quickly. I was shaking inside. "Bet I can race you to that fence," I heard myself blurt out dumbly. Even before I spun around on my heels, I knew the barbed wire fence was too high. But I ached with anger and helplessness. I ran toward my pain, toward my fall.

I did not even feel the iron barbs piercing my skin. It was only afterward, toppled in an unheroic heap, that I felt the pain riving me.

"What did you do that for? Ay, foolish child!" Shirley was at my side, poking at the torn skin. "Now look at what you've done. You are hurt!" she said angrily.

My head swam, my leg throbbed in the swell of the pain, and my breath came back hard. "I'm not!" I shouted. Savagely I flung her hand back. Then I was running again, running away, running blindly in the deepening dusk.

When I stopped, she was nowhere to be seen. I wished I had the courage to fight for my love. But then I could not force myself on her out of pride. Still, I should have tried, should have told her how deeply I needed her myself. Now it was too late.

The night had sucked away the bright colors from the world, and there were now only the massed gray-black shadows that seemed to stand back, huddled against the deeper darkness, without shape or name. Somewhere, the gecko was again crying *tuk-ko... tuk-koo...* But the evening was silent, unable to give even a hollow echo. The star apple trees in the yard stood motionless although I felt the humidity pressing down. Later a cold rain fell for quite a while.

In the morning I sent a wire to the registrar at MSU in Marawi. I said I was coming.

Crossing the street from the telegraph office, I vaguely hoped for some violent disaster to descend, some monstrous accident overtaking me. I would be struck down, crushed, torn in the street. But the faces bobbing beneath the freckled shadows cast by the trees would not change expression. Life would flow on undisturbed, in the bright untrammeled sunlight.

I did not die that summer. I saw May stretching beyond a rimless horizon. Then it was June, noisily announced by the sudden hubbub at Divisoria: salesgirls calling out their wares, mothers haggling over the price of ruled pads, pencils, notebooks.

I soon packed my clothes and things in the new suitcase: there was no escape from college.

In the Bukidnon Bus terminal, a strange world (which henceforth was to be mine) tightened around me while I stalled, uncertain and afraid. People were hurrying about in disarray. Passengers walked around looking at signboards, their brown bags scraping against their legs. A mother struggled with a wailing baby as she hailed a departing bus, but nobody paid her any attention.

The conductor took my new suitcase and heaved it expertly into the back of the bus. "Get in, hurry," he said.

All about me, the tide of humanity continued to wash and swell. Late passengers were clambering into the jampacked Ciento Doce, and already an elbow was in my ribs. Then I knew I must fight for a seat. I hoisted myself into the bus. I stepped on a few toes and I got stepped on in return. At one point an umbrella caught in my shirt, but I held my ground. Finally, I got my seat, between the window and beside a man wearing a kopiah. There the hard glare of the sun struck me like a fist.

I squinted at my watch, my first one, a gift from Uncle Kee Chuan, and composed my face. It was time to go.

"Take care, David," my erstwhile archenemy said, now merely my worried sister Lu. I noticed it was the first time she had not called me Boy.

"You can study here at Xavier U. You don't have to go," Auntie Tita repeated.

"You know I have to, Auntie. Don't worry, I'll take care of myself."

She smiled and gently touched my cheek. "Of course, David, I'm sure you will. Good luck, hijo, and don't forget to write."

"That's a promise," I said, in a voice that was steady and, I hoped, grownup-sounding. But my eyes were blinking furiously.

Rich, I thought suddenly. So long, old pal.

The motor started. The entire bus quavered, then the Ciento Doce began to ease toward the road.

"Bye, David!"

"Bye, hijo. Study hard."

"I will."

It did not matter that my voice had thickened to a curious timbre. I glanced at the swiftly diminishing figures of Lu and Auntie for one last time, then I looked ahead. The conductor came up and handed me my ticket. The amount P2.75 had been punched out. It was the fare for adults. ✤

Auring's Dilemma

Marily Ysip Orosa

*I*t was 1965, but you would think it was Spanish colonial times. On my 16th birthday, my father made it clear that I was not allowed to go out alone with boys, period. I dared not ask why. His word was law and no one was allowed to question it—certainly not a teenager whose social life depended on a parent's good graces.

My father, however, begrudgingly said that because I had finally turned 16, he would give me permission to attend jam sessions held in private homes, but only under certain conditions. First, I would have to abide by a midnight curfew; second, I could only be allowed to go to a party once a month; and most importantly, I would have to bring a chaperone.

He was in his den one Saturday afternoon when I gathered the courage to ask if I could attend Meldee's 18th birthday the following Saturday.

"Meldee's debut is coming up, Dad. Anne Marie, Ludy, Mary, everybody is going," I said in a gush. He pushed his chair back from his desk and stared at me. Our driver had told me that my father was in a lousy mood because he had lost to his friend Mario at golf. My timing was obviously wrong.

He frowned at the mention of "debut." I started to get sweaty palms. "You said one party a month, Dad, and this is the one I want to attend. Please."

He was scowling when he suddenly thundered, "Choose, Caesaria or Auring?" He was referring to our maids.

Caesaria was our cook of 14 years, a 40-year old Igorota from a remote town in the Mountain Province called Mayuyao where the rice terraces are said to be magnificent. She had a failed marriage and hated men. "I am disgraced," she told my mom, meaning she had a child out of wedlock. She had ballooned to 230 pounds and looked like an angry sumo wrestler.

Auring, on the other hand, was 23 years old, a devotee to the Sto. Niño de Cebu, a petite sweet barrio lass from Moalboal, Cebu. She cleaned, helped out in the kitchen and even washed and ironed our clothes. She had long black wavy hair that reached up to her waist. Because she braided her hair too tight, her hairline had started to recede, but she still looked pretty. My younger sister said she looked "virginal," as if coyness was synonymous with virginity.

"Auring," I replied, greatly relieved that my father actually let me choose my chaperone. Auring would be easier to escape from—and to bribe. She always seemed to be in need of a few extra pesos.

"All right then, give me the names of your friend Meldee's parents, their home address and telephone numbers," he added. With that, the conversation ended.

Being the eldest in a family of nine girls, I expected my parents to be very strict with me. I was their guinea pig, their human experiment, on how to bring up a proper young lady. In the '60s, girls from good families were expected to be "lady-like" or better still, "Mary-like," the buzz word in our all-girls school run by strict German nuns. I imagined that my mom had this same pressure when she herself turned 16 before the war. No un-chaperoned dates with those sweet-talking American GIs. No slow dancing. No vacations to Antipolo and Baguio without an adult. They were the same rules imposed upon me.

~

Saturday night came. I wore a pale blue sleeveless taffeta dress with a hemline that was an inch below the knee. Our car brought Auring and me to Meldee's big bash at her parent's sprawling home in La Vista in Quezon City. Jess, my 17-year old secret boyfriend of three months, a dashing 5'11" NCAA champion javelin thrower with black curly hair and smiling eyes, met me there. He winked at me as he surreptitiously showed me a crisp five peso bill, the bribe money for Auring, which he whispered was the going rate for chaperones. We both laughed. Auring, in her white pantsuit uniform, was oblivious to what we were laughing about.

I hurriedly brought Auring to the kitchen where the other maids, clad in similar white uniforms, sat, shuffling cards as they played pekwa. She didn't want to gamble so she opted to chat with the non-players, who were seriously discussing whose ward was the most difficult and which Fernando Poe movie was the best. I didn't care what she did or talked about. I was only too happy to be left alone with my boyfriend, be able to dance slow drag with him, and maybe even smoke a blue seal Marlboro cigarette or two. All three were absolute no-no's in my father's book of laws.

Meldee's debut had all the trimmings of a proper coming out party. The house was all lit up, and the garden decked with round capiz lanterns. The buffet, catered by some ritzy hotel, was a lavish spread. There was a cotillion, a brisk dance number like a quadrille, perfectly executed by 12 pairs of dancers who had religiously practiced with a highly paid choreographer every Saturday for six months. And playing The Beatles, Chubby Checker and Ventures music non-stop all night was a five-man combo called the Hi Jacks, a live band said to be the most expensive in Manila. It was obviously a pricey party but for me, it was run-of-the-mill, a me-too event much like other high-budget parties featured in the society pages. Jess and I wanted something different, so we decided to party hop to another affair in Valle Verde which is about 15 minutes away from Meldee's. I was nervous but happy to get rid of Auring. She had a way of spying on me to have something she could use to tell on me—or bribe me with.

Auring didn't notice that we had slipped away. Our destination was a soirée, where kids our age chatted and discussed literature, politics and everything in between. It was more highbrow and grownup. The soiree was held outdoors under a moonlit sky, and it felt magical and more exciting than the debut. Piped in instrumental music was kept to a low so as not to disrupt discussion of our school's forthcoming student council elections. I felt like an adult while I held a stemmed crystal glass filled with lemonade-rum punch and participated in the lively conversation.

The time passed quickly; we completely forgot my midnight curfew. It was Mary's phone call that jolted us back to reality. "Hoy, you better get back soon, Auring is looking for you. She's braying like a donkey and bothering the band with all the commotion she's causing," Mary half shouted on the phone. "Your chaperone's babbling that because of you she could be sent back to her fishing village, and may even lose her Christmas bonus!"

Jess and I frantically rushed back and arrived at Meldee's at 12:30. My nervous boyfriend had to bribe Auring ten pesos, not five, to keep her from reporting the incident to my dad. Poor Jess, it was his entire week's allowance. I begged a visibly irked Auring to take it because at first she was not inclined to but eventually, she relented. My grandfather once taught me a Spanish adage that would aptly describe her phony tentativeness: "*Hele hele, pero quire.*"

On the way home, Auring and I were both edgy, quietly concocting in our minds some excuse for being 35 minutes late. We decided to tell my father some preposterous story of bumper to bumper traffic on Aurora Boulevard at midnight because of a vehicular accident involving a calesa and five cars.

But our fear was greater than the actual encounter with my father. To my surprise, he summarily dismissed us with a wave of his hand after we regaled him with our story. Apparently, my father was in a good mood because earlier on that day, he had beaten his friend Mario at golf.

The ten peso bribe was effective. My parents never found out that I had escaped from one party to go to another.

Over the next few months, Auring continued to hold me hostage as she kept more and more secrets of my escapades, which earned her quite a bit of money. Jess and I often wondered why she needed so much cash. Was she sending her two young siblings to school? Or maybe she was helping finance her father's new motorized banca? Surely, we thought, her reasons were noble.

Caesaria, the biggest gossip that ever lived told us why: Auring had fallen madly in love with our next door neighbor's 20-year old gardener, Felipe, a dark-skinned man with a sharp nose and shifty eyes. Caesaria went on to divulge that Felipe had vices galore—cigarettes and beer—and worst of all, was totally addicted to a local numbers game called jueteng, the bane of millions of Philippine households. Auring, our sweet, virginal Auring, was not only smitten by his bad-boy looks, but was his willing source of funds. Sadly she had turned into Felipe's "co-dependent."

By this time, I had learned to mistrust and dislike Auring. She had become bossy and grouchy, and extremely money-minded. She had raised her chaperone "fee" to ten pesos. It was first degree extortion and black mail all rolled into one. I also discerned that one day soon—very soon—Auring would tell on me to my parents—surely for a handsome fee.

A week before Christmas, Auring surprised us all with her decision to resign from our employ. She bravely told my mom that she would be going home to Moalboal. To have peace and quiet, she added, with a melodramatic sigh, while casting a wicked glance at me

With great prodding, Caesaria disclosed the real reason behind Auring's sudden departure. I held my breath as Caesaria spoke. Images of my escapades came to mind like a Charlie Chaplin film in fast forward. Caesaria revealed that Auring, a devotee to the Sto. Niño, started getting nightmares that she would soon be banished to some desolate place—limbo, purgatory or the Sahara dessert—by the Sto Niño. He was very unhappy with her affair with Felipe. To appease him, Auring had to leave Manila to be separated from Felipe for good. It was to be the ultimate penance for all her sins.

With a sigh of relief, I totally agreed. ❧

Someone Else

Dolores de Manuel

*L*iana knows that somewhere in California lives a distant cousin—she sometimes thinks of her, jokingly, as her evil twin. The last anyone heard of her, she'd run away from home to join a Vietnamese gang. Her name is Chechi, and like Liana she has the Tala family features.

At family gatherings, from aunts and uncles exclaiming about how grownup she's getting, Liana always hears about her looks. And tonight is the biggest gathering in a long time--for her great grandfather Lolo Ito's 85th birthday. All the able-bodied and solvent members of the Tala clan, pulled in by family sentiment, by her aunts' eager phone calls and constant emails, are making their way to Toronto from around the continent and across the oceans: Massachusetts, Vancouver, Maryland, California, Rome, Manila.

On their drive from Montreal her parents chat about who's coming from where, eight of Lolo Ito's nine children, dozens of grandchildren and more great-grandchildren. Liana is thankful that their trip is just six hours. The ride in the Honda minivan is smooth enough for her to doze, and to review her sociology paper notes and the scores for the Mozart and Haydn pieces for next month's concert, and for her sister Toni to read her magazines. She'd rather be at the concert rehearsal but there's no getting out of this gathering, not this time. And though it's an ordeal to be confronted by all the exclaiming aunts and uncles, it's still not as bad as what her mom says her cousin Benny is facing–instead of driving up from Annapolis with Tito Ando, he's being deployed to Iraq.

Then again, thinking of earlier reunions where she's been commanded to make the rounds of all her aunts and uncles, she wonders whether Benny hasn't actually dodged a different kind of bullet. "Kiss Tita whoever" and "say hello to Tito whosit," navigating between the blood relatives and in-laws and the family friends called "Tita" and "Tito" as courtesy aunts and uncles has always felt dangerous to her. And then there's the chore of smiling politely and looking modest when they talk about how well she's doing in school, all her awards, Quebec provincial bursaries and scholarships, and trying not to clench her teeth when they say she's so grownup--what do they expect, when she's 18! And of course the talk about her looks.

The moment they're welcomed at the gleaming door of the McMansion, it starts: "Look at her, amor!" says Tita Bootsie, her mother's sister, to her husband Tito Bitoy. "Liana, you look just so, so much like the Talas!" The strong jaw, high cheekbones, slightly pointed nose, olive skin: all of them are reminders of the family legend that one of their ancestors was a Moorish pirate. A Corsair, maybe-- Liana pictures him standing proud and gallant on the deck of his ship, handsome like Tito Ray, the best-looking of her uncles. But she knows she's being too romantic; aren't pirates just thieves and marauders on boats?

With the Tala looks they're sometimes taken for Indians, sometimes American Indians—or First Peoples, to use the Canadian term that Liana likes. Ojibwe, Cree, Navajo— some of the guesses her cousin Mel heard when he was going through what he called his "native" phase, growing his hair long so he could braid it, wearing cowboy boots and string ties. And right in the entrance hall is Tito Moro, dark and bearded, telling a favorite from his repertoire of stories— the one about airport screeners at LAX, looking at his passport, asking him if he's a Muslim and if he has contacts with Abu Sayyaf in Mindanao. "They just kept on hounding me, I couldn't say anything to get them to give up. Then I remembered I had St. Anthony prayer cards from Mama in my wallet, and the Miraculous Medal of Our Lady around my neck. I pulled them out and asked, "Do you see Osama holding any of these on his 'WANTED' poster?"

The 'WANTED' poster. That reminds her of Chechi, whom she hasn't seen since they were little. They last met at another family gathering, in San Francisco, when Liana and her parents were on their way from Manila to Toronto, part of their clan's gradual migration. She remembers the exclamations about their looking like sisters, even though they're just third cousins, and the unease she felt looking into Chechi's face, strange yet familiar, and seeing a hostile glare. They even have the same name, both of them Cecilia, for their great-grandmother Lola Chiling. But Liana, Cecilia Ana, thinks her nickname is so much more elegant—it's a great relief that she hasn't gotten landed with one of those Filipino nicknames that sound so dumb to her. Chechi and her branch of the family aren't mentioned much by the rest of the family anyway—they'd rather talk about the successful businesses, the accountants, dentists and law students, while Chechi's dad is flipping burgers. Whenever he can, he and his brothers will make a pilgrimage of sorts, to their own holy of holies, to Las Vegas, driving through the night, eight hours across hills and deserts, to gamble away whatever earnings they've managed to save.

Of course, the family gathering is like a pilgrimage too, thinks Liana as they file into the living room behind a group of earlier arrivals. "Don't forget, you have to make mano!" her mother murmurs to her and Toni, who grimaces. Lolo Ito and Lola Chiling sit in the overstuffed velvet armchairs, as if enthroned, in state. Liana watches the two as they hold out their hands for the grandchildren and great-grandchildren to take and touch to their foreheads, and can't decide whether with their dignity and twisted, bony hands, the benign smiles on their hollow cheeks, they look grotesque, or regal, or both. As Liana bends her head to Lola Chiling's hand she notices the heavy gold bracelet, with its medal of St. Cecilia with her harp, which has fascinated her since she was little. When November 22, St. Cecilia's day, comes around, Liana gets a call or an email from her grandmother, Lola Chiling's eldest daughter, wishing her a happy feast day. And four years ago, when the clan celebrated Lola Chiling's 80th birthday, it was Lola's saint's day as well, and with Saint Cecilia being the patron of music they put together a sing-along and a musical recital for her. Tita Bootsie, organizing as usual, asked Liana to play her flute and to sing but she thanked a kind fate that she had a school award presentation that she couldn't miss. Not that she minded performing, she was good enough, but—"saint's day...feast day," for goodness sake, she thinks, surely, like making mano, a somewhat primitive, atavistic tradition? Although after her Tolstoy phase last year it doesn't seem so bad to her any more—for weeks she read and reread *Anna Karenina* and *War and Peace*, and looked for commentaries and film versions. The scene with the lovely young Countess Natasha Rostov's feast day party reconciles her. She laughs as she realizes that she's casting herself as Natasha, but then if Natasha has a feast day party then Lola Chiling, by all accounts a beauty in her day, can have one too, and include Liana in the celebration.

Sometimes Liana envies the Countess Natasha and wishes herself back in the days of ballrooms, chaperones and even arranged marriages—the ones that bloom into romance, of course. She hates the murky world of her classmates' crude groupings, the cynical "friends with benefits" transactions, the casual hooking up, whether accompanied by drunken binges or not. She's seen enough to know that's not for her, to want to hold aloof. Toni jokes that the only men Liana is really interested in are Harry Potter and Jane Austen's Mr. Darcy—and to tell the truth either of them would be far more appealing than some of the boys whose coarse whispers or casual, "Do you want to...." invitations she's heard. The worst was in biology class last month—Neil, sitting next to her, took to passing her his drawings of genitalia, with captions like: "c u after class" and "can't fool me I no u want it." As if that was supposed to interest her?

She knows that no Prince Andrei is going to come along for her as he did for Countess Natasha, but sometimes she wishes that it were still all right to marry one's cousins. Like her great-great-grandparents, Lolo Peping and Lola Diday, first cousins—even in the fading sepia photographs it's clear that they both have the Tala features. At least that would be safe and familiar, and then maybe she'd marry Justin, her favorite cousin, everyone's favorite. He's a year younger than her, but somehow he seems more grownup—kind, confident and collected, the

Student Council President, the leader of the youth group at Our Lady of Hope, a clean, flashing smile. With his warm golden glow he's always surrounded by friends— on other stays in Toronto, Liana has enjoyed hanging out with them, singing with Mike and Ryan and Nick as they play their guitars. She moves through the rooms full of relatives wondering where Justin is, thinking that as usual nothing happens at these family gatherings—just eating and trying to avoid difficult aunts. After a while, getting impatient, she decides to try and find a quiet corner to work on the sociology paper that's due in a few days.

Liana realizes that Chechi is on her mind because somehow, by some strange twist of fate, she's ended up writing about the sociology of gangs. From the first class, she's been so impressed with Dr. Dumont, the sociology professor, that she's considering a sociology major instead of literature or art. She's tried hard to please her, and it's worked. Dr. Dumont, treating her like the prize student, suggested the gang topic, not Liana's first choice, but she didn't want to say no, and now she's gotten into it. As she writes about the Tiny Rascals in California, the Red Bloods, Blue Crips and Bo Gars of Montreal she rolls her eyes at the gang names and laughs to imagine a WANTED poster for Chechi with a photo on it that could be taken for her, goody-goody, law-abiding Liana. It was almost funny, how Dr. Dumont, usually so incisive, turned all tentative last week when giving Liana the *Montreal Mirror* article, on Filipino gangs in Cote-des-Neiges.

"Ummm...I don't know if you've heard anything about this in your family and community...but, in any case, this is an article that you could use." Her tone was so cautious, as if not knowing just how tactful to be, wondering how close she was to an uncomfortable topic. Liana could practically see a thought bubble over Dr. Dumont's head. What did it read–maybe, "I know you can't be one of the Filipinos who hang out in gangs, since you've made it into a select Montreal college, but just maybe your brother or cousin is and you're the good one who's managed to escape." She wishes she could just have told Dr. Dumont, "They're nothing to do with me, I'm not one of them." But then there was no accusation made. And that would be one of those things you can't say plainly anyway. It would be coming too close to upsetting a delicate balance in a country that values its multicultural heritage--or something like that.

Looking at the faces in the article photos, she's reminded of the clique of Filipino kids in her grade school that often brought in rice for lunch, the ones who spoke Tagalog to each other. Technically, she supposed, she was one of them, born in the Philippines, but she didn't hang out with them. After a few years in Canada she'd forgotten her Tagalog—they always spoke English at home, even in the Philippines—and was starting to think of herself as Canadian. Then she noticed they were calling her "Boom-buy" behind her back—at least that's what it sounded like, until she went home and asked, "Mom, what does "Boom-buy" mean in Tagalog?"

"It means people from India, you know, Bombay, and it usually means the Indian vendors, they'd go around selling umbrellas and mosquito nets. When we were little the maids would try to scare us by telling us that a big bad "Bombay" would grab us and put us in his sack if we didn't watch out."

After that she just hung out with Canadian friends and it was a relief to move on to a special high school with a Gifted Education program, where there were more kids like her.

The gathering swirls on around her as she moves from room to room, looking for relatives she likes and trying to steer clear of the others. It works until she hears a high, complaining voice behind her. "Bootsie, where's Justin?" calls out Tita Mely. As usual, her tone is accusing as she continues, "Why isn't he here? Everyone else is here."

My least favorite aunt, asking about my favorite cousin, thinks Liana. But she's right, why isn't Justin here?

Tita Bootsie smiles apologetically. "He just went to bring a book over to Mike Timbol's house, he should be back soon...he should be back by now..." she trails off with a worried frown.

"Those Timbol boys?" Tita Mely jumps in. "You know, if Justin is 17, he's just the age to get mixed up with a bad crowd. I think I saw one of the Timbols with some of those kids who hang out in Malvern Town Centre. Those kids— their families were just kanto boys and tambays in Manila, why should they be any different here? They're still kanto boys here." Seeing Liana's puzzled face she explains, "Kanto is the street corner and tambays are the kind who just stand around, looking for trouble. Even a girl like you can get pulled in. You're staying out of trouble, right, Liana?" She sweeps away before Liana can open her mouth to protest, of course I stay out of trouble! And what she's saying about Mike and Ryan Timbol is just unfair.

Dinner is served and the clan swoops down on the lechon, a plump roast pig, the skin shiny brown and crunchy, savoring it, congratulating Tita Bootsie on having found the right place to buy it. The party goes on with a special karaoke production and a huge birthday cake for a gently smiling Lolo Ito, serene in his chair. Liana is uneasy, though; Justin still hasn't turned up and other relatives have been wondering where he is. She drifts into the kitchen on the way to the back coat closet, to put her sociology notes away with her bag. The phone rings, and Tita Bootsie, loading the dishwasher, asks,

"Can you pick that up, please Liana darling?" She glances at the caller ID and sees the readout, 42 DIV POLICE STN. What could they want? She picks up the receiver and hears a hum of background noise—the police station must be crowded, she thinks—and then a shaky voice, words coming in a rush:

"Hi, it's Justin, who is this? Liana? Liana, please, tell my dad, he has to come and pick me up. The police station on Milner and Morningside. Right away, please, I've been here for hours and they're just letting us call now. I'm OK, just tell him to come now, I can't talk. Tell him right now. Please."

Liana feels her mouth gaping open and raises her hand to cover it. What have they done to Justin, why should he need to be picked up from the police station? She walks over to Tita Bootsie, who stares at her—her lips are moving but she can't make any sound come out of her mouth. Finally, when she pulls her over into the laundry room, where nobody will overhear, and whispers to her, the words come tumbling out. Then, leaving a stunned Tita Bootsie, she slips into the dining room where Tito Bitoy is chatting at the table and whispers, "Come quick, Tito, it's urgent!" Back in the kitchen she spills out the story. Without responding to her, he sticks his head back into the dining room and calls out to another cousin: "Tommy, come a minute, please?" Liana wonders why and realizes, of course, a law student, just in case there are any legal issues. They huddle briefly in the kitchen and start out the back door. Tita Bootsie comes quickly too, trying to be unobtrusive, but Tito Bitoy holds out his hand. "No, stay, hon, you have to stay, people will wonder what's wrong if they see us both leaving." She bites her lip and nods. Liana can see she's trying not to cry.

As the men slip out, Liana hurries behind, without waiting to ask, and slides into the back of the car. Sociological research, I'm doing field work, to see how the rest of the world lives, that's her first line, and she realizes that she's still holding the folder with her paper notes. But that's a comforting cover-up. She has to find out what's wrong with Justin—she doesn't want to worry but she's sure that something has happened.

They drive a mile in tense silence, before Tito Bitoy notices that she's in the car. "What are you doing here, Liana?"

"Please let me come along, Tito, please?"

"A police station is no place for a girl. You should have stayed at the house. I don't have time to drive you back, you'll just have to wait in the car while we go in. I don't want you coming in so you just stay put."

"What kind of antiquated idea is that, what about all the female police officers in there?" But the question is unspoken. His tone is sharp; she can tell that it's a final decision and there's no point in protest.

They're pulling into the huge parking lot in front of the police station, a white building that looks like it's made of giant snow blocks, before Tito Bitoy breaks the silence again. "What do you think the situation is, Tommy?"

"We have to find out if he's been charged. We'll call a lawyer right away if he has. But they might have just picked him up for something minor and not charged him, and they're letting him go now. Let's hope that that's all it is."

Once they're parked Tito Bitoy strides out, bracing his shoulders, Tommy following. She watches as they walk in the door, holding themselves taut and ready for whatever there is to face.

Ten minutes, fifteen minutes, half an hour. Liana takes out the articles for her report and has them spread out on her lap but can't focus on the words. Instead she looks out the car window at the police station, trying to decide whether it's worth it to risk Tito Bitoy's wrath and go in. Finally she sees them emerging, Tommy holding a sheaf of papers, Tito Bitoy with his jaw set. Behind them, Justin stumbles, pale and wide-eyed. He gropes for the car door handle, nods to Liana and slumps down into the back seat with a sigh.

Tito Bitoy sighs too. "All right, son, you were lucky, they didn't charge you. I don't like what they were saying, though, about suspected gang activity. Now tell us what you were doing, what happened. Not what you told the police, what really happened."

Justin turns even paler and shakes wildly, almost like a wet dog. Liana tries not to stare, but this boy with pain and fear in his eyes can't be the same collected Justin she knows. It feels like a door to a strange land is opening on a desolate pitch black landscape, with a cold howling wind pushing and pulling at her. Even Justin's stammering whisper feels like an icy wind.

"I told them the truth, Dad. I wasn't doing anything. I was with Mike Timbol. He wasn't doing anything either. And they shot Ryan, his brother. I...I think...it looked like...he's dead." He shudders, convulsed.

"What? Who shot him? Another gang? Where were you? What happened?"

"We thought they were part of a gang. They were dressed like bikers. But...but...they were the police."

"Undercover officers," says Tommy. "Where were you? What were you doing?"

"We went to find Ryan. Mike heard that Ryan and his friends went looking for some kids who beat up one of their cousins yesterday. These white kids...they called them stupid little rice-eaters and yelled stuff like "white power." Mike wanted to stop Ryan, he didn't want him to get hurt. We followed them to the schoolyard." His voice cracks.

"Did they have any weapons?" asks Tito Bitoy.

"They had a few sticks and bats...I didn't see anyone with a knife or anything. But a bunch of Ryan's friends were there, and just a few of the white kids. Then a car came along and a couple of the white kids jumped in. The rest started to walk away too. We thought that was it."

"Then they came back?"

"Then a black sports car pulled up right close to us and a couple of guys in leather jackets jumped out. One of them was really big. He looked tough, like a biker. We thought he was a friend of the white kids or something. We didn't know who he was."

"He didn't show a badge?" asks Tommy.

Justin shakes his head. That starts him trembling again. "They didn't say they were cops or anything. And then the big guy pulled out a gun. Mike said we'd better run. We saw Ryan start to run too. I...I don't know why... but he jumped on Ryan. You know, the cop was huge, Ryan is just 5'3". We saw them struggling...Ryan pulled away... and the cop shot him. He shot him in the back."

Justin's chilling whisper goes on, whispering the details--police cars arriving, sirens, ambulances, being brought to the police station.

But Liana can hardly hear any more. A dark wind seems to be swirling around her. Because this kind of thing isn't supposed to happen, not to people she knows, not in civilized Toronto, not here in tolerant Canada. Somewhere else, maybe, to someone else. Somehow, she's stumbled into a world she doesn't know. Who knows what bleak, terrifying land she's been blown into, and when she'll stop shaking inside.

She hears Justin's tone change. "The Timbols...Dad, this will kill them. How can we help them, what can we do for them?"

Tito Bitoy takes a deep breath. He starts the car. "I don't know, son. We'll do what we can. We'll think of something we can do."

As they drive back to the gathering, Justin muses aloud about gathering the youth group, finding ways to help the Timbols. Liana hears him coming together, starting to sound more like himself. But she's still lost in a land of dark wind, trembling with cold fear and rage. She tries not to think of a boy lying dead, shot in the back. She tries not to ask just what anyone can do. She looks down at her lap and sees her notes, an article, pictures of faces. This time the faces look familiar. Maybe they're people she knows. They look like Justin, like Ryan. Maybe they look like her. 🐚

Something Like That

Dean Francis Alfar

Before you leave for your classes, you read the newspaper headline: Girl Dies in Fire. And you shake your head and think "Poor girl" or "Poor parents of the girl" or something like that. It's not a unique circumstance. Fires happen all the time in Manila. People die, life goes on.

But you look at the accompanying photo and see the girl, half-burnt, sprawled in her bathroom, partially covered by singed towels that were soaking wet when she entrusted her life to their questionable abilities. The bathtub is intact, which makes you think "she must have been too terrified to climb in" and maybe you're right.

Or maybe not.

Maybe she didn't want to get boiled.

Or something like that.

The black-and-white photo reveals more details: a cracked mirror, remnants of her medicine cabinet, the lidless toilet. The shower curtain is missing, but you think that, of course, it must have melted away, yes, because plastic does that. You reread the article and discover that when she was found, the girl was almost obscured by steam. That she couldn't escape because the windows were bulletproof glass and locked from the outside. That she used her mobile phone twice: to call and to text for help.

You think about yourself, about what you would do, who you would call when hope for rescue was still strong. And who would you text goodbye when hope faded.

She was a politician's daughter, which explains the need for windows that denied gunshots. But she was also a young girl, which explains why her parents hoped that she was out with her friends when the fire consumed the house. The sad fact was that she wasn't at out singing at a videoke or dancing at a club or something like that. She was home, which makes you think about statistics and fire safety and how you will get away from an inferno when it threatens your own home. After all, it's most likely you'd be home too. If a fire occurred.

You think about calling the mother or the father of the girl. Not that you knew her, not that you knew them, not that you know what to say. It's the thought of connecting, the thought of the thought that counts or something like that.

But you think it's stupid or maudlin or ill-timed and put down your own cell phone, not that you even know the phone number of anyone involved. But at least, you think, you would have called. At least.

You look at the newspaper photo of the burnt bathroom again and picture the girl screaming or crying or praying or unconscious or hidden under wet towels and scalding steam, then turn the newspaper page looking for something, anything else, to read.

Anything but that. 🐚

The Veil

Maria Victoria Beltran

When a woman crosses the invisible line of innocence, it does not always mean that she will reach the goal of wisdom. But then perhaps, she does.

Ayesha wakes up before dusk is replaced by the soft glow of sunrise. She stirs, sits on the dormitory bed and heads for the wash room. She cleans herself for Silaat or Muslim prayer. A few minutes later, she comes back to the room she shares with Teresa. She takes out a clean mat from her cabinet and carefully places it on the floor near the window facing the rising sun. Just as carefully, she puts on a white hijab or veil to cover her hair. She takes out her slippers, faces in the direction of Mecca, stands erect, head down, hands at the sides and arranges her feet so that they are evenly spaced.

Allaahu Akbar! Allaahu Akbar...

She starts to intone silently, afraid that her roommate would wake up from her prayers. Teresa knows the ritual by heart. They have been roommates in the dormitory for almost three months now. She has learned to pretend to sleep throughout these prayers not wanting to embarrass Ayesha or disturb her. She watches silently as Ayesha stands in attention and brings her hands to her ears with palms forward and thumbs behind her earlobes. Ayesha is now engrossed in Qiyam—the opening plea. She places her right hand over her left hand at chest level then she drops her hands to her sides. She bends from her waist with her palms on her knees with her back parallel to the ground. She looks at her feet while bending.

Ayesha rises from her bent position and stands with her arms at her sides. Placing her hands on her knees, she slowly lowers herself to a kneeling position. Then she touches the ground with her forehead and nose while placing her palms on the ground taking care that her elbows do not touch the ground. Finally, she bends her toes so that the top of her feet face the Qibla or direction of Mecca.

"Subhaana rabbiyal' Alaa! Subhaana rabbiyal' Alaa...

Somehow, the chanting lulls Teresa into another world inhabited by women in chadors, mosques, camels and clusters of dates in an oasis. The two students are freshmen at the University of the Philippines in Diliman, Quezon City. They met at the start of the semester during the orientation for all the freshmen students in Kalayaan Dormitory. They would not have recognized each other again in the sea of faces in the auditorium except for the fact that they found out later that they were roommates. Besides, Ayesha stands out in the crowd because of the veil that she wears to cover her hair.

"Which province do you come from? In Mindanao?" Teresa asks.

"I grew up in Riyadh but my mother is from Cebu and my father is a Tausug from Zamboanga." Ayesha answers quickly. She must have been asked the same question a number of times.

"How about you?" she continues.

"I come from the northern Mindanao city of Butuan, where they discovered the Balanghai boats," Teresa retorts proudly.

"Do you know that Butuan was ruled by a Tausug prince in the 14th century? My father says this is the reason why there are a lot of similarities between the Tausug and Butuan dialects," Ayesha informs her new friend.

"I can understand Butuanon but I don't speak it fluently," says Teresa.

"That's okay, I don't speak Tausug," Ayesha chides her.

That was the start of an uneasy friendship between the two. There is something in Ayesha that Teresa finds disconcerting. For one thing, she prays five times a day. In addition, she does not eat pork, shrimps, and crabs. She always wears loose pants or long skirts and long sleeved tops and she never goes out without a veil on her head. Also, she neither drinks alcohol nor smoke cigarettes. Ayesha is never tempted to stay too long in the dormitory cafeteria to chat with the others. There is an aura of aloofness about her that seems to say yes, we can be friends but not too close, please.

Teresa is not a stranger to the Muslims of Mindanao. They roam around her city selling brass wares, batik, and malong. Some have stalls in the market where they also offer exquisite South sea pearls. As a child, her yaya used to scare her that a Muslim warrior in a vinta boat would snatch her away from her family if she didn't behave. She has always been warned by family and friends to be careful with the Muslim people. Her mother tells her they cannot be trusted in business and that sometimes their men run amok brandishing the Kris, their favorite weapon. Their women stay in their houses or mind their stores in their signature malongs, veils and beautiful jewelries. These people largely stay among themselves. Teresa wonders where they have been hiding their children. Thinking about it now, she does not have a classmate in school back home who is a Muslim. Ayesha is the first Muslim girl she comes very close to.

As Salaamu 'alaikum wa rahmatulaah...

The chanting stops. Ayesha pauses for a moment as if gazing at the minaret of a mosque in Riyadh outside their window. She looks at Teresa who smiles at her.

"Did I wake you up?" Ayesha asks her.

"Yes, but it's fine. We have no class in English today; we are going to a film showing, instead," Teresa reminds her.

"Yes, I remember and this coming weekend, we will go to Matabungkay Beach".

"So, Ayesha, everybody is curious if you will still be wearing your veil when you go swimming."

"I know. I will bring my Muslim swimming clothes so that they can watch me."

"I always wonder how your mom takes it, living in Riyadh. You told me she is Christian?"

"But she has converted to Muslim a long time ago. My mom is a better Muslim than my dad now." Ayesha laughs.

"That is strange; I always thought that women are treated as the weaker sex in your religion. Your mom swallows that?"

"It is not true, Teresa. There are a lot of misconceptions about our religion. In fact, we believe that women have a very special place in our society."

"Sorry for all my questions, it is not my intention to question your beliefs."

"I guess you are just as curious as everybody else what I will be wearing in Matabungkay Beach," Ayesha says cheerfully, without sarcasm.

The two girls start giggling. They are both majoring in Bachelor of Science in Biology at UP Diliman. It is a block section which means that they have exactly the same schedule. It has become a habit to wait for each other when they go to school and back to the dormitory again. Conveniently, they go to the cafeteria together for their meals and to the study room when they prepare for their examinations. They have also gone to the shopping center in the campus and to some eatery in Area 1 and 2 on their free time a couple of times. The arrangement suits both girls.

"Hurry up, everyone. You can board the bus now."

The house mother walks around like a hen exhorting her wayward chicks inside the pen. Ayesha's hijab glares under the morning light. Beside her is Teresa clad in blue jeans and a baby shirt. Her belly ring peeps out of her navel. The students are in a festive mood. They line up to board the bus that will take them through the tree lined streets of the campus to the audiovisual room in the College and Arts building.

"You don't feel hot in those clothes and veil?" Teresa asks.

"I am so used to these clothes; it feels like second skin already. Perhaps I would feel naked without my hijab. In Riyadh, we wear chadors but that would look really weird here," says Ayesha.

"Don't you ever feel like wearing clothes like mine?"

"I don't know; it does not cross my mind. This is me. I

happen to be a Muslim woman and as such I wear clothes that don't reveal anything except my hands and my face."

"You are not uncomfortable that you look different from everybody else? Somehow I feel lucky that I can wear a veil and take it away anytime when I want to!"

"No, Teresa. I don't feel uncomfortable. It just never ceases to amaze me. As much as people preach the importance of accepting differences, they still stare when I walk through the door. It's the same old reaction every time."

The bus slows down in front of the College and Arts building and like children going to an excursion, everybody scrambles to exit the bus. The two girls silently join the queue. Ayesha exits the bus first. She waits warily for Teresa. She sees Fernando in the entrance of the corridor, talking to the other students, who always gather around him before and after class. They exchange the usual smile of salutation. In his smile, she saw her smile, his lips invisibly pressed to her cheeks. Ayesha immediately blushes. She feels a touch on her sleeve and turns to find Teresa beside her.

"I can see that you and Fernando have already met," Teresa whispers to her.

"Of course, he is in our block section."

"And he is my charming town mate."

"Come, let's go to the audiovisual room, I don't want to miss the film showing." Ayesha grips Teresa's hand.

Ayesha left Manila at the age of three. Her father worked as a computer programmer in a Riyadh company. He had brought his family to the Middle East and they have lived there ever since except for the annual holidays to the Philippines. The children attended the International School in Riyadh. Ayesha was not a stranger to the Christian way of life; her classmates included children of expatriates coming from all over the world. Back in Riyadh, it was unthinkable to feel any admiration for the opposite sex; this was not encouraged. But Manila gives her the urge to socialize. It does not matter if he is a Muslim or Christian, Ayesha reassures herself.

On the way to the audiovisual room, there is a whiff of anxiety in the air. Something is up, Ayesha tells herself. She can feel that the students are staring at her veil more than usual. She sees fire spreading throughout the campus and it is threatening to engulf her. The two enter the dark audiovisual room.

"Class, please calm down. Something is happening in New York and we are suspending the film showing for now," Miss Fabular, their English teacher says. "Instead, we will watch the CNN report. Please take your seats."

The small television set that is hastily placed in the middle of the room comes alive with a picture of an airplane crashing into a building interspersed with the grim faces of the reporters narrating the attack. And right before their very eyes unfolds the second plane that crashes into the neighboring skyscraper. The crowd gasps. Ayesha closes her eyes.

In the next few days, the horrible events in New York become the subject of discussions and speculations in the campus and everywhere else. Osama bin Laden and Al Qaeda are thrust into infamy. Every day, the horrors of September 11 are shown on TV and written about in the newspapers.

"You should stop wearing your veil, some people are really uncomfortable with it." Fernando tells Ayesha.

"I am not a terrorist!"

"We are just trying to help you," says Teresa.

The three classmates sit on a bench in the sunken garden. They come from the library where a group of students heckle at them when they pass by. It is not an isolated incident. Sometimes, people just stare at Ayesha with accusations in their eyes. The incident that happened thousands of miles away pains the young student.

"Veiling goes beyond religion for me. No matter how my faith fluctuates, veiling is something I just don't compromise. There wouldn't be any sense in wearing it one day and throwing it away the next day. When I walk around without my hijab, I always feel bare," Ayesha explains to her friends.

Teresa and Fernando look at each other. There seem to be no way their friend will listen to them. They just hope that things will settle down in the next days.

"Let us walk back to the library, we still have to finish our research," Fernando tries to change the subject.

They stand up silently and when they come close to the student hecklers, Ayesha slowly takes off her hijab. She uncovers her neck and then her hair. She folds the veil ceremoniously and places it in her bag.

Her long, black hair catches the red glow of sunset. 🌺

Shiny Black Boots

M.G. Bertulfo

"**I**f you enlist, the first casualty will be me because it will kill me!"

That's my Ma. She has, you know, a flair for drama. She didn't take the news well. Whadduya expect? There's not much we talk about and then when I do tell her about the most important decision I ever made in my life, it's met by this skirmish:

"O! Anak, naman! You are too young. You don't know what you are doing! Are you sick, Noel?" She slapped her palm on my forehead to take my temperature, which, I guess, was normal.

Then she stormed my room. "Hey, Ma! Whatcha doing? Don't you see the sign?" The sign on the door was in caution-yellow decorated with a large black skull and cross-bones. It read: MY STUFF. NO TRESPASSERS. A nice bit of free-hand art, if I do say so myself. She hated that sign.

"Just looking, OK?" came her answer, shrill. She threw open my blue footlocker and stood hunched over it.

"For what?" I yelled from the living room.

"Drugs."

I almost can't believe she's my mom when she accuses me of stuff I'm not doing. What kind of kid does she think she raised? The apartment felt hot, cramped. Through the doorway, I saw my gear fly everywhere—CD's, concert stubs, ball-caps, shoes. She pulled posters from my walls.

Okay, if she wants to play it that way, I thought. "*Pa* would've wanted me to sign up," I shot back my volley. "He got me more than you ever will."

"Don't you talk back to me!"

Bingo. I'd hit a nerve.

She started on my dresser drawers, pulled them out, and over-turned them. "We didn't come to America for you to fight. Your Pa did enough service so you won't have to. Stupid, stupid!"

Whenever she gets like this, there's no talking to her, as if there ever was. *The Battle of Telling Ma in the Living Room.* A good soldier knows when to retreat and regroup. So, without saying another word, I snagged her keys and snuck out the back door of our four-flat.

~

I could've taken the EL, trained it into the city instead of taking her car without permission. Sometimes, a man's gotta do what a man's gotta do. This man has never been so clear in his whole life. I'm gonna join up, serve my country. Drive Ma crazy, too.

My destination was Lake Michigan, usually a quick twenty minutes away on weekends. I drove my parents' beat-up old Corolla east down the Congress Expressway, alongside the Sears Tower, Columbia College, through the edge of Grant Park. I was almost past Buckingham Fountain when I hit a snag, a big line of bumper to bumper traffic. I'd wanted to catch a glimpse of the Lake before I met with the recruiter; I always forget my troubles there.

Lake Shore Drive's the best street in the City to take to Lake Michigan. You get a sweep of the skyline, the beaches, and the water at the same time. And did I mention the color? Icy blue on a clear day, like some kind of cool gem. Sometimes, I liked to pretend it was the Atlantic. "Don't you want to see the world, son?" Pa used to ask. His eyes always lit up when he talked to me about traveling.

See, Pa, he grabbed life by the horns. He'd been to Greece, Portugal, Spain, and Italy when he served in the navy. Pa and his Pinoy buddies were stuck on galley duty making chow for the men. They weren't allowed to do much else back then. Still, he made enough in U.S. dollars to send home to Lola. His paycheck supported our whole family in Manila. When he joined up, he was 17, my age. You've gotta respect that. My Pa, he did whatever it took to make sure our family was all right.

~

Today it was gonna be tough even turning onto Lake Shore Drive. I craned my neck to see what was causing the snarl. A mass of people thronged onto the drive. What was it? A marathon? Nah, they were all walking, real slow. And with police escorts.

Then I noticed banners and picket signs. I could make out the closer ones: "War is Not the Answer." And "No Blood for Oil." Protesters, thousands of them. They were bundled in coats, scarves, and caps against the end of winter. I cracked my window open an inch and heard drums and chanting, "This is what Democracy looks like!"

Where do they think they are? San Francisco? This is Chicago. Seems like no one told them. Bearded grandfathers, wiry grandmothers, nuns, students, punks, suits and dresses, even kids snaked up the drive. Whoa. They're shutting down the busiest street in the City. Where'd the peace-niks come from? And what do they know about sacrifice? Have any of their dads served?

I managed to pull the car onto a small side street to avoid the crowd, parked and walked toward Navy Pier. It would take longer to hoof it; that didn't matter. More than ever, I needed to be there, stand right at the edge of the water.

As I picked my way through Grant Park, I saw weird black birds on the ground, totally still, like statues. I got closer. It turned out they weren't birds, but boots. There were hundreds of black boots, unlaced, worn in places, and tongues hanging down. They stood in rows and looked out-of-place, kinda sad. There were tags with the names and ages of the guys who'd worn them. A lot were only a year or two older'n'me. A sign read, Eyes Wide Open Exhibition. To honor the 504 American soldiers killed in Iraq.

I walked through the rows of boots, American flags, flowers and photos. It was so still; didn't feel natural. I stared into the gaping dark hole of someone's right boot, someone I wasn't gonna have the chance to meet. A boot never looked so empty before. A chill crept up my arms, the kind you get when you stand in the middle of a cemetery. It made me shiver. I hurried through the rest of the park, making faster time for the Lake.

~

My feet were sore and tired when I finally reached Navy Pier. Pilots and sailors used to train here during World War II. Now it's got a Ferris wheel, a kids' museum, an IMAX theater, a coupla schooners, and tons of food stalls. In the summertime, Pa and I used to ride the Blue Line to the Loop and walk to the Pier for Chicago dogs. Beef franks on steamed poppy seed buns, tangy mustard, peppers, and a slice of pickle. We'd hang out on the boardwalk and watch tourists. People came here from the world over. They spoke Hindi, Japanese, Spanish, Russian, even Tagalog. They asked us the same thing, "That's a Lake? You can't see the end of it!"

It's true. That's another thing I love about the Lake. It goes on forever, like staring at your future. Wide open. "The Lake's your crystal ball," said Pa. "It tells you everything you need to know."

Pa's one of those guys, short and walks with the Filipino strut. Even though his real name was Rudy, his buddies called him Rooster 'cause of the way he walked around all proud. He was strict, like Ma, but he always heard me out in the end. Sometimes, if I squint, I can still see him in our kitchen sizzling up some tapsilog. Or slapping mahjong tiles down onto the kitchen table.

Pa told these corny jokes, the kind you roll your eyes at and wish they didn't make you laugh. He'd get that I've-got-a-good-one spark in his eye and call me over. "O, Noel, what do you call a crazy rooster? Coo-coo-doodle-do! Why did the rooster cross the road? It was the chicken's day off!" He always did stuff to make me laugh.

Lunch at school last Thursday, an army guy, a recruiter, showed up. He laughed at my jokes, even the lame ones. He was lean, decked out in fatigues and shiny black boots, not a crease on them as if they'd never seen action. Come to think of it, there was something creepy about his boots. They reminded me of vultures, the way they walked around and around me when he talked. Still, the recruiter was friendly and real eager.

We talked ball, Sox versus Cubs, that kind of stuff. He was interested in knowing all about me. I made an appointment for Monday. Tomorrow—

A boy squealed. "Daddy, can we go on the Ferris wheel?" His chin pointed up at the looming ride. The boy's baby voice had snapped me out of my thoughts. He was throwing a tantrum 'cause his dad had said no. I used to tug at Pa, beg him for candy and money for rides. That little guy has no idea how lucky he is. I'd give my front teeth, my side teeth, and my molars just to be standing here with Pa, again.

I turned toward the Lake. The fresh wind felt good against my face, cooled me down from my fight with Ma. But there weren't any answers for me in the water today, not for the hard questions.

What would Pa think? I wondered. Would he really have wanted me to enlist? I used to ask him, "Hey Pa, tell me about the Navy." Most of the time, he'd just shrug, pull out his deck of cards, and try to distract me. But once, he said, "Pays the bills when there's mouths to feed, i-specially big ones like yours." I took one last look at the boy holding his dad's hand. An awful feeling of heaviness weighed on me, enough to sink me.

Pa, do I really have it in me to kill someone? What if I don't want to?

~

The peace-niks wound their way up Lake Shore Drive as I walked slowly to the car. I had Ma to face. She could shock'n'awe George W. himself if she wanted to. She'd be furious that I split on her. And took the car without asking. I'm toast.

I scrounged for change. Nothing I can do about the dents and dings or the rust on her car, but at least I could get the winter road-salt washed off it. Maybe that would soften Ma's barrage. My hands accidentally bumped the rosary she'd hung on the rear view mirror. She'd been praying a lot more, lately. She looked haggard, too, older than I'd ever seen her. Maybe it's because she's working double-shifts at the hospital now. My books, lunch pass, prom—stuff gets expensive.

After the car wash, I stopped by Ramel's Asian Market, and bought Ma a package of hopia, her favorite. I guess I felt guilty for messing with her earlier. I also didn't wanna deploy for a tour of duty, my first and possibly last one, and have us mad at each other. A truce with Ma would sure be nice.

I got back just after sunset, lay the hopia on the kitchen table, then returned Ma's keys to their peg. The lamps were off in the hallway and the kitchen. Our apartment felt cold in the dim. There was a faint light coming from under my bedroom door.

That's where I found Ma, still in my room. My posters had been pinned back on the walls. Torn corners were carefully taped. None of my empty pop bottles lay around on my dresser. My room was cleaner than when I'd left.

Ma's eyes were red-rimmed. She sat with something clutched in her hands. On the bed beside her, my suitcase lay open. Clothes were neatly folded and packed inside. She gave me a defeated look. "Go, if you have to," was how she greeted me.

"I won't need my clothes, Ma," I told her. "They'll gimme all that. And money, too." I sat beside her on my bed, rested my head on her shoulder for the first time in a long while. "I can send it home to you." The room got real quiet. I felt myself rise and fall with her breathing.

Ma handed me what she'd been holding, a framed photo of Pa in uniform. We both stared at him. She sat real stiff. I wasn't sure what to do; I never am when she's this quiet. Even though she was right next to me, she felt a million light years away, in the next galaxy. Ma made a few sniffling sounds and I knew the moment was almost gone. She'd probably get up, start cleaning my room again. Or go ballistic about the car.

But, instead of yelling or calling me an idiot or ransacking my room, she took my face in her hands and kissed my forehead. "I know you're a good boy," she said softly. "You're like your Pa."

She fumbled for more words. Maybe they got stuck in her throat 'cause something was sure sticking in mine. "Keep yourself safe, anak. Out of harm's way, hah? You're all I've got, now."

Then she left and closed my door.

~

I sat on my bed for a long time holding our photo of Pa. Will I keep the appointment on Monday? I dunno. The vultures are circling and there's a lot to think over. I looked down and noticed my sneakers. They were ratty and old, but they stood solidly on my family's hardwood floor. I wiggled my big toes to check I was still around, still in my skin. Alive. I felt the fullness of my shoes.

I've got time, I thought. All the time in the world to decide. ✤

Yellow Is for Luck

Rebecca Mabanglo-Mayor

S ister Bernadette brought me two flats of primroses today. Pink, yellow, purple, blue, all sorts with fat green leaves. And a new pair of work gloves spotted with white dots and a new spade with an orange handle. She said it was going to be a pretty day out, once the fog cleared, a perfect day, she said, for putting new plants in the ground for springtime. I think it's too early for primroses and I'm suspicious of them. They don't look quite right, these flowers with their bright faced blooms. All the other flowers in the garden are still asleep and I wonder if I'll wake them up if I plant these primroses. Bad things can happen when you do things at the wrong time or forget to do the right things at the right time. But they came from Sister Bernadette and my nanay—my mother— says I have to do what sister says when I'm at the school.

Sister wants me to plant them around the statue of Our Blessed Mother. She says that Our Mother has waited a long time for spring and will be happy to see the blossoms at her feet. I wonder about that, because it seems to me that of anyone, Our Mother would know when the blooms will happen. The ground is soft today, not hard with frost like last week, and there are buds on the rhododendrons, but then again, rhodies are silly flowers prone to bloom in late winter if the weather has been mild. Then it turns cold and their leaves turn black with frost, and the blooms die before they have a chance to see the sun. So I think maybe if I plant the primroses near the Blessed Mother, she will watch over them and tell them not to peek their heads out when the frost comes back, and I think maybe the Sister Bernadette is right to have me plant them there.

Sister is right about a lot of things, my nanay says, because she's my special teacher and doesn't laugh that I'm bigger than the other kids in my class, and doesn't mind that I don't know the things they know about numbers and books. Sister tells me when it's time to eat lunch and when it's time for paints and when to wait for Nanay to pick me up and take me home. She knows how to pray and she knows how to sing, but I don't think she knows the secrets my tatay— my father— told me about the primroses. I don't think even Nanay knows because he only told me.

"Remember, Juana," he said one day when I was smaller. "always plant primroses in your front yard for luck. When I first came to America, my luck was terrible. I was only a little bit older than you are and I wasn't good in school either. I couldn't understand what people were saying and the other children laughed at me at school. Then our neighbor told me about primroses and gave me a yellow one to plant near our front door. I felt better right away! I started to make friends and do better on my tests and ever since, I make sure I have primroses in my garden."

"So many colors," I said as he turned the soil with a small spade. "Why, Tatay?"

I felt brave that day, brave enough to ask questions. He didn't get angry like Nanay does when I ask questions like about the moon being made out of cheese and where you can buy wooden nickels.

Tatay knelt on the ground next to me and pointed to each one.

"The purple ones are for keeping healthy, and the red ones are for strength," he told me. "The blue ones are for the ones that we have lost and the white ones are for remembering that we are from God. But none of these are as important as the yellow ones, Juana. No matter how poor you might be, always get at least one yellow primrose to plant in your garden. Yellow is the color of gold and planting a yellow primrose is like planting gold in your garden. When it blooms you will be rich all your life. You must always remember to plant yellow ones and take care of them in the summer when the sun tries to steal the blooms."

"I promise, Tatay," I said, and I decided that day that yellow was also the color of my father and as long as there were yellow primroses, he would always come home to us.

That was a long time ago, I think, because I'm much taller now, taller than Nanay, and we don't have primroses at home anymore. Not since the big buildings came down somewhere far away and Tatay had to go even farther away to keep us safe. Not since Nanay started crying every night and left me at school every day to work at the grocery store. Not since Sister Bernadette told me to stop watching the news even if I liked what the man said about the weather.

Before I start to plant them, I check the primroses one more time. Pink, yellow, purple, blue. Some with yellow hearts, some with white ones. It was very thoughtful of Sister Bernadette to get two of each color. Once she only brought me one of every color she could find, but then the primroses couldn't decide who they wanted to be planted next to. The pink with a yellow heart said she didn't want to be near any of the blues no matter what color their hearts were. The white with a yellow heart didn't think the pink was nice for saying such things and refused to stay near her. The blues wanted to be with the yellows, but the yellows wanted to be by themselves. I pleaded with Sister Bernadette to get me more primroses so I could please them all, but she said there wasn't time, there wasn't enough room. But when May Day arrived and all the primroses had wilted brown from the spiteful words they whispered to each other at night, Sister Bernadette promised she would do better this year. Two whole flats of primroses! I feel happy and full of primroses. I like the feel of their wispy roots when I tap them from their green plastic containers. The primroses like it too, that they are finally free of their tiny homes. Sometimes, even before I tamp the soil back around their waists I can feel them reaching through the ground to find water. Maybe they have lost a father or a brother and when they reach out through the ground, they find the roots of another rose and they think, ah, here they are! They were never lost, they have been here all along.

I can feel the rain through my new gloves, except it isn't rain anymore, is it? It's water and dirt and growing things soaking in to touch my fingers. I rest my fingertips against each other and make a church steeple with my hands. I can see the primroses I've planted between my palms and I know they will be all right this year, because they are at Our Mother's feet and I have prayed for them beneath the chapel roof. They are all there in neat rows and angles, pinks, blues, purples, all of them except the yellow ones with yellow hearts. It makes me a little scared that I have not planted these last two primroses at Our Mother's feet like Sister Bernadette had asked me to. I don't want Sister to be angry with me, or to disappoint Our Blessed Mother, but I know yellow primroses must be planted in front of the school, because that is what Tatay taught me before he left. I'm not supposed to be out front, because if Nanay catches me there, she might pull me up the stairs and into the school to the door that leads to the basement. She might open the door and tell me that if I am not good, the next time she goes to work, she might leave me in the basement. And I do not want that. It is dark down there, and the walls are cold and damp. It is like being planted upside down with your feet in the air trying the reach the sun and your head in the ground and you're trying to breathe and you can't, and you promise that you'll be good, Nanay, just don't put me in the basement.

A cool wind shivers the birch tree nearby and I realize I have my eyes closed tight. I blink and wipe wet tears from my face as I look around. I feel the sun on my head warming my scalp, and I can feel the Blessed Mother smiling and telling me that everything will be okay. She will help me plant the primroses because she knows Tatay would want it that way. I peek over the laurel hedge toward Sister Bernadette's room to see if she is there. The window is empty and I don't see anyone else in the courtyard. My stomach growls and I know that it will be snack time soon. They will be looking for me. I know I must hurry, so I take a deep breath, pick up the two yellow primroses and run to the wood fence that separates the courtyard from the front of the school. There's a gap in the fence near the building and I push the primroses to the other side. I crouch on my hands and knees and at first I am not sure I can fit through the gap. It's a tight fit and I have to shimmy my hips to get through. I feel my dress tear on a sliver, but I keep moving before Sister catches me gone.

Before I stand up, I pick up the primroses and suddenly realize that I've left my spade near the Blessed Mother. I chew my lip for a moment, then take another deep breath. I feel the Blessed Mother tell me I'll have to dig the holes with my hands. The front yard of the school is a grassy place cut in the middle by a path to the front door of the school. I run quickly to the edge of the path where a naked dwarf maple tree sleeps. Above me the sky is darkening and the wind is colder. My fingers cramp as they try to make holes in the dirt and my heart is starting to pound. Sister will be looking for me soon.

Finally, I take the yellow primroses out of their packages and plop them into the new holes. I push the dirt around the waists of each rose and brush the bits from my fingertips. Dirt falls from my gloves onto the roses and they look sad all of a sudden. I didn't think to bring any water to wash them off and when I try to brush them clean, some of the petals pull away and fall to the ground. I am frightened, I've broken the rules coming to the front of the convent to plant these roses, and now they are falling apart. The sky is getting darker and the wind is getting colder, just like the day I fell from the sky, the night Tatay was hurt.

At least I think it was nighttime. I couldn't be sure because I was in the playground, swinging on the monkey bars with Helen and Teresa. I was dangling upside down and I could feel the bright spring sun against my knees and face.

"I can see your underwear!" said Teresa from somewhere above me. "They're white with pink flowers!"

I tried to push my skirt up between my thighs but I was laughing too hard, and then it was dark, and cold and rainy, and I didn't know where I was all of a sudden. I slipped off the monkey bars and landed in a heap.

"You okay?" I heard Helen say from somewhere near Teresa. But their voices didn't sound right, like they were far away and there was a terrible popping sound all around me, like the ones I'd heard on the news. I crouched low and found that I was sitting in a muddy pool, and when I looked around again, I was in a trench and there were strange men, yelling all around me. I screamed when one came close enough to touch me and then I was sitting in the school infirmary with Sister Bernadette pressing an ice pack against the side of my head.

"You had a nasty fall, Juana," she said, "but you're going to be okay."

And I looked into her dark brown eyes and her clean face, and then her face wasn't clean any more but streaked with dirt and sweat, and it wasn't her anymore but the man and he's asking me what I'm doing there. I struggled against his grasp and wriggled free and ran down the trench as quickly as I could. There were men everywhere trying to catch me. They were holding guns and every once in a while the sky would light up with fire or lightning. I couldn't tell which, but I ran and ran and ran, and I knew if I could just find my tatay, he would tell me what was happening.

I asked Sister the next day when my tatay would come home and she told me he was gone, and I couldn't understand, because Tatay was always going somewhere and he was always going to come back, so why was everyone crying? And why was Nanay always holding that American flag to her chest while rosary beads slipped through her fingers?

But that was a long time ago, maybe last week and now I have to make sure the primroses are planted so Tatay can come home safe.

I look down at the primroses; they are all torn up, and in my hands are their muddy yellow faces, and I try to put them back, but they won't stick and I hear the Blessed Mother scolding me, telling me I've been bad.

"I just need some water," I tell her as she starts to shake me. But it's not really the Blessed Mother, it's my nanay and she's shaking me and crying.

"I couldn't find you anywhere!" she cries. "You're supposed to stay inside the school, Juana!"

I try to make her understand that I just need to water the primroses, then their faces would be okay, everything would be okay.

"Let go, let go!" I scream and I push her to the ground. Suddenly arms wrap around me and I tumble to the ground with Sister Bernadette. We land hard and I hear her cry out in pain. I try to wriggle out of her arms, but Nanay is there holding down my legs.

"Juana!" she cries. "Juana, what are you doing?"

"I have to water the primroses," I say mournfully. "I have to make them better, Nanay, or Tatay won't come home. The maple tree will wake up and swallow all Tatay's luck and then he will never come home. Never and it will be my fault because I wasn't here to take care of them like I had promised him."

I cry even harder, and I can feel my whole body shuddering and shaking. I start to rock side to side and my stomach tightens with every sob.

"Juana," Nanay says, her voice soft like the Blessed Mother, "your tatay is gone. He was hurt very badly and he won't be coming home."

And I remembered Nanay had said he was hurt somewhere called Iraq and I couldn't remember a part of the body called Iraq, because it sounded like a place not a part, but how could Tatay be hurt in a place that wasn't his body?

I decide Nanay is wrong, that Tatay is just lost and needs more luck to come home to us. Tomorrow, I think, tomorrow, I'll ask Sister for more primroses, all of them yellow, and I'll be more careful and I'll be more good, and Tatay will finally come home. 🌼

Neighbors

Katrina Ramos Atienza

*H*e had come to the house, as it were, entirely by accident. That is, as 'accidental' as it could have been, knowing that the girl's sister's daughter's party was in the same village. In the invitation the name of the street leapt out at him. He had known, precisely, that it was the street in which he had lived. But years of pretending otherwise dulled his knowledge—or perhaps he had wanted it dulled, so much so that as he and the girl (not his wife) pulled into the village, his skin reared and tightened into little bumps of gooseflesh as his eyes looked upon what had been his village, a long time ago.

For example, here was the narrow, garbage-choked street that led into the village, the tricycle's last stop before one could take a jeepney into 'civilized' territory. Electrical wires dipped and sagged along the route. The jeepney would pass by a squat, square church with a blue roof, which never seemed to be open; an empty lot pocked with garbage and dry, scrubby grass; and a ceramic-toilet factory. After the piled-high stacks of toilets in their boxes, there came a low building tacked with glaring neon signs advertising massages and bars, and then there was a bank, and then a furniture store, and then a row of pretty restaurants, this time without any glaring neon lights. Then came the park, and the office building, and the grocery with the twin cinemas and the nicer church (all ocher and white and turrets), and the nicer village, which did not have garbage-choked narrow streets nor empty lots and certainly no ceramic toilet factories. It was a five-minute jeepney ride away, and it was also a world away.

He had passed what was once the grocery and twin cinema, and it was now a massive mall. The rolling green lot that had surrounded it was now devoured by restaurants and cars and drugstores and a rusty beige shelter facing an army of jeepneys. The twin cinema expanded to 10 movie houses, and it jutted out a hulking blue flank into where he and his friends used to sit, underneath an old acacia tree that was felled by one of the big typhoons that came every year when he lived in this place.

He was silent as he drove, past the mall, approaching the office building (now multiplied by 10) and the park (nonexistent) and the bank and the restaurants and the girlie bars and the factory, with still the same sagging, dipping electrical wires guarding the skies, into the narrow, garbage-choked street that led into the village. It was a short drive away, and it was a world away.

"What are you thinking about?" she asked. She had bangs and blunt-cut hair and a tasteful blue blouse and well-cut jeans. Very pleasant.

"Nothing," he answered. In his mind he was nine, and his mother had allowed him to take the jeepney by himself, for the very first time. His two classmates met him at the newly opened convenience store at the edge of the narrow, garbage-choked street. How they had marveled at the smell of new paint, the brightly lit wall of refrigerators promising a multitude of fizzy drinks. They pooled their coins together and bought the store's signature drink, something fizzy and large and mixed with crushed ice, tasting of artificial strawberries and the red of a lollipop tongue. The large cup—as large as his forearm—smelled of playing cards.

Twelve pesos.

They took turns sipping the drink as they walked into the waiting jeepney. Excitedly they handed the fare to the driver, and happily they passed on other passengers' fares. Grinning, they saw the grocery come into view. They chorused: "Para—stop!"

They scrambled down the jeepney and rushed into the twin cinema, intending to watch a movie starring a ghoulish family with a Frankenstein monster as their butler. But the ticket lady would not let them in. PG-15, she said. They pleaded and cajoled and begged, but she was not amused, and the guard threatened to call their mothers. So they went to the grocery, to the section outside the main cash registers that carried liquor and cigarettes, stationery and candy. They bought cinnamon-flavored gum that resembled a pink roll of scotch tape and a packet of sand-like candy that exploded in their mouths, which they ate under the old acacia tree near the church. His classmate told them that if they drank soda while there was exploding candy in their mouths, their throats would burst. His other classmate scoffed, but none of them dared to prove their friend wrong.

They passed an hour telling each other stories. Some—he had to admit—were cobbled together from the things whispered to him by his little sister's yaya, about the Satanists who wore shades and sat outside school gates, waiting to kidnap unsuspecting children. What they did to the children he didn't want to imagine. In his story, his cousin had been kidnapped, and his aunt and uncle never saw the child again. Then his classmate told them that one time, as he waited for the tricycle to pick him up from school, he walked outside to look for the fish ball vendor, when a tall man, also wearing shades, offered him a stick-on tattoo. He refused and ran back inside the school, but stayed long enough to see a young girl accept the trinket. She licked the tattoo and slapped it on her arm (it was a goldfish, he said) and swooned. The man in shades picked her up and carried her to a waiting van.

Of course, he had no such cousin, and his classmate saw no such thing. The goldfish stick-on tattoo was, as it was described, exactly the same goldfish as one of the stickers that adorned the inside of the window of the tricycle that picked his classmate up every afternoon. He had hitched with this classmate before, when his mama had dengue fever. The classmate insisted on sitting behind the driver, leaving him to sit inside, marveling at the garishly colored stickers. There were women with full breasts and tiny waists and round, round thighs, with yellow hair that curved as sensuously as their bodies. The women exhorted him to pay only with coins in the morning, and to pay before leaving the sidecar. One beautiful woman curled atop a sign that said, Basta Driver Sweet Lover, an expression of delight on her cartoon face.

A few nights ago he had seen the ghoulish family movie on cable. The movie was funny and pleasant, and he could not understand why, at the time, the rating for PG movies jumped from 13 to 15 just when they had been allowed to see a movie on their own. He had hoped his friends would pass for 13, but 15 was an impossibility, a whole other age, a world of coolness and things that only teenagers did. How he had longed to be a teenager. He thought of his neighbor Mark, who had invited him to play in his house (which he had remembered as an honor, as Mark was his only neighbor with a real swing in their tiny pocket garden, bordered by desert roses and santan bushes). Then one day Mark stopped calling him over to play. He peeked through his gates at Mark one day, so suddenly tall, buying pandesal with other suddenly tall boys, loudly joking in deepened voices of things that only teenagers could understand. The swing rusted and sat idly, and he always peeked through the gates, staring at it, wishing Mark would call him over, again.

"Turn here," said the girl, but he was already turning into the street, named after a pungent Philippine fruit. Instinctively he stiffened as he turned the corner past the green house where an old man once tended to cages full of furious lovebirds, one of which pecked his finger hard when he poked it, on a dare.

A row of cars were parked on the sidewalk in front of the girl's sister's small, rented home. The house was the washed-out color of what would have been an obnoxious pink. Five tiny monoblock tables were set in the driveway, balloons bobbed atop the tiny chairs. The sister greeted the girl with a warm smile and winced as he was introduced. All the adults sat in the wrought iron garden set in the pocket garden. They talked among themselves as the children were monopolized by a clown with a loud karaoke machine. He, however, was steadfastly ignored by the girl's sister. He cleared his throat and said he would step out for a smoke. The girl nodded.

"So what if he's rich, he's not annulled. Technically they're still..." the sister's voice trailed, drowned out by the children participating in the clown's contest to see who could say "Happy Birthday Tesssssaaaaaaaaa" the longest.

He lit his cigarette and walked aimlessly. Ah, but there it was: in the midst of it he knew exactly where he had wanted to go. Two blocks from the sister's house, and there it was, facing what had been Mark's old house (the swing set must have rusted and fallen apart a long time ago, and the house now sported an extension where the old garage had been). What had happened to Mark, he wondered. He lost touch with everyone in the old village after they moved.

The house (he could not think of it as "his") stood abandoned in a garden overgrown with tall grass and weeds. He laughed to himself – his mother was no gardener, and often the house was this shape when they had lived here. The porch ceiling, which sagged in his boyhood, now hung in strips: flat wooden stalagmites. The gate was still black, but rustier. He stubbed out the cigarette on the sidewalk, recalling how it had annoyed Manang Tansing, Mark's spinster aunt. His father had painted the sidewalk yellow on the eve of the 1986 revolution. They woke up the next morning to see it covered with red paint. Manang Tansing loudly exhorted Marcos' virtues in Ilocano as she gardened across the street. His father laughed and laughed.

He recalled how, one stormy morning as his mother futilely hailed tricycle after tricycle to take him into school, he looked down to stretch his aching calves when he saw a severed snake's head near his shoe. An evil yellow eye stared back at him. He had jumped and screamed, but his mother said the cat had probably killed it. He dreamt of that feverish yellow eye for several nights.

He shivered and pushed the gate open.

The cracked driveway was now littered by rusted cans, the screen door on the kitchen hung by one hinge, and the brown front door, which they had never opened as it was too close to the gate, was riddled with holes and water stains. The mango tree was chopped down. He had loved the tree—

he had climbed it every day that he stayed here, either in the morning before school or in the afternoon. Like greeting an old friend. He had a favorite spot where bough and branch formed a perfect seat, and he sat here, dreaming, escaping. He wished his papa would build him a tree house, and his father promised, but the tree house was never built. To compensate they hung a plastic tarp over the lower branches of the property's other tree, an aratiles, at the edge of the backyard, but the smell of the berries overpowered him, and large red ants always swarmed, and that was where they threw the shit. The toilet always backed up, and they had no money for repairs. His mother found an old paint can and hung a plastic bag over it, making him shit there. Then they knotted it and walked to the middle of the backyard and threw it as far as they could, where it inevitably landed with a soft thump on the roots of the aratiles tree. How badly he felt about it, shitting in a paint can. He felt so oafish and cumbersome that not even the toilet would accept his waste.

There was a bench, at the side of the garage. He had spent part of a night there sobbing uncontrollably. His mother found out he had given his sister's musical toy to a neighbor, and she yanked him outside the bathroom and pushed him out the house, refusing to let him enter until he went to the neighbor and asked it back. He was naked and afraid. His father intervened an hour later. His sobs then were like animal yelps, struggling out from a region in his chest he could not locate.

His mother had raged in that house.

His father's business improved, and he was older, and he thought he could understand the news, but all that he knew was that times were better. They were moving to a new house, with new things. His mother would no longer rage, like the time when the men came and took their Betamax as he watched the Transformers movie for the third time in a row. It was just after the part when Optimus Prime died, and the first time he and his papa saw it they had teared up, just a little, and then the men opened the front door without knocking and began pulling wires out the wall. His mother was composed as she asked them what the matter was, but that night he could hear her voice from behind the wall of his room, urgently raging at his father.

They had packed and moved their things that Christmas, but there was a problem with something in the new house, and they spent Christmas Eve in the old. He and his sister folded together three phonebooks and taped them against the wall, making a Christmas tree. They spread a woven mat in front of the yellow paper tree and ate refrigerator cake and fried chicken and grapes. "This house is gloomy," said his uncle, who had helped them pack. "The spirits know you're leaving and they're excited to take it back."

The first time they arrived in the house he was four, and he clearly remembered seeing a mound of earth beneath a tree, rising up and down like a sleeping person's chest when he breathes. He had stood in front of it, transfixed, until his mother called him inside. He hadn't known if it was a dream or if it was real. Or if it was something that, like many other things in this house, he had pushed back far away.

He lit another cigarette and walked outside. How small this house now seemed, and how it loomed over him before. He had been suffocated under its weight in the past, drowned by its expanse, unable to fathom how it stretched onwards. Now he saw it again, and it was insignificant. ❧

Editor

Cecilia Manguerra Brainard is the multi-award author and editor of 14 books. Her awards include: a California Arts Council Fellowship in Fiction, a Brody Arts Fund Award, a Special Recognition Award from the Los Angeles Unified School District, a Certificate of Recognition from the California State Senate 21st District, a 1998 Outstanding Individual Award from her birth city, Cebu, Philippines, and the respected Filipinas Magazine Award for Arts in 2001. She also received several travel grants from the USIS (United States Information Service).

She has lectured and performed in UCLA, USC, University of Connecticut, University of the Philippines, PEN, Beyond Baroque, Shakespeare & Company in Paris, and others. She teaches creative writing at the Writers Program at UCLA-Extension.

She is married to Lauren R. Brainard; they have three sons. Her website is ceciliabrainard.com and her blog is cbrainard.blogspot.com.

Contributors

Dean Francis Alfar is Filipino playwright, novelist and writer of speculative fiction. His books include *Salamanca* (Ateneo Press), *The Kite of Stars and Other Stories* (Anvil Publishing), *Siglo: Freedom* (Kestrel) and *Siglo: Passion* (Kestrel). He edits the annual *Philippine Speculative Fiction* series (Kestrel) with Nikki Alfar, now in its third year. His literary awards include the Don Carlos Palanca Memorial Awards for Literature — including the Grand Prize for Novel in 2005— as well as the Manila Critics' Circle National Book Award and the Philippines Free Press Literary Award.

Katrina Ramos Atienza graduated from UP Los Baños with a degree in Communication Arts, major in Writing, in 2002. She has worked as a P.R. writer for the Enrique Zobel Foundation, as a copy editor for a trade media company, and currently as a P.R. associate in one of the world's largest law firms.

Her short stories have been published by the *Philippines Free Press,* the *Manila Times* and the *Philippine Graphic,* and were included in the *Muse Apprentice Guild* and *Warm Bodies* literary anthologies. She is the writer of four chick lit novels, *Pink Shoes* (2006), *The Hagette* (2006), *If the Shoe Fits* (2008), and *Shoes Off* (2009), which were published by Psicom Publishing, Inc.

She lives in Manila with her husband and son.

Maria Victoria Beltran was born and raised in Butuan City and currently resides in Cebu City. She graduated from the University of the Philippines, Visayas, Cebu, with a Bachelor of Science in Biology. She is a member of the writers' groups Bathalad and Women in Literary Arts, Inc. (WILA). Her fictions, essays and poems have been published in various local and national publications and anthologies. Also a visual artist, she has joined various group exhibits and has mounted two solo painting exhibit. She is also a member of the Board of Trustee of PUSOD, Inc., an open organization of visual artists. She is currently involved in making independent Cebuano films as scriptwriter, producer, and actress. She is an awardee of the Komisyon sa Wikang Filipino (KWF), Gawad Komisyon for Cebuano fiction in 2007 and 2008.

M.G. Bertulfo was raised by a family of Pinay healers and Pinoy warriors. Now, she lives a train ride from the Sears Tower in Chicago. She's written for CBS, Pearson Education Asia, *Sierra Magazine, Chicago Wilderness Magazine* and more. You'll often find her doing field research for her historical novel: exploring a caravel, sailing on a lake, or paddling a canoe down-river. Otherwise, she's lost in some archives with her nose in a book or surfing the web for paintings of old barangays (Filipino communities). She wrote "Shiny Black Boots" to honor her younger cousins, their parents, and her friends who had to struggle with how and whether to support our fighting wars after September 11th. She's carried a lot of picket signs for peace. M.G. hopes her story gives you a moment to pause—so you can do whatever's right by your own light within.

Amalia B. Bueno is a poet, writer and researcher. Born in Quezon City, Philippines and raised in Hawaii, she has been published in *Bamboo Ridge Press, University of Hawaii's Katipunan Literary Journal: Voices of Hawaii, Our Own Voice,* and Meritage Press. Her poetry and fiction is forthcoming in *Bleeding on the Page* (Spinster's Ink Press) and *Honolulu Stories* (Mutual Publishing). She was recently selected to attend the Voices of Our Nation's Arts summer creative writing program at the University of San Francisco.

Max Gutierrez is a third generation Filipino-American born and raised in Vallejo, California. Graduated from San Jose State University in Political Science. Currently working on a documentary about the history of Filipinos in Vallejo, California. He is studying the art of Escrima while trying to maintain his day job as a waiter in Fisherman's Wharf in San Francisco. Began writing in college--mostly poetry and in his journal. "Uncle Gil" is dedicated to his late uncle Gil.

Leslieann Hobayan is a writer-mama learning to balance parenting with writing, among other things. Currently teaching at Rutgers University, she has served as a writing mentor for youth at Urban Word NYC and has taught creative writing at UC-Santa Cruz and Montclair State University. Nominated for a Pushcart, her work has appeared in *The New York Quarterly, Phati'tude, Babaylan: An Anthology of Filipina and Filipina-American Writers, and Pinoy Poetics.* She is currently at work on a novel and a manuscript of poems.

Jaime An Lim was born in Cagayan de Oro City. He finished his Bachelor of Arts in English at Mindanao State University, Marawi City, his MA in Creative Writing at Silliman University, Dumaguete City, and several post-graduate degrees, including a PhD in Comparative Literature, at Indiana University, Bloomington, Indiana. His fiction, poetry, and essays have won various national literary awards. He is currently the Dean of the Institute of Arts and Sciences, Far Eastern University, Philippines.

Paulino Lim Jr. is professor emeritus of English at California State University, Long Beach. He has a Master's degree from the University of Santo Tomas (UST) and a Doctorate from the University of California, Los Angeles, (UCLA). He was a Fulbright lecturer in Taiwan, and visiting professor at De La Salle University in Manila for more than a decade. He received a National Endowment for the Humanities grant at Indiana University, spent a sabbatical at Göttingen, Germany, and was the first prize winner of the *Asiaweek* Short Story Competition of 1985.

He is the author of a scholarly monograph, *The Style of Lord Byron's Plays.* His other published works include: two short story anthologies *(Passion Summer and Other Stories, & Curaçao Cure and Other Stories)*; a quartet of political novels *(Tiger Orchids on Mount Mayon, Sparrows Don't Sing in the Philippines, Requiem for a Rebel Priest, & Ka Gaby, Nom de Guerre)*; and two dramas *(It's All in Your Mind, & Ménage Filipinescas).*

Rebecca Mabanglo-Mayor received her MA in English with honors from Western Washington University in 2003 for her thesis "Notes from the Margins," a mixed work of memoir and fiction. Her poetry and short fiction have appeared in the *Katipunan Literary Magazine* and the online magazine *Haruah*. In addition, she has served as a freelance writer and editor for several trade journals. Currently she is working on her first novel, and she performs regularly as a storyteller in her local area. Her blog *Binding Wor(l)ds Together* can be found at wordbinder.blogspot.com.

Dolores de Manuel was born in London, England, the daughter of a Filipino diplomat, and grew up in England, Mexico, Argentina and Israel. She has a Bachelor of Arts in English from St. Paul College of Manila, an MA in Philippine Literature from Ateneo de Manila University, and a PhD in English Literature from Fordham University, New York. She has taught for many years at Ateneo de Manila University, Manhattan College, and currently, Nassau Community College, where she is an Associate Professor in the English Department.

She lives on Long Island, NY, with her husband, George Kraus, her daughter, Elena and her son, Anthony. Since 1990 she has been spending several weeks a year in Canada, where her parents, siblings and extended family have settled.

She has written many scholarly works and reference articles on Asian American literature and has been awarded National Endowment for the Humanities Fellowships at several universities, including University of Michigan and Harvard. It's been a while since she has had a piece of fiction published, and writing "Someone Else" has been a welcome change of pace.

The story "Someone Else" is dedicated to the memory of Jeffrey Reodica, 1987-2004.

Rashaan Alexis Meneses is Filipina/Chicana born and raised in the seismically diverse and fractured landscape of California. She is currently working on a collection of short stories based on the "invisible" Los Angeles. Her stories focus on people often seen blurred into the backdrop of this metropolis. In 2006, she earned her MFA from Saint Mary's College of California's Fiction, Creative Writing Program. She received her Bachelor of Arts in English, with a specialization in Fiction, from UCLA. A 2005-2006 Jacob K. Javits Fellow, her publications include *MARY, Amerasia Journal, Filipinas* magazine and *Coloring Book: An Eclectic Anthology of Fiction and Poetry by Multicultural Writers*, from Rattlecat Press. She is currently based in the Bay Area, CA.

Veronica Montes was born and raised in the San Francisco Bay Area. Her short fiction has appeared in the anthologies *Contemporary Fiction* by Filipinos in America (Anvil, 1998), *Growing Up Filipino* (Philippine American Literary House, 2003), and *Going Home to a Landscape: Writings by Filipinas* (Calyx Books, 2003), and in the literary journals *Prism International, Furious Fictions, Maganda*, and *Bamboo Ridge*. Her blog, Nesting Ground, can be found at vmontes.blogspot.com/.

Charlson Ong, resident fellow of the Institute of Creative Writing and fictionist/scriptwriter/singer extraordinaire, was born on July 6, 1960. He obtained a Bachelor of Arts in Psychology from the University of the Philippines in 1977, and currently teaches literature and creative writing under UP's Department of English and Comparative Literature. He has joined several writers' workshops here and abroad, and has acquired numerous grants and awards for his fiction, including the Palanca, Free Press, Graphic, Asiaweek,

National Book Award, and the Dr. Jose P. Rizal Award for Excellence. His novel, *Embarrassment of Riches* published by UP Press in 2002, won the Centennial Literary Prize. In addition to this, Ong has served as co-editor of the Likhaan Book of Poetry and Fiction. His latest novel *Banyaga* won the National Book Award for Fiction.

Marily Ysip Orosa is president of Studio 5 Designs and Studio 5 Publishing, two multi-awarded companies that are known for their high-end and memorable design work. Her coffee table books have been recipients of the National Book Awards for Best Book Design, and her company's work for corporate clients have also yearly won Anvil Awards of Excellence here and abroad, as well as Gold Quill Awards of Excellence and other prestigious awards. Her stories and essays are widely anthologized. She continues to tandem with Maryknoll College chum Cecilia Brainard on a series of anthologies, one of which, *A La Carte Food & Fiction* won an international Gourmand World Award (Literature Category) in 2008, a first for the Philippines. Marily has a blog at marilyo.multiply.com.

Kannika Claudine D. Peña graduated cum laude from the University of the Philippines, Diliman, with a degree in Creative Writing. The story "Be Safe" is from her undergraduate thesis, an interconnected collection of young adult short stories entitled *Thursday's Child*. Most of her stories are set in the province where she grew up in, Bataan, and in the future she hopes to put her hometown in the Philippine literary map.

Oscar Peñaranda left the Philippines at the age of 12. He spent his adolescent years in Vancouver, Canada and then moved to San Francisco at the age of 17. His stories and poems and essays have been anthologized both nationally and internationally. In 1980, his play *Followers of the Seasons* was performed by the Asian American Theater Company in San Francisco. In 2004, two of his own collections of writings were published, one a collection of poems (*Full Deck, Jokers Playing*) and the other a collection of interrelated stories (*Seasons by the Bay*).

Seasons By the Bay won the best fiction category for 2004 for the Global Filipino Literary Award, a literary organization based in Singapore, Paris, and Washington, D.C. It also won the award for fiction for PAWA (Philippine American Writers and Artists) for 2005, and *Full Deck* won the poetry category. It is the first and only time so far that the same writer won both fiction and poetry award from PAWA for the same year.

Edgar Poma's short stories have appeared in publications such as *Growing Up Filipino: Stories for Young Adults*. He is a Filipino-American writer born and raised in Sacramento, and a graduate of the University of California at Berkeley. He lives in San Francisco and Honolulu.

Tony Robles is a writer and activist, whose work is highly influenced by his family, culture, and the working class community. His poetry has appeared in numerous journals and magazines, including *DisOrient Journalzine, Pinoy Poetics, The Asian Pacific American Journal,* and the anthology *Seven-Card Stud* and *Seven Manangs Wild* (2002).

In his first children's book, *Lakas and the Manilatown Fish*, Tony Robles found inspiration from his own son, Lakas, and his uncle, poet Al Robles, one of the original Manilatown manongs.

Tony Robles's latest book, *Lakas and the Makibaka Hotel,* stars the same indomitable youth. Through both books, Robles hopes children will learn about the power of imagination and understand their own power to create new possibilities.

Born and raised in San Francisco, Anthony 'Tony' Robles continues to live there.

Brian Ascalon Roley is the author of *American Son: A Novel* (W.W. Norton), which was a New York Times Notable Book, Los Angeles Times Best Book, Kiriyama Pacific Rim Prize Finalist, and winner of the 2003 Association of Asian American Studies Prose Book Award. His work has been widely anthologized, and appears in a variety of magazines. Most recently he received a Lawrence Foundation Award for the title story in a collection-in-progress, *Blood of Jose Rizal.* "Old Man" is a chapter from a novel-in-progress that began with a piece written for Akashic Books' *Los Angeles Noir* anthology. He is a half-Filipino and was raised in Los Angeles. He now lives in Cincinnati with his wife and sons and teaches in the graduate creative writing program at Miami University of Oxford, OH. His website is www.brianroley.com.

Jonathan Jimena Siason holds an MFA in Creative Writing from the De La Salle University. His stories have seen print in the *Philippines Free Press, Philippine Graphic, Story Philippines,* and the anthologies *Bul-Ol: The First Tamaraw Anthology of Stories for Children, Philippine Speculative Fiction Volume 2, Heartbreak, A Different Voice: Fiction by Young Filipino Writers.* In 2008, he was a finalist in the Philippines Free Press Award for fiction. Currently he is an associate professor at the Ateneo de Zamboanga University.

Aileen Suzara is the daughter of Filipino immigrants from Bicol and Pangasinan. She grew up in Hawai'i and California. Drawn to the interconnections of identity, history, and environment, she graduated from Mount Holyoke College with a BA in Environmental Studies: Culture and Colonization. Aileen is currently based in Oakland, and is a board member of the Filipino/American Coalition for Environmental Solidarity (FACES). She turns to storytelling in all its forms -- from family narrative to recipes -- as a way of decolonizing the mind.

Geronimo G. Tagatac's father was from Ilocos Norte. His mother was a Russian Jew. Geronimo has been a Special Forces soldier, a legislative consultant, a dishwasher, cook, folksinger, computer system planner, a modern and jazz dancer and a roofer. His short fiction has appeared in *Writers Forum, The Northwest Review, Alternatives Magazine, Orion Magazine, The Clackamas Literary Review* and *The Chautauqua Literary Review*. He's received fellowships from Oregon Literary Arts and Fishtrap. His first book of short fiction, *The Weight of the Sun*, was a 2007 Oregon Literary Arts finalist. Geronimo lives and writes, in Salem, Oregon.

Marianne Villanueva is the author of two short story collections, *Ginseng and Other Tales From Manila* and *Mayor of the Roses: Stories*. She has co-edited an anthology of writings by Filipino women, *Going Home to a Landscape*. Her book reviews and fiction have been published in *Puerto del Sol, Hyphen, Sou'wester, The Threepenny Review*, the San Francisco Chronicle Book Review, and the *Women's Review of Books*. She has just completed her third collection, *The Lost Language*.

Acknowledgements

"How My Mother Flew" is a revisioning of "Into the Morning" which first appeared in *The Kite of Stars and Other Stories* (Anvil Publishing, 2007). Copyright 2007 by Dean Francis Alfar. Reprinted by permission of the author.

"The Music Teacher" is an excerpt from "Six From Downtown" which first appeared in *The Kite of Stars and Other Stories* (Anvil Publishing, 2007). Copyright 2007 by Dean Francis Alfar. Reprinted by permission of the author.

"Vigan" first appeared in *Going Home to a Landscape* (Calyx Books, 2003), edited by Marianne Villanueva and Virginia Cerenio. Copyright 2003 by Cecilia Manguerra Brainard. Reprinted by permission of the author.

"Nurse Rita" first appeared in *Philippines Free Press*, October 6, 2007. Copyright 2007 by Paulino Lim Jr. Reprinted by permission of the author.

"A Season of 10,000 Noses" is reprinted by permission of the author. Copyright 2009 by Charlson Ong.

"The Price" is part of the collection *Seasons by the Bay* (Tiboli Publishing, 2004). Copyright 2004 by Oscar Peñaranda. Reprinted by permission of the author.

"Old Man" is a chapter from a novel in progress by Brian Ascalon Roley. It began with a piece written for Akashic Books' *Los Angeles Noir* anthology. Copyright 2008 by Brian Ascalon Roley. Reprinted by permission of the author.

"Black Dog" is part of the collection *Mayor of the Roses* (University of Miami Press, 2005) by Marianne Villanueva. Copyright 2005 by Marianne Villanueva. Reprinted by permission of the author.